"It's nice to share the worry with someone."

Cecilia spoke softly as Adam opened the car door for her. "You can't imagine how good it is to talk to you and know you understand."

"Don't get so caught up in your family and your store that you forget to be a woman, too," he said, touching her smooth, cool cheek with his fingertips.

Cecilia met Adam's eyes, dark and searching, and a thousand thoughts converged as she felt him lower his head to hers. His lips were soft and warm, and instinctively she moved closer to him, wrapping her arms around his neck.

For endless moments she stopped thinking entirely, aware only of Adam's hands in her hair, of his chest broad and hard against her breasts.

They had only kissed, and yet Cecilia's whole body quivered in the aftershock. Even as Adam released her, she knew there was and had always been an almost tangible bond between them.

Tonight was far more than just a casual dinner with an old friend.

ABOUT THE AUTHOR

Virginia-based authors Sally Siddon and Barbara Bradford got the idea for *Spring Thaw* when a former boyfriend of Barbara's decided to look her up after more than twenty years. That meeting set the team's creative wheels in motion, and the result is this poignant love story about two people reclaiming the riches of their past. Barbara, a former teacher, and Sally, a former journalist, are best friends, as well as coauthors. *Spring Thaw* is the second Superromance published by this award-winning duo.

Books by Sally Bradford

HARLEQUIN SUPERROMANCE
281—THE ARRANGEMENT

Spring Thaw

SALLY BRADFORD

Harlequin Books

TORONTO • NEW YORK • LONDON
AMSTERDAM • PARIS • SYDNEY • HAMBURG
STOCKHOLM • ATHENS • TOKYO • MILAN

Published July 1989

First printing May 1989

ISBN 0-373-70365-1

CHAPTER ONE

SNOW FELL from a windless sky, filling footprints and dusting the trees with white. Adam had forgotten how beautiful winter could be in Spokane. Rubbing frost off the inside of his car window, he drove slowly toward the outskirts of town, hoping he was on the right road. So much had changed in twenty years.

The sight of the old frame house on the hill brought a quick smile of recognition, and Adam turned his Bronco into the gravel driveway that was packed deep in snow. He paused before getting out of the car, reaching back in his mind toward his childhood and letting the memories settle. The basketball hoop that hung over the garage door was rusted now, with only a piece of net hanging from the rim. But the tree house was gone, and bare, outstretched branches of the maple were etched against the winter sky. Adam climbed the porch steps, hesitating a moment before he lifted the worn brass knocker. Maybe he shouldn't have come at all.

The man who answered the door was stoop-shouldered with a fringe of white hair around his balding head. He peered out at Adam through wire-rimmed glasses, a puzzled look of half recognition in his vibrant blue eyes. "What can I do for you?" he asked.

"I'm Adam Campbell, Mr. Riley. Do you remember me?" It was a rhetorical question. Adam knew that Joe

Riley would never forget him, not after what had happened.

The door opened wider and Joe Riley leaned forward to get a better look. For an instant a barely perceptible shadow crossed his face. Then he stretched out both hands in welcome. "My word, boy, come in out of the cold. Let me have a look at you!" With a grip that was still firm, he grasped Adam's shoulder and examined him from head to foot. "You've grown into a man, no mistaking that," he pronounced, "and with all you've been through it couldn't be otherwise. Come on into the kitchen. I've got some hot coffee."

Sensing acceptance, Adam relaxed slightly. He could already smell the coffee, along with the odors of pipe tobacco and pine-scented air freshener. They were familiar smells, long forgotten. Feeling nostalgic, Adam followed Joe Riley through the cavernous front hall. This old house had been his second home during his childhood, and much of the time he'd felt closer to the Rileys than his own fragmented family. The house was quiet now, without the laughter and shouts of children. Over the years the hall carpet had grown threadbare, and the forest scenes on the wallpaper had faded to a greenish gray, but otherwise, nothing had changed. The old house had aged gracefully, Adam decided, very much like the man who lived there.

"Now tell me what brings you back to these parts," Joe Riley was saying as he poured two mugs of coffee and added a jigger of whiskey to each.

"I'm slated to be the new wing commander at Fairchild," Adam explained as he sat down at the table.

"Running the show at Fairchild Air Force Base, are you? That means they're grooming you for general." The old man's gaze was direct and curious. He couldn't help but wonder if there wasn't more to the relocation than that. Someone with Adam's background could have chosen from a half a dozen commands, including others that might have been even more prestigious. And yet he'd come back to Spokane.

"I'm just taking things one step at a time." Adam unzipped his leather jacket and draped it over the back of the wooden kitchen chair. He considered telling Joe Riley the rest of his plans and decided against it. As he'd just said, one step at a time. "I appreciated you sending me that letter," Adam added to fill the silence.

"The letter," the old man repeated. He set the coffee mugs on the red-checked plastic table cloth and sat down across from Adam. If that letter was still on his mind, Adam obviously did have other reasons for coming back to Spokane. "So you did get the letter," he mused, studying the younger man carefully. "I'd wondered about that off and on over the years."

"Yes, I got it, and I thought about it a lot during those years in Viet Nam," Adam told him. "I'm sorry I never answered."

"I didn't expect an answer," Joe Riley replied softly. "There was a long time there when we weren't sure we'd ever hear from you again." His eyes were filled with compassion. "All those years as a prisoner must have been hell for you, boy. We heard the stories about the POW camps and what they did to the Americans. We did some praying for you."

"Thanks, Mr. Riley," Adam said quietly. He took a drink of coffee, letting the heat and the whiskey burn his throat. "That's a part of my life I've put behind me." As he spoke the words, he realized there were several segments of his life that fell into the same category. But not for much longer. "So tell me about the family," Adam said, purposely changing the subject.

The vibrant blue eyes twinkled. "Anyone in particular you're wanting to hear about?"

"Well, I . . ." Adam hadn't expected him to be so direct.

"My guess is you're asking about Cecelia." Joe Riley opened the top drawer of a small chest near the kitchen table and dug down under a stack of envelopes. "I've got a picture of the whole lot of them from when they were here at Christmas. . . ." He laid a hazy photograph in front of Adam. "I guess you remember them all. Mike's a doctor now," he said, moving a gnarled finger from one face to the next, "and Bob's got himself a restaurant out in Kansas City, and Jim is running some sort of computer service—never did quite understand what he does . . ."

Adam listened with interest to the news of the boys he'd grown up with, but his eyes were searching the faces of the women in the picture. Joe Riley had been right. Cecelia was the one he wanted to know about.

"The girls are kind of hard to tell apart," the old man continued. "There's Jeannie and Bridget . . ." He paused. "And Cecelia's over there on the right."

Adam already knew. He'd picked her out instantly and had been studying her. She had the same petite figure, but her thick, dark hair was cut short. He could tell she'd been laughing when the shutter snapped, but the camera had been too far away for him to see much more. Yet he kept staring at the tiny image. "How is Cecelia?" he asked as casually as he could manage.

Joe Riley looked directly at Adam with kindness in his eyes. He sensed the younger man's hesitation and knew it was time to put the past to rest. "It's all right, boy. What's done is done."

No, Adam thought, *it's not done. At least not for me.*

Joe Riley settled back in his chair. "Cecelia's had a rough go of it since she lost her husband."

"She lost her husband?" Adam repeated, totally unprepared for what he'd just heard.

The old man took a well-used pipe from the side pocket of his sagging brown cardigan sweater. "Must be twelve years or so now since Tom died. Just dropped dead one day when he was cutting the grass. Doctor said later it was a problem with a blood vessel—an aneurysm I think he called it." He scraped a wooden match along the bottom of the table and lighted his pipe.

Adam listened silently, still staring at the photograph. What Joe Riley had just told him changed the entire situation. Cecelia was a widow, still young and obviously still very attractive.

"Cecelia was real broken up after that—they all were," Joe Riley continued. "She pulled herself together and opened a shop, sells kids' clothes. Got her sister, Jeannie, working with her. They're doing all right," he added proudly. "Funny thing how fast the years move along. I can't believe Cecelia's thirty-nine years old." Joe Riley puffed on his pipe. "That must make you forty-three. Seems impossible."

Adam was only half listening. "You said 'they were broken up'...she has children?" He hoped the answer would be yes.

"She's got a houseful. And fine kids, they are, too— every one of them. Say, Adam..." The old man studied him across the table. "I think it would be all right if you looked her up. That is one reason you've come back to Spokane, isn't it?"

"In a way..." Adam paused. That was true. From the beginning he'd planned to see Cecelia. But he'd expected to simply be asking for information about another man's wife. Now that he knew she was free, he was even more anxious to see her.

Joe Riley walked Adam to the door and stood watching until the Bronco disappeared around the turn in the road. He couldn't quite figure what the boy was really after. *The boy.* He shook his head as he closed the door. Adam was a man by any measure and he might be good for Cecelia. She'd been alone for too long now, and that wasn't right for a woman. Of course, she might not see it that way.

CECELIA'S HAND TREMBLED as she hung up the phone. Pop's words still echoed in her ears. Adam Campbell was back in town. Memories she had successfully hidden away long ago came rushing back, overwhelming her. *"He looks good...said he might look you up..."* Cecelia ran her fingers through her short, dark curls. Pop must have known what that news would do to her, which was no doubt why he'd called to prepare her.

"I won't see him," Cecelia said aloud, as she paced across her bedroom. "When he calls, I'll tell him no." Standing by the bedroom window, she looked out at the moon shadows as the wind rocked the branches of the old oak tree that had stood beside the house for nearly a century. She tried to picture what Adam must look like now, but the old images were locked in her mind. She hadn't thought about Adam or about what had happened for a long time. The pain was still there. Knowing he was in Spokane brought it all back.

Cecelia went to her dresser and picked up the small framed photographs of her children, one by one. She carefully studied each of their faces. What would they think of her if they knew? And how about Tom? Gently she touched his picture, taken on their honeymoon. Would he have married her if he had known about her past from the very beginning?

Twisting the gold wedding band on her finger, she paced back and forth across the room, stopping to watch moonbeams shimmer on the fresh snow. Finally she turned toward the old trunk at the end of her bed. Thirty years of memories were stored there.

After taking the key from under the velvet liner in her jewelry box, she knelt down and ran her fingers along the edge of the leather bindings and across the mellowed brass hardware before she unlocked the trunk and raised the heavy lid. As it opened, the pungent odor of cedar filled the room. Purposefully, she removed several wool blankets and set them on the floor beside her. Then, taking a deep breath, she reached deep into the trunk where she kept her journals.

No matter how late the hour, or how tired she was, Cecelia wrote a few lines every night. She'd followed the ritual since she was ten years old. All her memories, some wonderful and some painful, were faithfully recorded. Her writing over the years was like a patchwork quilt, each tiny piece a part of the whole.

Patiently she searched through the books. She rarely read her journals, but she knew that if she wanted to she could recapture the past in a matter of moments. The newest journals were covered in soft pastel fabrics and the oldest were black and white composition notebooks from her childhood. But the one she was looking for was leather, red leather, with a broken lock. She finally found it buried at the bottom of the trunk where she had hidden it a long time ago. Opening the book to the first page, she read her name, "Cecelia Anne Riley." And beneath it, "Age seventeen." The entries began on the first day of January.

> This is a brand new year and it's off to a great start! Adam came for dinner tonight. I've seen him every day since he got home for Christmas leave. He is very good looking, especially in his Air Force Academy uniform. I know he has been watching me a lot. I think he knows that I'm grown up. Now maybe he will think of me as a real girl, not just Jim's kid sister.

Despite her apprehension, Cecelia laughed softly and flipped through the next several pages which were filled, as she had expected, with nothing but thoughts about Adam. "Adam smiled at me"; "Adam held my hand when we went ice-skating"; "Adam put his arms around me when we were tobogganing." Finally, a few days later:

> Adam took me to the movies tonight. Afterward he kissed me! I really liked it!

And later in the week:

> Adam and I parked out at the river tonight. We kissed a lot. I got all shivery and I told him it was because I was cold. But that wasn't true. I shiver when he kisses me like that.

She turned the page:

Adam touched me tonight, first through my blouse
and then underneath. I know we shouldn't be
doing that, but it feels so good. I think I love him.

Following this were three blank pages before the
simple entry that said nothing and everything:

Adam and I were snowed in at a ski cabin in the
mountains. We love each other so much.

Cecelia wrapped her arms around her legs and leaned
her head on her knees, remembering. The rest of the
story wasn't recorded because she hadn't known what
to say. How could a seventeen-year-old girl write about
making love for the first time? How could she possibly
have written about the exhilaration, the fear, the wonder of it all? The belief that no two people in love had
ever experienced the intensity she and Adam had
shared?

Cecelia lifted her head and began to read again. After his leave had ended, Adam had gone back to the
academy, and she had missed him terribly. Page after
page was filled with her longing for him, until the beginning of March.

My period hasn't come since before Christmas.

Shaking, the way she had shaken when she had written those words twenty years before, Cecelia couldn't go
on reading. When she had told Adam she was carrying
his baby, he had determined he would drop out of the
academy and marry her. But, as young as they were,
Cecelia and Adam knew they were not ready for marriage. They loved each other in that exciting way that

new love is, but neither had the greater sense of a commitment strong enough to last a lifetime.

Together with Cecelia's parents, they had decided that Adam would finish at the academy, and Cecelia would go to a home for unwed mothers before her pregnancy showed. When the baby was born, it would be given up for adoption. The secret would be kept from everyone else.

With trembling fingers she turned the pages of the journal—through the spring, the summer, and into early fall where she found the entry that tore at her heart.

I had a baby boy today. He weighed six pounds, 12 ounces. I will never see him again.

For a long time after she'd placed all the journals and the blankets back in the old trunk and locked it, Cecelia cried softly, watching the tip of an icy branch rake across the window pane. Finally, close to sleep, she opened the drawer of her nightstand and took out her current journal. Curling up against the gentle warmth of the down comforter, she wrote two lines.

Adam is back but I won't see him. He belongs to the past.

DANNY MITCHELL PARKED HIS CAR across the street from the Mahoney house and tried to decide what to do. He'd thought Angela might want to help with posters for the demonstration, but now that he'd come, he wasn't so sure anymore. She wasn't as committed to the cause as he was, but then, lots of people started out that way before they really got into it.

Danny watched with interest as the front door of the Mahoney house opened and a scraggly brown dog streaked outside and rolled in the snow. Two boys were close behind him, a matched set jogging down the front steps in high-top sneakers, gangly kids with carrot-red hair. They must be the thirteen-year-old twins Angela talked about, Danny decided. A girl with dark hair followed them. That would be Kim. And the one flipping her blond ponytail and stalking across the porch had to be Mary Beth, the sister who kept getting in trouble. Angela came last, wearing her Eastern Washington State sweatshirt, her long, dark hair loose across her shoulders as she hurried down the steps. She was yelling something to one of her brothers who had opened the tailgate of an old station wagon parked in the driveway.

Danny had never met any of the Mahoneys except Angela, but he'd listened carefully when she talked about them and wondered what it would be like to have brothers and sisters and aunts and uncles and a grandfather—a real family. In the three months since his father had died, he'd felt as if he had no family at all, even though he was still living with his mother.

A woman with short, dark hair appeared in the doorway and called to the children. Danny opened his window slightly so he could hear her. "Bring those groceries in the back door so you don't track snow through the house," she was saying. "And somebody catch Bingo."

The boys responded in unison, chasing the dog. It dashed away from them, while the girls laughed and cheered their brothers on.

Closing his window, Danny started the engine. Angela was busy with her family. She wouldn't have time to help him. And he didn't really need her, anyway. He didn't need anyone.

FROM THE FRONT DOOR of the turn-of-the-century white frame house, Cecelia watched the old Ford roar down the street. Wishing teenagers didn't find it necessary to drive so fast, she took a last look at Bingo romping in a snowdrift and then went inside.

Winter was a losing battle, but at least February was almost over. A few more weeks and the sun would be warm and they'd see the grass again. And by that time Adam would have called if he were going to. Cecelia paused, thinking about Adam as she had daily since the night Pop had told her he'd come back. That had been a week ago, and she'd still heard nothing. At first she'd jumped every time the phone rang, which some evenings was nearly constantly. But in the past day or two, she'd begun to think that Adam might not contact her after all.

The sound of Sean's stricken voice brought her reverie to an abrupt halt.

"Hey, Mom, what's going on?" he shouted from the direction of the kitchen.

Cecelia didn't even stop to answer. All of her maternal instincts warned her that her son's cry demanded an instant response.

"Mom!" he bellowed again.

Not daring to think about what might be wrong, Cecelia ran to the kitchen. "Oh, no!" she gasped as she came to a horrified stop in the doorway, taking in the entire scene at a glance.

There was water everywhere. The grocery bags that had been set down inside the back door were already soaked. The floor was flooding fast, and within minutes the water would spread out of the kitchen and into the rest of the house. Cecelia searched frantically for the source of the problem. The faucets at the sink were turned off, but as her gaze dropped she saw water pouring out from around the door of the cabinet below. Then the door burst open and water shot out like a geyser.

"Damn!" she exclaimed. This was what the plumber had warned her about last month. Old pipes. In need of replacement. Cecelia tried to think logically. Sean stood immobilized in front of the refrigerator, still clutching two brown sacks of groceries as he watched the water swirl around his sneakers. He wasn't going to be of any help. *The main valve,* she suddenly remembered.

"Quick, Sean!" she shouted. "Go to the basement and shut off the water valve behind the washing machine. Run!" She sloshed across the kitchen floor and grabbed for the broken pipe in a futile effort to stem the flow. Water spurted in all directions, soaking her from head to toe in an icy rush.

At that moment Mary Beth burst through the back door and Bingo streaked past her, running full speed into the kitchen and skidding across the flooded floor.

"Get that dog out of here," Cecelia ordered. "Sean," she yelled, "haven't you found that cutoff valve yet?"

Mary Beth surveyed the kitchen in horror. "Mom, what happened?"

"Pipe burst," Cecelia answered tersely. "Go down and help your brother find the cutoff valve."

"But I'll get my new shoes wet," Mary Beth protested.

"Take them off!" Cecelia exploded. She forced the cabinet door shut, but water still gushed out. Bingo ran back and forth, barking at the water.

"I'll get Bingo instead," Mary Beth offered. "Here, Bingo," she called, not budging from the doorway. Finally the old pipes whined, and the water rushing out the door became a trickle.

"Did that do it, Mom?" Sean called from the basement.

Cautiously Cecelia opened the cabinet door to look. "Victory," she called to her son. She leaned against the counter contemplating her dripping jersey dress, trying to decide what to do next.

"Let's build a swimming pool," Sean suggested, clomping up the stairs from the basement.

"Super idea," agreed Kevin, who, along with Kim and Angela, had joined Mary Beth near the back door. "We can sell admission."

"This isn't funny," Mary Beth shrieked. "We've got to get the water on—I have to wash my hair."

No, Cecelia thought, watching the water creep toward the hardwood floor in the dining room. *It isn't funny, and it's going to take hours to clean this mess up.*

A loud knock at the back door startled all of them and sent Bingo racing through the water, barking furiously.

"You don't suppose that could be a plumber?" Kevin asked hopefully.

"No chance," Cecelia sighed. "Tell whoever it is to go away and let's get this cleaned up," she instructed. "Everyone to the basement for buckets, rags, mops, anything you can find that will soak up water. I'm going to—'' She stopped in mid-sentence, suddenly aware of an eerie silence in the kitchen.

As she turned around, Cecelia's eyes rose to meet the puzzled gaze of a man standing in the doorway. For several moments she stared at him, unable to move. At first she almost didn't recognize him. Then she knew, and her lips silently mouthed his name. Adam Campbell.

Bingo whimpered softly, but otherwise there was no sound in the kitchen except the icy wind gusting through the open door. Adam and Cecelia stood facing each other, their eyes locked together, their bodies motionless. Seconds ticked by. Bingo whimpered again.

"Cecelia?" Adam said quietly.

Suddenly she saw him in detail—still ruggedly handsome, but now with fine lines etched across his forehead and around his deep brown eyes. His hair wasn't really blond anymore. It was darker, more of a sandy color, and it was longer than she'd remembered. He stood solidly in the doorway, towering over her as he always had. His body was still trim, but he'd filled out and his leather jacket emphasized the breadth of his shoulders. He looked older, she realized, but of course he would. Twenty years was a long time.

"Adam!" Cecelia whispered softly. "What are you doing here?"

He clicked the door latch shut behind him, and the sound echoed in the silence. "I stopped by to see you," he said as naturally as if he had been there only yesterday. His eyes left hers, and his gaze swept the kitchen. "But I seem to have come at an awkward time."

An awkward time, she thought. Yes, he had come at an awkward time. She looked down at her soggy dress and at the water pooled on the floor. Of course the flooded kitchen was what he meant. But the broken pipe, which had been such a crisis moments before, seemed trivial to her now.

"You look like you could use some help," he suggested gently.

"Yes," Cecelia said vaguely. She realized she was still staring at him as she tried to mesh the past and the present in her mind. "A pipe under the sink broke," she heard herself explaining. "We were about to get this cleaned up and call a plumber."

Adam sensed her discomfort and silently chastised himself for arriving unannounced. He should have kept calling no matter how many times the line was busy. He'd planned the visit for a week, so he could have given her some warning. He'd owed her that. "Cecelia, I'm sorry to just drop in like this," he apologized. "If you'd like me to come back some other time..."

"No, that's all right," she murmured, but inside her a voice cried out: *No, don't come back. Don't do this to me. Let me go on just like I was. Don't make me remember.* Cecelia glanced at her children, who were silently watching the drama unfold and then at Adam who was looking curiously at the assembled group. She realized she had yet to introduce them. "These are my children," she said, ignoring the instincts that warned her against bringing together the two parts of her life she had managed to keep totally separate.

"I'd like you to meet Kevin and Sean," she began.

Adam shook hands with the two boys, thinking of how much they looked alike, even to their mouths full of silver braces, and of how much they looked like their mother in spite of their carrot-red hair.

"And this is Mary Beth," Cecelia continued.

She's different, Adam thought, her facial structure, her body build, everything about her. Maybe she resembled her father, he decided.

"And Angela—"

Adam's smile widened as he took Angela's hand. The girl was an exact duplicate of a teenaged Cecelia.

"And this is Kim," Cecelia concluded, watching her middle daughter shyly shake Adam's hand.

Adam searched Kim's face. She resembled her mother, too, but not nearly so much as Angela. Her eyes were dark, unlike Cecelia's, and she seemed very reserved. He wondered what she was thinking.

"This is Adam Campbell," Cecelia was saying. "He's a . . ." She hesitated for only the briefest instant. "An old friend," she finished smoothly. She caught a brief look that passed between Angela and Mary Beth, but she ignored it.

"And this is Bingo," she added. The dog responded to his name by wagging his tail furiously and spraying water on Adam's gray slacks. "Well, that's the whole family." Cecelia paused, not sure what to do next.

Adam wasn't sure either. His eyes held hers, questioning. He saw her down the tunnel of the years, her image slowly replacing the old memories. The long hair that had flowed below her shoulders was now brushed back in short dark curls. Her face was fuller with a few lines and deeper dimples, Adam noted, as he saw the first hint of a shaky smile touch her lips. And her body, under that wet green dress that clung to every curve, was fuller too, and more shapely. There was a dimension to the blue eyes that hadn't been there before. The girl had become a woman. That much was easy to see. But he couldn't tell whether she was angry or merely surprised to see him. Since she stood surrounded by her children, he certainly couldn't ask her.

Adam cleared his throat. "I believe when I interrupted, you were in the middle of organizing a cleanup brigade," he said tentatively. "I'm pretty good with a mop."

"What we need is a plumber so we can turn the water back on," Mary Beth interjected. "I have to wash my hair."

Adam laughed. "I'm afraid I'm not very good at plumbing, but I can find someone who is if you'll guide me toward the phone."

Everyone looked expectantly at Cecelia, and she forced herself to take stock of the situation. Adam didn't show any signs of leaving, and there wasn't anything she could do about that at the moment. The water had to be cleaned up immediately, and someone needed to call the plumber. Ignoring the rush of thoughts and emotions that threatened to paralyze her, Cecelia took charge.

"Kevin, why don't you take Mr. Campbell to the phone in the front hall," she suggested, "but go around the outside of the house so you don't have to walk through all the water."

Kevin grunted and opened the back door.

"And show him where the list is with the plumber's number on it," Cecelia added.

As they left the kitchen, she heard Adam's deep voice. "Never mind 'Mr. Campbell,'" he was saying. "Call me Adam."

Cecelia was aware of the other four children staring at her curiously. She could easily guess at some of the unspoken questions, but she wasn't about to answer any of them. She'd already explained that Adam was an old friend. That was absolutely all they needed to know. "All right," she began briskly, "everyone to the basement for mops, sponges, rags—whatever you can find that will sop up water."

Mumbling among themselves, they all left, except for Mary Beth. "Who is that dude? I mean who is he really?" she asked in a conspiratorial tone.

"I've already explained," Cecelia answered evenly. "Adam is an old friend, someone I knew when I was growing up."

Mary Beth gave her mother a penetrating look. "You must have known him real well, the way you were staring at each other," she shot over her shoulder as she hurried down the stairs.

Yes, Cecelia thought, *I did know him very well. But that was a long time ago.*

CHAPTER TWO

CECELIA STRIPPED OFF her wet clothes and wrapped her body in a soft, thick towel. From downstairs she could hear the clanging of the pipes as the plumber worked and the rise and fall of voices from the kitchen. One deep, resonant voice stood out from the others. She leaned against the bathroom vanity, her whole body shaking. With all her heart she wished that Adam Campbell hadn't come.

She tried to slow her racing mind. Did he know she was a widow? What was he thinking when she stood there introducing her five children? Was he remembering, wondering? Did he have children, too? A wife?

Shivering, Cecelia tried to focus on the moment. The critical question was why Adam Campbell had, in fact, come back. The obvious way to find out was to ask him, but that might not be as easy as it seemed. Voices again drifted into the bedroom accompanied by much banging and punctuated with laughter. She felt a sudden need to dress quickly and go back downstairs.

When Cecelia reappeared in the kitchen, she was greeted by a question from Mary Beth. "The plumber fixed the pipe and he's gone—can I go wash my hair now?"

"Not until the cleanup is finished," Cecelia answered automatically.

"I'm going to be late," Mary Beth grumbled.

"So get busy and do some work," Sean prodded. "All you've been doing is standing around, anyway."

"That's not true." Mary Beth snapped.

Cecelia thought she saw Adam wink at her, but she wasn't sure. "How about we order some pizza and celebrate a dry floor?" Adam suggested tactfully.

Cecelia noticed that Mary Beth joined in the rousing cheer that greeted his suggestion and even began drying off some of the canned goods while Adam went to call the pizza parlor. Surveying the kitchen, Cecelia realized that within another half hour things should be in good shape. That was about when the pizza would arrive. Adam's timing had been good.

As she helped wring out rags in the sink, Cecelia felt strangely detached from the flurry of activity around her, almost as though her body was in the kitchen and the rest of her was somewhere else. She found herself watching Adam, sometimes seeing him as a stranger and sometimes catching glimpses of the boy she'd known. She felt as if she was trying to fit the pieces of two different puzzles together in one.

The doorbell rang just as Cecelia returned from taking the last of the buckets and rags to the basement. She looked around for her purse, but Adam was ahead of her. "My treat," he said as he insisted on paying the delivery man. She decided not to argue.

"Wow!" Kevin exclaimed, setting the boxes on the long, pine table. "Three pizzas. Mom only lets us order two." Sean dragged a dining room chair into the kitchen and everyone sat down.

Cecelia joined them, feeling strangely out of control. The kids were all talking at once, especially Sean and Kevin, and always with their mouths full of food.

Adam seemed comfortable. He probably had teenagers of his own, she decided.

"Adam's the new wing commander at Fairchild," Sean said. "He told us while we were cleaning up. And he said when he takes over he'll give us a personal guided tour of the base."

As Sean's words sank in, Cecelia's stomach knotted. She felt Adam's eyes on her, but she didn't look at him. If Adam was the wing commander, that meant he'd be living nearby. And if he hadn't even assumed command yet, he hadn't wasted any time in coming to see her. She stole a sideways glance at Adam. What in heaven's name did he have in mind?

But Adam's attention was focused on Kevin. "You really flew F-4's in Viet Nam?" Kevin was asking, wide-eyed.

"I sure did, and B-52's afterward."

Cecelia shifted her position slightly so she could see Adam without actually looking at him. She studied him, the square jaw, the thick, wavy hair, the fine, white scar that ran the length of his right cheek. The scar was probably a remnant of Viet Nam.

But that was past history. Viet Nam had been over for American soldiers since the early seventies. Where had Adam been since? Cecelia glanced down at his hands. He wore an Air Force Academy ring on his right hand; his left was bare. Of course, because a man wasn't wearing a wedding ring didn't necessarily mean he wasn't married.

The pizza was almost gone when Kim excused herself to go upstairs and work on a computer program. Angela quietly joined her. Mary Beth glanced at the clock and stood up abruptly. "My date's due in twenty minutes and I've still got to shampoo my hair," she exclaimed.

"Hold it, Mary Beth," Cecelia called out as her daughter rapidly exited the kitchen. "Exactly what are your plans tonight?"

Mary Beth spun around, her eyes defiant. "Why do you always pick on me? You never even ask Angela."

"You're sixteen and Angela's eighteen," Cecelia answered patiently. "Besides, she didn't stay out until two in the morning when she was supposed to be in by eleven. Now, let's try again. What are your plans, Mary Beth?"

"Roger is picking me up at eight and we're going—" her hesitation was almost unnoticeable "—to a movie," she finished quickly. "Does that satisfy you?"

"Not quite," Cecelia answered. "Make sure you do exactly what you've told me you'll be doing and be home—in the house—by eleven."

"Now you're accusing me of lying!" Mary Beth stormed, her eyes flashing with anger. "My *real* mother would never treat me like this." She ran out of the kitchen and stomped up the stairs, her angry footsteps echoing in the silent kitchen. Cecelia took a deep breath. She hated the inevitable confrontation every time she challenged Mary Beth.

"She's really ticked," Kevin observed. "Sorry, Mom," he apologized when Cecelia glared at him.

"Mary Beth's always like that," Sean explained to Adam. "She's allergic to rules."

Adam didn't answer.

"As long as the pizza's gone, why don't you clear out and give me a chance to talk to Mr. Campbell?" Cecelia suggested to the twins.

"Aw, Mom, he was just starting to tell us about how planes are refueled in the air," Kevin protested.

"I'll tell you all about that next time I see you," Adam interjected.

"On your way, guys," Cecelia said firmly. Grudgingly both boys stood up, scraping their chairs sharply against the floor. They wandered out of the kitchen toward the family room.

Adam watched them disappear. "They're nice kids, Cecelia—all of them," he told her. "It looks like you've done a hell of a good job with them."

"Thank you," she murmured, even more unsettled than she had been before. Nervously she closed the lid of an empty pizza box. She'd wanted the children to leave, but now that she was alone with Adam, she realized everything had been easier before.

"You must have had a rough go of it by yourself," Adam said.

So he did know about Tom. "It is hard sometimes," she admitted, "but we've done all right."

"Hey, Mom," Mary Beth yelled from upstairs. "My hair dryer's broken, and Angela's using hers, and Kim's isn't strong enough. Can I use yours?"

Cecelia frowned, annoyed by the interruption. Normally the answer would have been no, but she didn't want to argue just then. Mary Beth probably knew that. "Yes, but put it in my bathroom when you're finished," Cecelia called back. She saw Adam smile.

"You've really got your hands full with that one," he noted, "but she's got a lot of spunk. I like her."

"I could settle for a little less spunk," Cecelia replied.

"Not in the long run." He gave Cecelia a searching look. "I heard her comment about her 'real mother.' Is she adopted?"

"Yes, when she was a baby," Cecelia explained.

"When you adopted her, did you—"

Cecelia interrupted him, not wanting to hear his question. "We chose to adopt because we had only Angela then, and we both really liked children."

"Yes, but did you think about—"

"Mom?"

Cecelia saw Kevin standing in the doorway. "Later, Kevin," she said impatiently. She turned back to Adam, willing Kevin to leave quickly before he overheard something he shouldn't.

"Sorry, Mom," Kevin persisted, "but it'll only take a minute. I just talked to Andy and he and Pete Timmons are going to bring over a video. Do we have any popcorn?"

"Kevin!" Cecelia exploded. "Can't you give me even a few minutes to talk to someone without constantly interrupting?"

Kevin's eyebrows shot up and he stared at his mother. "Jeez," he muttered, turning away. "All I asked was whether we had any popcorn."

Cecelia rested her face in her hands. It wasn't Kevin's fault his timing was bad. "I shouldn't have yelled at him," she said, half to herself.

"With five of them, I'd think you'd be yelling most of the time," Adam observed.

"I do my share."

"Now, what were we talking about?"

"We were about to change the subject," Cecelia answered.

"Would you rather I go?" Adam asked quietly.

Cecelia pressed folds in the napkin. All she had to say was yes. Slowly she raised her eyes and met, not the laughing eyes of the boy she'd known twenty years before, but solemn, serious eyes, deep with compassion.

"Why are you here, Adam?" she asked him. "What do you want after all this time?"

Adam wasn't ready to tell her all of it. Not yet. He wasn't even sure he could, because from the moment he'd seen her, his reasons had changed. "When I knew I was coming back to Spokane, I thought about you," he began slowly, not looking at her. "Then, when I got into town, it was all so familiar. I kept remembering the places and the people, all sorts of things from growing up that I hadn't thought about for years. The past was like a magnet that kept pulling at me, and so one day last week I went to see your father—"

"I know. He called to tell me."

"I figured he would. He looks great, Cecelia. Except for the white hair and a few wrinkles, he hasn't changed at all. He gave me a good slug of his version of Irish coffee and all the latest news about the Riley clan."

The image of Pop made Cecelia smile. "That's his favorite subject."

"I know." Adam looked up as Sean strolled past him toward the refrigerator.

"Don't mind me," Sean said. "I'm only getting ice cream."

"Oh, no, you're not," Cecelia corrected him. "We just had dinner."

"But Mom—"

"Out!" She pointed at the door and he left, scuffing his sneakers against the floor.

"Do you ever get to carry on a conversation with anyone?" Adam asked.

"Occasionally. It's usually not quite this bad."

As far as Adam was concerned, the situation was impossible. Now that he'd seen Cecelia again, he wanted to talk to her, really talk to her, which wasn't going to happen as long as her kids were around. "Why don't we take a walk?" he suggested.

"A walk?" That was one more step toward familiarity. But simply sending him away was no longer realistic. As long as he'd come, she had to talk to him. She could settle things between them tonight, and then she wouldn't see him again. "Well, I suppose we could take a walk," she agreed. "Let me tell the kids where I'm going."

Cecelia had given the boys ground rules for the evening and was on her way to get her coat when Angela stopped her in the front hall. "Mom, I'm leaving for the meeting now." She turned toward a tall, slightly built boy with a peace symbol earring visible beneath his shaggy blond hair. This is Danny Mitchell. He's giving me a ride."

"Nice to meet you, Danny," Cecelia said, extending her hand. The boy looked different from most of Angela's other friends. His hair, his clothes—everything about him seemed radical. She tried to remember exactly what kind of meeting Angela had said she was going to and wished she'd asked more about it.

Danny took Angela's mother's hand, noting her grip was firm and warm. He liked her. Some people were put off by his appearance, but she didn't seem to notice. That meant she wasn't into making snap judgments about people, which gave her lots of points in his book. "I'm glad to meet you, Mrs. Mahoney," he said politely.

At least he seemed well mannered, Cecelia noted. It was hard to tell much about young people by looking at them.

"I shouldn't be late," Angela said as they went out.

Cecelia didn't answer. Even though she still lived at home, Angela was eighteen and attending college. That meant she needed more freedom, and Cecelia was working hard to let her daughter go. She turned to find Adam behind her, pulling on his jacket, and for just a moment wished she had someone to share all the family decisions that were so tough to make alone.

Snow was still falling lightly when Adam and Cecelia started down the front steps, but the wind had died and the night air was more crisp than cold. Adam glanced over to see Angela and Danny getting into Danny's car. "Isn't that your daughter?"

"Yes, she's on her way to a meeting," Cecelia told him.

"And that's her boyfriend?" He'd caught only a glimpse of the unkempt youth as the car pulled away.

"No, he's just someone she knows from college. I think Angela told me he has a girlfriend who is studying abroad."

"I'll bet you're glad of that. He doesn't look like someone you'd want to cultivate."

Adam's comment put Cecelia on the defensive, even though she'd had roughly the same response to Danny. Making a judgment from thirty feet away seemed unfair. "At that age a lot of kids look weird," she replied. "I think it's a stage."

They walked in silence for a few moments, their boots crunching the snow-packed sidewalk. Adam realized he'd been making small talk for most of the evening. Actually both of them had. Discussing important matters was hard after so many years, especially with a houseful of kids and a flooded floor. But now that they were finally alone, he didn't seem to have any of the right words. He supposed he could come right out and say what was on his mind, but that didn't seem to be the best approach, either. "There's so much I want to know, Cecelia," he said finally, "but I'm not sure how to ask you. I don't know where to begin."

"Neither do I, Adam." Cecelia looked up at him and in the light from the street lamp she saw the once-familiar profile. He looked as confused as she was. "Exactly what did Pop tell you?" she asked cautiously.

"Well, he said you and Jeannie have a children's shop and you've made quite a success of it. He's very proud of you, you know."

Cecelia nodded, wondering what else they'd talked about.

"Let's see," Adam continued, "he said you have a houseful of kids—"

"So you were prepared."

"Not quite."

"I suppose it would be hard to prepare anyone for five teenagers."

Adam hesitated. "He told me about what happened to your husband. I'm sorry, Cecelia."

"Thank you, Adam," Cecelia answered quietly. "It sounds as if you got the whole news bulletin. There's not much else to add."

"But that's all it was, just a news bulletin." He looked down at her and thought of how fragile she seemed. The woman she'd become was even more lovely than the girl he'd known. He wanted to tell her so, but it didn't seem appropriate. Maybe if they kept talking, he'd find an opportunity.

"I don't know a thing about what's actually happening to you," he continued. "You must be lonely. Your husband has been gone a long time—why didn't you remarry?"

"Remarry? With five children?" Cecelia laughed softly. "You must be joking. Between the kids and getting the shop going, I didn't have an ounce of energy left."

"And now?"

Cecelia hesitated. Remarrying wasn't even a consideration anymore. "I don't know whether I'd want to be married again," she told him honestly. "The shop is doing well and the children are growing up. My life is settled now. Marriage wouldn't fit in. Besides," she added, "there's no one I want to marry." She looked up at him. "How about you, Adam? Do you have a family?"

"Nope." He shook his head. "Same reasons. With life in the air force, it didn't fit in."

"That's funny," she mused. "The way you relate to teenagers, I'd have thought you had some. Most military men I know do have wives and families."

Adam's silence told Cecelia she'd hit a sensitive spot, and she backed away. They kept on walking, their steady pace taking them south along Grand Boulevard. For a while they talked about Cecelia's family and about Adam's military assignments, safe, impersonal topics. She knew he'd wanted to bring up their past, back at the house. But he seemed to have changed his mind, and as far as she was concerned that was just fine.

"How long has it been since you went to a movie?" Adam asked abruptly.

"You mean in a movie theater?" That was an odd question. Cecelia thought for a moment. "I don't know. A long time."

"Me, too," he told her. He nodded toward the theater marquee across the street. "Want to go?"

"Well . . ." Going to a movie certainly wasn't what she'd expected. But if they didn't have anything to discuss, why not? "Sure," she agreed. "I'll go call the kids."

By the time she'd finished talking to Kim, Adam had bought their tickets. As they walked into the darkened theater, Cecelia realized that once upon a time she and Adam had gone to lots of movies together. That seemed very long ago.

Two hours and a box of popcorn later, they emerged into the snowy night. By now Cecelia felt more relaxed and less threatened by Adam. "I wasn't so sure about going to a movie, but it was fun," she told him.

Adam barely heard her. After spending the past two hours sorting out his thoughts, he had finally come to grips with the reason he was having so much trouble talking to Cecelia. He still felt so damn guilty about walking out on her. Every time he looked at her, every time they got beyond the weather or her kids, he felt as if a knife were stabbing him. He hadn't expected to react to her that way. But that was before he'd been with her and seen how lovely she was and how very vulnerable. There was no way he could make things right, but at least he could face up to the past and tell her how he felt. He owed her that.

"Do you mind if we walk home?" he asked, knowing they would have no privacy once they were back at her house. "I know it's a long way, and if you're cold we could call a cab—"

"I don't mind," Cecelia answered.

As they fell in step together, Adam tried to decide how to begin. "Look," he finally said somewhat awkwardly, "I need to talk to you."

"Adam..." Cecelia stopped him. She should have insisted on the cab. "Adam, please don't talk about what happened before." A note of urgency crept into her voice. "Can't we begin here? Can't we go from this point forward like two people who just met?"

Adam shook his head. "That's pretty unrealistic."

She didn't answer. Of course he was right. They couldn't erase the past by pretending it didn't exist. Too much had happened. She felt his gloved hand over hers. If they could only begin again... Cecelia swallowed hard. "What were you going to say, Adam?" He was still holding her hand.

"Mostly I wanted to tell you I'm sorry," he answered haltingly. "I walked out on you when you needed me most. I left you to have a baby alone." His voice broke but he went on. "I was young, and too caught up in myself, but that's no excuse. It took three years in a POW hellhole in Viet Nam to finally figure out what I'd done."

"Adam, don't. It's all over."

"That doesn't make it right." He couldn't look at her. "I did love you, you know, even if we were young and it wasn't for very long."

"Adam, please...we did what seemed right at the time."

His voice droned on, his words twisting inside Cecelia until she wanted to scream for him to stop. She began walking faster, taking her hand from his and stuffing it into her jacket pocket. He didn't know what he was doing to her. He *couldn't* know.

"When I had time to think, I realized how stupid I'd been. I wished a thousand times I could have those choices back so I could make them differently," he continued doggedly. "I kept thinking about what you'd gone through, alone and frightened.... But by then it was too late." He turned to her, shielded by the darkness. "I abandoned you, Cecelia, and I abandoned the baby. I didn't mean to, but I did."

"Please stop, Adam," Cecelia pleaded in a shaky voice.

Adam paid no attention. "I decided when I was in Viet Nam that if I ever got back, I'd find you and I'd marry you if you'd still have me. It was all pretty irrational. Everything was, then." He kicked at the snow with the toe of his boot. "When I did get home. I found out you were already married."

Her own anguish momentarily overshadowed, Cecelia listened in astonishment. He'd suffered, too. She had never considered that. Over all those years, she'd never thought about his feelings. "I don't know what to say," she answered slowly. "I guess it didn't occur to me that you had any regrets." Cecelia looked up to find his face was drawn and sober, his eyes focused straight ahead. In some strange way it helped to know she hadn't been totally alone in her grief. And maybe it also helped to know for sure that once he had really loved her.

"You don't owe me anything," she finally answered. "I want you to understand that."

"Do you still hate me for it, Cecelia?"

She met his eyes, wishing she could have somehow known through all those awful times how much he'd cared. "I never hated you, Adam. I only hated myself."

"But I was the one—"

"No, I was the one who gave up the baby." She stopped. She'd never before said the words aloud.

"We made the decision together," he argued.

"No, Adam, the final choice was mine. I've spent the rest of my life trying to forget." She walked slowly beside him, her head down. "That's why I didn't want to see you. I've buried the past and I knew you'd bring it back again."

"And I've done exactly that, haven't I?"

Her words were deliberate. "Yes, Adam, you have." She didn't seem angry, only resigned.

"I couldn't have stayed away," he told her. "I had to make sure you were all right."

Cecelia stopped walking and put a gloved hand on his arm. "Then you've done what you came to do." Her eyes were bright with tears. "I know it's been a long time, but I don't think the pain will ever go away. Please don't make me think about it anymore." Her eyes pleaded with him. "Adam, don't talk about the baby."

Adam looked away. The baby was the very reason he'd come. He needed all the information she could give him. Maybe the best thing to do was wait.

They walked for almost a mile with each of them lost in private thoughts. Cecelia was beginning to see a different Adam Campbell, a man far more compassionate and thoughtful than the boy she'd remembered. Probably she affected him differently now, too. As they neared the porch steps, Cecelia started to say goodnight, but Adam grasped her shoulders and gently turned her toward him. "I want to see you again, Cecelia. Would that be all right?"

She met his eyes, unsure whether the emotions she saw there were an offer of friendship or something else. She was equally unsure of herself. She was standing so close to him that she could feel the moist warmth of his breath that hung white in the chill air. His hands, still firmly on her shoulders, conveyed a warmth of their own.

Reason told her that even a casual friendship could prove to be a big mistake, if a casual friendship between them was possible. "I don't know," she replied. "You were right when you said we couldn't escape the past. It's always going to be there, every time we're together. I'm not sure I can deal with that."

"I think it's time we faced what happened. Like your dad told me, what's done is done."

Hearing her father's words of forgiveness came as a surprise. "He told you that?"

"He did."

Cecelia lowered her eyes. "I guess I need to think about it. I just don't know."

The silence continued until they reached her front door. After saying good-night, she went inside and then directly to bed. Sleep eluded her for a full hour. Turning on the light by her bed, she took out her journal and read the entry she had made a week before, then began to write.

I said I wouldn't see Adam, but I had no choice. Now that it's done, I'm not sure I'm sorry.

CHAPTER THREE

IT WAS NEARLY A WEEK since he'd seen Cecelia. Adam leaned back in his swivel desk chair and stared at the maps and charts on the wall of his office without really seeing them. The past kept haunting him. What if he'd married Cecelia and they'd kept the baby?

He could still remember finding out that Cecelia was pregnant. It had been a blustery day in early spring when everything had been going his way. Then the phone call had come and he'd felt the cage doors closing around him. Initially he'd resigned himself to a wedding. But when her parents said they were too young, and he'd been given an out, Adam had taken it and run. For a while he'd had no regrets. When Cecelia's father sent the letter telling him the baby had been born, all he'd felt was relief that it was over.

Now he saw everything differently. What really mattered, although he couldn't see it at the time, was that Cecelia had given birth to a son—his son. That had been all that was on his mind when he had come back to Spokane. Then he'd seen Cecelia again. She'd matured into one hell of a woman. He let her image float through his mind, savoring it, and then he looked down again at the note he was holding in his hands.

"The roses arrived tonight," she had written, "just after I got home from work. I've put them in a vase on the hall table where we can all enjoy them. You should see them—they're absolutely lovely.''

Her response was rather formal but still basically what he'd hoped for when he'd sent the flowers. He'd wanted her to keep thinking about him. She'd simply signed the note "Cecelia." He read the last line one more time, trying to decide whether she was saying in an oblique way that she'd made up her mind to see him again.

Adam tilted the chair forward and dropped the note on his desk. He should have given her more time before he'd discussed their son. At least he'd had the good sense not to make a pitch for finding him. But, dammit, the baby was what was on his mind, and it was on hers too. There was a child out there somewhere, actually a young man by now. And wherever he was, he was part of them both.

Adam tapped his pencil rhythmically on the edge of his battleship-gray, government-issue desk, picturing Cecelia after the movie, with the white fur of her parka softly framing her face. He could still see traces of the girl he had known so long ago, but what attracted him now was the woman she'd become. When he had taken her hand while they were out walking, he had felt her vulnerability. And she had pulled her hand away because she knew he had. He began to shuffle through the pink memos and phone messages on his desk. He was going to call Cecelia. He wanted to see her again.

The intercom buzzed, and Adam answered it. "Colonel Lathrop has scheduled a meeting for 1600, sir."

"Did he give any indication of what it's about?"

"No, sir. But—" The young voice on the other end hesitated.

"Go ahead, sergeant," Adam said impatiently.

"It could be about the demonstration, sir."

"Demonstration?"

"Yes, sir. About two hundred students are marching outside the front gate, sir."

Adam groaned. "Thank you, sergeant," he muttered, checking his watch. He still could call Cecelia before the meeting and, knowing Lathrop, they'd be out of the office by five. That would leave plenty of time to go home, shower and change, and still pick up Cecelia at seven for dinner. If she would go. If he handled it right, he was betting she would. Adam picked up the phone.

"TELEPHONE FOR YOU, Cecelia," Jeannie called. The younger of the two sisters was sitting in the office in the rear of The Kangaroo Pouch, where she was nursing five-month-old Benjamin.

Cecelia groaned. She had a dripping paintbrush in one hand and a tuna sandwich in the other. It was Friday, the end of a very busy week, and she was fixing up a wicker cradle she'd bought at an auction. She did not want to stop for a phone call.

"Take a message and tell them I'll get back to them later," Cecelia said. "Unless it's Angela," she added. "I need to talk to her." After all that conversation at breakfast about a peace demonstration, and after meeting Danny Mitchell the other night, Cecelia wanted to know exactly what her oldest daughter was up to.

"Sorry to interrupt," Jeannie said as she came out of the office with Benjamin snuggled against one shoulder. "But there's someone on the phone who insists on talking to you personally." Cecelia's sister had a perplexed look on her freckled face. "Actually it's a man.

I tried to get him to tell me what he wanted, but he was very insistent.'' She patted Benjamin's back gently.

"Probably that salesman who's been bugging me," Cecelia muttered. "I told him last week we aren't interested in factory-made baby clothes." She laid the paintbrush across the top of the can and made her way around several baby carriages, past some tricycles and into the office where she picked up the telephone. "This is Cecelia Mahoney," she said briskly.

"Sorry to take you away from what you were doing." The caller didn't say who he was, but he didn't have to.

"Adam!" she exclaimed. Ever since the roses had arrived, she'd known he would phone, but she hadn't expected to speak to him at the shop. Not that it made any difference. She'd already decided what to do.

"I'm glad you liked the flowers," he continued.

"They are beautiful, Adam," she said, her tone guarded.

"I'd like to see you. How about having dinner with me tonight?"

Cecelia took a deep breath. "I don't think so, Adam."

"Well, if you're busy tonight, how about tomorrow?"

She'd have to be direct. "It isn't that I'm busy. I'm just not sure it's a good idea for us to see each other." Cecelia heard the hesitancy in her own voice and hoped he hadn't. The palm of her hand was damp against the phone, and her mouth was strangely dry.

"Look, Cecelia, I don't blame you for being annoyed that I showed up unannounced like I did," Adam countered. "It wasn't the best beginning."

"That's not the problem and you know it, Adam." Cecelia's voice faltered, but she went on, knowing that what she was doing would ultimately be best for everyone. "This can't be a beginning," she told him. "We ended the chapter twenty years ago. There's no place to go from here."

Adam didn't answer. Over the phone line, Cecelia heard a buzzer in the background, once, then again.

"Hold on a minute, Cecelia," he said, irritation in his voice. Moments later he was back. "Look, I'm late for a meeting, but I want you to think about this some more. I'm not willing to believe it's that simple. Besides, all I want is to take you to dinner. Is that so much to ask?"

"Adam, I've already told you—"

"I have to go, Cecelia. I'll stop by your house at seven and we can finish this conversation then."

"But Adam—" Cecelia stared at the phone until she heard the dial tone. Then she walked slowly into the shop.

"What's the matter?" asked Jeannie, who had tucked Benjamin into a carriage and taken over painting the cradle.

"Nothing, really." Cecelia rocked Benjamin's carriage gently. "At least nothing important."

"Bull!" Jeannie retorted. "You look like you're in a daze. Out with it. Who was on the phone?"

"Adam Campbell."

"Adam Campbell?" Jeannie repeated. "You mean the Adam Campbell who was a friend of Jim's? The one who was a POW in Viet Nam all those years?"

Cecelia looked over at Jeannie, startled by her sister's reaction. But of course that was how she would remember Adam. She didn't know the rest. No one did, except their parents. Her mother had taken the secret to her grave and Pop had never talked about the baby.

"The same Adam Campbell," Cecelia answered, forcing a half smile.

"So what did he say? Is he back in Spokane?"

"He's the new wing commander at Fairchild."

"That's absolutely wonderful!" Jeannie exclaimed. "Didn't you have a few dates with him?" She paused, wrinkling her forehead. Then her face brightened. "No, I remember now! You had a giant-sized crush on him for a while because I remember you crying a whole lot just after he left—right before that summer you spent at Aunt Nellie's."

"You've got a pretty good memory," Cecelia observed.

"Adam Campbell was a real hunk in those days. I wonder what he looks like now." Jeannie's bright blue eyes twinkled. "Maybe he'll take you out to dinner and you can find out."

"Funny, going out to dinner tonight is exactly what he suggested," Cecelia answered slowly.

Jeannie stopped painting and looked directly at her sister. "So why don't you sound happier about it? Is he married or something?"

"No."

"At least you got all the pertinent information in one phone call. I assume you're going?"

"Maybe...I don't know." Cecelia was tired of being pressured. The decision was hard enough as it was. "Look, Jeannie, I'm not in the market for a man— Adam Campbell or anyone else. My life is just fine the way it is. I don't need any complications."

Jeannie laughed and returned to her painting. "Been out of circulation so long you've got a case of the jitters," she diagnosed. "Don't worry about it. Look at

it as a free meal and a few hours with an old friend. Just
forget he's a man."

"Sure thing," Cecelia answered, knowing that even
if she could forget everything else, there was no way she
could ever forget Adam Campbell was a man.

"Hey, it's already after four." Jeannie stood up and
closed the paint can. "Why don't I close up the shop
and you can go home and get ready. Soak in the bathtub for a while—that'll make you feel better."

"I don't need to soak in the bathtub," Cecelia replied irritably. "Besides, I was hoping to hear from
Angela."

"Oh, I'm sorry. With all this talk about Adam
Campbell, I forgot to tell you she called while you were
out."

"And?"

"She said just to tell you she'd decided to go to the
demonstration after all and she'd either be home by
seven or she'd call you."

"Damn," Cecelia muttered.

"You didn't want her to go?"

"Not really. It's that antinuclear weapons demonstration she's been talking about for a week. I suppose
it won't do her any harm to walk around for a few hours
with a picket sign, but still—"

"Of course it won't," Jeannie said. "When I was in
college, I practically majored in demonstrations. Kids
nowadays are really missing out."

"I hope you're right." Cecelia smiled at her sister.
Jeannie's brand of wisdom was good for her. The five
years that separated them were just enough to help
Jeannie understand teenagers in a way she couldn't.

"Of course I'm right," Jeannie assured her. "Now
quit worrying about Angela and go home and take a

bath. And promise me you'll go to dinner with Adam Campbell and have a good time. After all, it's only dinner.''

"I suppose." That was the same thing Adam had said. *Just dinner.* She thought about Adam for a moment, not about the boy but about Colonel Adam Campbell who'd come to see her that snowy evening a week before. Maybe when she got to know him better the past would fade. Maybe. She would go to dinner, Cecelia decided, aware of the smile on her lips as she went to get her coat. If it didn't work out, she'd say no to him next time. Or the next.

AS HE PULLED HIS CAR off to the side of the highway, Danny Mitchell glanced in the rearview mirror and watched the string of cars behind him follow his head. Anticipation surged through him. "This is our biggest demonstration yet," he announced to the six students wedged into his beat-up Ford. "We'll get some attention today."

"What do we do next?" Angela asked him as the car doors opened.

"Get the signs out of the trunk and get going," he told her. "The air force base is right up the road."

Behind them more cars were pulling in, all of them packed with protestors. They were a noisy, festive bunch, gathering in small clusters on the highway so that the sparse traffic had to pull off onto the shoulder to pass. Danny handed out signs and black arm bands and then took several small packets out of the car trunk and distributed them to the drivers of the cars just behind him. The group was hyped just enough, he decided as he made his way through the milling crowd. This time they were going to make a splash. He grinned at the pun. If everything went as planned, they'd be home just in time to watch themselves on the evening news.

"Everybody stay together," someone shouted, and the motley procession began to move forward.

"No nukes, no nukes." Someone began the loud chant and others picked it up like a football crowd cheering the team. Danny knew that many of them didn't have any deep commitment to the cause, but that didn't matter. They were bodies, and the more of them there were, the more impact they'd have. In reality he wasn't even sure there were any nuclear weapons at Fairchild, but that didn't matter, either. Nuclear weapons were part of the insanity of the whole military establishment, and as long as they existed anywhere, the fight against them had to go on.

"This is really exciting," Angela said, falling in step beside Danny. "I didn't know there would be so many people."

"Your first demonstration?" He could tell by her face, enthusiastic but apprehensive, that she wasn't sure of herself.

"I almost went once last year and then I didn't." She said it almost like an apology.

"You should have. Everybody should. If we don't do something, we're not going to have any world left to do it in."

Angela frowned. "But what about having nuclear weapons as a deterrent? I've read—"

"Don't tell me you're letting them suck you in," Danny scoffed. "Even if nobody ever dropped a bomb, the nuclear waste is going to poison the environment until the world isn't worth living in."

"I guess." Angela hesitated as they approached the front gate of Fairchild. "What do we do now?"

"Stay together and march. The leaders all have black arm bands. Just do what they tell you."

Several airmen closed and locked the front gate as the group approached. The demonstration leaders yelled epithets and encouraged the marchers to chant louder. As Danny cut back into the crowd, he saw Angela catch up with two other girls she seemed to know. She was a good friend, but she was naive as hell and however much he worked on her, she'd probably never develop a real commitment. At least she was concerned and she was there. That was what counted. When the news teams arrived, reporters were going to find exactly what they'd been promised.

ADAM CHECKED THE CLOCK. Almost six already, and Lathrop was still going strong. Adam had heard all he wanted to hear about contingency plans and potential threats to national security. In his opinion, that group marching outside in the snow was nothing but a bunch of misdirected teenagers. If everyone simply ignored them, they'd go back to college where they belonged. A few hours with a history book might give them a little perspective, he thought irritably.

"Now, gentlemen, does anyone have any pressing business off base tonight?" Colonel Lathrop asked the group.

Adam frowned. "Yes, as a matter of fact, I do."

"If you can put it off, I'd recommend it. Anyone going off base could incite that mob and create an incident. If you must leave, be prepared to come back to wing headquarters tonight in case this demonstration turns into a security problem. Staff cars are available for your use.''

Adam watched Lathrop pick up a small, black, two-way radio commonly called a ''brick'' because of its characteristic size and shape. The radio could summon any commanding officer at any moment, which was one reason it was often referred to as ''that damn brick,'' especially in the bedroom.

''Don't forget to have your bricks with you at all times,'' Lathrop directed. ''That's all, gentlemen.''

Adam stood up, but Colonel Lathrop's voice stopped him.

''Colonel Campbell, may I see you for a minute?''

Adam waited until the others had left the room. As wing commander and base commander respectively, he and George Lathrop scrupulously observed military formality whenever they were on duty. But they'd been friends since they were at the academy together, and in private the walls came down.

''You got time for a drink, Adam?'' Lathrop asked after the office door was shut.

''Not tonight,'' Adam told him. ''I'm supposed to be somewhere by seven and I'd like to get cleaned up first.''

''Hot date?''

''Not exactly. Just a girl—actually, a woman I used to know. She's not a girl anymore.''

Lathrop stroked the spreading bald spot on the back of his head. ''Yeah, I guess we're all grown up. Sometimes I think how nice it would be if we could go back. I can always see so much more clearly looking back.''

''That's true,'' Adam agreed. He waited, somewhat impatiently, for Lathrop to work his way around to whatever was on his mind.

"Any way to postpone this date? This situation out at the front gate doesn't look good."

Adam chuckled. "Come on, George, those are just college kids out there. Some professor got them all stirred up after that nuclear reactor scare. Hell, half of them are just doing it for a lark—they probably don't even know why they've come."

"From what I hear," Lathrop answered, "there's a hard core of them ripe for a confrontation. The scuttlebutt is they've called the media and they're hoping a TV crew will show up. If it does, you can bet they'll be looking for some way to get on the air."

Adam wasn't about to give up his date with Cecelia for a bunch of demonstrators. "I can't see us hiding in headquarters like prisoners just because some fool kids are walking around outside the gate with picket signs."

"No," Lathrop agreed, "neither can I. That's why I didn't close the base. Hell, I'll get to you on the brick if it's necessary."

"I'm sure you will, George." Adam picked up his radio. A squawking brick wasn't exactly what he had in mind as a dinner companion.

Adam's stride was brisk as he left Colonel Lathrop's office and headed for his staff car. He pulled his overcoat up around his neck and put on his fur-lined gloves. On top of everything else, those demonstrators had to be crazy, he thought. They were freezing their butts off. He checked his watch, noting it was almost seven. That left no time to shower and change out of his uniform. He thought about stopping to call Cecelia to tell her he'd be late but rejected the idea. Better he should avoid a phone call. He didn't need to give her another opportunity to say no.

The chants of the demonstrators grew louder as
Adam drove his staff car along the snow-packed road
toward the main gate. Cutting his headlights, he slowly
approached the guardhouse, noting the two Air Force
police cars parked nearby. Part of George Lathrop's
added security, no doubt.

Instead of waving him on through, the guard at the
gate held up his hand, and Adam rolled down his window. "We have been instructed to warn anyone who
leaves the base that he is doing so at his own risk, Colonel," the guard informed him.

"I know, I know," Adam answered. "Open the gate,
airman."

"We have been further instructed to say that the base
commander discourages all personnel from going off
base tonight, sir."

Adam looked at the airman's face. He wasn't much
older than the demonstrators outside, maybe younger
than most of them, but he could teach them a thing or
two about responsibility. "I've already talked to Colonel Lathrop," he said more patiently. "And when I see
him again, I'll tell him you did your best. Now wave me
through."

"Yes, sir." His face expressionless, the airman saluted sharply, then stepped back into the gatehouse and
picked up his walkie-talkie.

Aware of the activity inside the fence, the demonstrators' voices grew louder. "No more nukes, no more
nukes," they chanted, walking back and forth with their
picket signs.

As the gate swung slowly open, Adam turned his
headlights back on, spotlighting the milling bodies
outside. The reports had said there were about two
hundred demonstrators. Adam decided that estimate

was conservative. He also saw several policemen, some with their nightsticks drawn. The empty echo of their bullhorns warned the demonstrators to keep the road clear.

Maybe George Lathrop had been right, he thought, but it was too late now. The best thing to do was to start driving and keep driving, very slowly, and hope some idiot didn't decide to throw himself on the road in front of the car.

As soon as he was outside the fence, the gate closed behind him. Mobs of demonstrators swarmed along the road on both sides of the car, yelling and waving hand-lettered signs, reading Peace in our Lifetime, Nukes Suck, War is a Bomb. When his headlights hit them, he could see their faces clearly. Some looked excited, a few were laughing, others appeared serious, even angry. But they were kids, he reminded himself, just kids who needed somebody to take them by the collar and give them a good, hard shake.

Adam was nearing the main highway when he caught the eye of one demonstrator with shaggy blond hair and a black band tied around his head. The boy stared directly at him, his eyes hard and hostile. Instinctively Adam knew the boy was one of the ringleaders. Tightening his hands on the steering wheel, he kept driving, his eyes still locked with the demonstrator's.

Adam's arrival was just what Danny had been waiting for. He couldn't see the man's face very well behind the glare of the headlights, but he'd caught a glimpse of the officer's uniform. Danny's eyes narrowed. Only moments before, Danny had seen the TV van unloading. There'd been just about enough time for the cameraman to get set up. Danny reached into the package secured inside his jacket.

Adam saw the boy's arm rise slowly, fingers knotted in a fist, poised for action. He kept driving, his senses on edge. When his car pulled within a few feet of the boy, Adam ducked instinctively. An egg splattered on the front windshield, followed rapidly by another and then another, until the glass was nearly covered with a slimy, spreading mass. As Adam turned on the windshield washer he saw the police move in, nightsticks raised. He blasted his horn and kept on driving, inching his way onto the main road and free-dom.

"Rotten kids," he muttered, his vision blurred by the freezing egg smeared across the windshield. Whatever the police did to them was no more than they deserved.

THE FRONT PORCH LIGHT was on as Adam pulled up in front of Cecelia's house. His anger had subsided slightly, but only slightly. His windshield was clean, but his car was still splattered with patches of frozen egg. Worse than that, he was nearly a hour late because of a bunch of troublemakers. As he shut off the engine, he saw a snowman on Cecelia's front lawn, complete with matching red scarf and a hat and a wide black smile. Probably Sean and Kevin's work, he decided as he walked up the sidewalk. They were the kind of kids who were going to grow up with better things to do than yell obscenities and throw eggs.

Even before he rang the doorbell, Adam heard Bingo barking inside. When Cecelia answered the door, the dog danced happily, wagging his tail. But Adam saw only the woman. Her eyes were welcoming and he knew she'd been waiting for him. Her dark hair waved softly back, accentuating her fair skin which seemed to have escaped any indications of age except for some fine lines by her eyes that disappeared when she smiled.

"You look beautiful, Cecelia," he said, stepping inside. "I'm sorry I'm late." His eyes moved from the diamond pendant at her throat to her deep-blue dress that draped gently across her breasts and flared out from her slender waist. "What made you change your mind about dinner?"

Cecelia smiled. "I thought about what you said and realized you're right. It's only dinner. That can't be too dangerous." But as she looked at him, she wasn't so sure. Seeing Adam in uniform brought back memories and some of the old feelings along with them. She could still remember exactly how she'd felt the first time he'd appeared proudly at their front door to show off his new Air Force Academy uniform. That had been long before he'd even noticed she was alive. But she certainly had noticed him. He was so handsome and so mature. She'd hated herself for being a gawky kid, but that hadn't kept her from dreaming.

"I thought we'd try a little country inn about twenty miles from here," Adam said. "The food is supposed to be excellent." More important, he'd been told the atmosphere was intimate, the dance floor was very small and the music was slow.

"That sounds wonderful, Adam." Cecelia started to get her coat and then remembered the roses. She turned toward the bouquet on the hall table. "Aren't they beautiful?"

"They are," Adam agreed, giving the flowers a cursory glance. He was studying her face. This woman had borne his son and yet he barely knew her. Or did he? People didn't really change very much, at least not inside. "I wish I'd sent the roses before I came the first time."

"And have them arrive in the middle of the flood?" Cecelia asked lightly.

Adam laughed, and all at once he wanted to take her in his arms and hold her. "The house is awfully quiet." He looked around. "Where is everyone?"

"They've all gone out. It's only Bingo and me." Although Adam barely moved, she knew what he was thinking, maybe because she was thinking the same thing. "But not for much longer," she added quickly as she bent to pat Bingo. "Angela should be home at any minute. Actually I expected her before now."

When she stood up, Adam was beside her, his hands firm on her shoulders as he turned her toward him. "Cecelia, as long as we have a moment alone—"

He was going to kiss her. Even if she couldn't have seen his face or felt the warm pressure of his hands, she'd have known. She met his eyes, and what passed between them transcended reason.

"I've been wanting to do this ever since I saw you last week—" At first he'd been afraid she might pull away, but now he knew she wouldn't. Her lips were as warm and sweet as he'd thought they'd be. What he hadn't realized was how quickly their touch would make him want more. It was as though kissing her had released all the emotion he'd denied from the moment he'd learned she was married. He pressed his cheek against hers and felt her tremble. He'd been right. People didn't change, and relationships left unfinished didn't die.

"Maybe we'd better go," he said, fighting the urge to kiss her again.

"Yes, I suppose we had." Cecelia's voice wavered. *"Just dinner—forget he's a man,"* Jeannie had told her.

And now she was having a hard time thinking about anything else. "I'll get my coat," she said, slowly moving away from him.

As Adam held her coat for her, the grandfather clock chimed eight. Angela was an hour late. Cecelia hoped Jeannie's advice on demonstrations was more accurate that what she'd said about Adam. Of course Angela was no longer a child . . . She noticed Adam picking up a black box from the table near the roses. "What's that?" she asked curiously.

"That's my brick. Whenever we have a problem out at the base, I have to be available. And tonight we have a problem."

Cecelia buttoned her coat, still half thinking about Angela. "I hope it's nothing serious."

"Just a bunch of obnoxious kids walking around with picket signs." Adam opened the door. "With any luck, the police will give them what's coming to them."

The cold blast of air through the open door was nothing compared to the chill that ran through Cecelia. She didn't move. "Adam, are they college kids demonstrating against nuclear weapons?"

Cecelia's face was suddenly pale. She obviously knew about the demonstration. Adam closed the door. "Don't tell me Angela is involved in this thing?"

"I'm afraid so," Cecelia answered slowly.

"Why the hell did you let her get mixed up in a demonstration?"

Cecelia tensed. "Angela is eighteen years old. Besides, Jeannie said demonstrations are a good experience."

Adam thought about the youth pelting his car with eggs. "Jeannie doesn't know what she's talking about.

Take off your coat and I'll phone headquarters and see what's going on."

"You think there are real problems?" Even more apprehensive than before, Cecelia unbuttoned her coat.

Adam picked up the phone. "That's what I'm about to find out."

Cecelia listened as Adam talked to George Lathrop, but his responses were mostly one syllable and his expression gave nothing away.

"There's something going on that you're not telling me," Cecelia said when he hung up. "Exactly what has happened?"

Adam considered what to say to her. If he told her the truth, dinner was probably out of the question. But he really didn't have much choice. "Lathrop says the thing broke up after the TV cameras left. The kids were throwing eggs—the police were involved. Lathrop doesn't know whether they took some of the kids down to the station or simply sent them home."

Cecelia stared at him. "You mean Angela might be in jail?"

"Possibly, but unlikely. Was she one of the ringleaders?"

"Of course not...well, at least I don't think so." Cecelia tried to remember exactly what Angela had said about the demonstration. Then she thought about Danny Mitchell. "She has a friend who was pretty heavily involved, but I think Angela was just along for the ride."

"Then she's probably fine," Adam said reassuringly. Maybe the evening wasn't lost after all.

"Adam—" Cecelia hesitated. "Would you mind terribly if we didn't go out tonight? I could fix us something here."

"You're worried about her, aren't you?"

"Yes, I am worried," Cecelia admitted.

Adam put his arm around her shoulders, and it was comforting having him there to share her problem. So often she had to handle things alone. "Do you think if we called the police, they could tell us anything?"

"Probably not. Frankly, for the moment, the best thing to do is wait and see if she comes home."

Cecelia nodded. "When they're eighteen, they're almost more difficult than when they were ten. At least when they're little you have some control."

Adam looked at her thoughtfully. "You realize, Cecelia, that you were eighteen when—"

"Yes, Adam," she interrupted. "I remember being eighteen, and I'd really rather not talk about it."

"Sorry I brought it up." Maybe her own mistake was part of the reason she was so protective of her oldest daughter, Adam realized. She'd been pregnant at Angela's age.

"I'm willing to give Angela an hour, and then we call the police," Cecelia said. "Now let's see what we can find for dinner." She paused, thinking over the contents of the refrigerator. "Sean and Kevin ate the spaghetti, but there should be eggs and there's always peanut butter."

Adam followed Cecelia into the kitchen with Bingo at their heels. He watched the gentle sway of her hips, as he walked behind her, and imagined sipping wine with her in a candlelit restaurant and dancing long into the night. "Peanut butter," he muttered to himself. "Damn that demonstration."

CHAPTER FOUR

DANNY FELT GOOD. The demonstration had been a success, better than he'd ever dreamed. As his last two passengers climbed out of the back seat of the Ford and slammed the door, Danny turned to Angela with a victorious grin. "We did it!" he exclaimed. "We're on a roll. You want to grab a sandwich and watch us on the news at my house?"

"Thanks, but I don't think so, Danny," Angela answered. "I've got to get home."

Disappointed, he gunned the engine and pulled away from the curb. "You realize you're missing good times. We really scored tonight. We're almost guaranteed a spot on the local news, and if it's a slow night, we might even get a shot at the network." He glanced at Angela, not sure why she wasn't more impressed. "Don't you understand what that means?"

"I guess not," Angela answered slowly. "I thought we were marching to protest nuclear weapons at Fairchild, not to get on television."

Danny sighed and turned down the radio that was blaring hard rock. She really didn't have the big picture. "The name of the game is publicity, Angela. The more attention we get, the more effective we'll be."

"But did you have to do it by throwing eggs?" she shot back. "You'd obviously planned it, but you didn't bother to mention that part."

So that was the problem. They pulled up to a red light and Danny turned toward her. "Look, Angela, we didn't hurt anybody. Organizing a demonstration is like staging a play. You have to build up to a climax."

Angela shook her head. "I still don't like it. With the police swinging nightsticks, somebody could have been hurt."

"But no one was," Danny pointed out. The light changed and Danny turned down Angela's street. "It's all relative, anyway. Nuclear bombs, or even nuclear waste can destroy the whole world."

"There's no excuse for breaking the law."

Danny pulled the Ford in front of the Mahoney house. "Does that mean you won't work with us anymore?"

Angela hesitated. "No, I still believe in what we're doing, but if demonstrating means getting mixed up with the police, count me out."

"You disappoint me, Angela," Danny said as they got out of the car. "I thought you had more guts."

"I'm just as gutsy as you are, Danny Mitchell," she said, turning to face him. "But there's a right way and a wrong way to do things. I'm not into breaking the law."

Danny shrugged. "Suit yourself." He fell in step with her. "You're not mad?"

"No, I'm not mad. Come on in for a minute and I'll give you the flyers I picked up at the printer yesterday."

BINGO STREAKED past Cecelia's feet barking loudly. Relief surged through her as she heard the front door open. That had to be Angela. At least she wasn't in jail. Cecelia was certain everything was all right, she intended to have some stern words with her oldest daughter.

"Excuse me, Adam," she said as she stuck the knife squarely in the center of the peanut butter. "I'll take care of this as quickly as possible."

Cecelia arrived in the front hall just as Angela walked in. The girl's eyes glistened with excitement and her cheeks were red and chapped from the cold. She had obviously been having a good time. "Hi, Mom, I'm home," she announced.

Cecelia's relief suddenly turned into irritation. All her worrying had obviously been unnecessary. "I thought you were going to be back two hours ago," she said, her tone making the statement an accusation. "Where have you been?"

Angela stared at her. "So what's wrong? It isn't even nine o'clock."

"That's not the point. Adam said there were problems with the demonstration and the police intervened."

"It wasn't that big a deal. Nobody got hurt or anything. Anyway, you remember Danny, don't you?"

"Hello, Mrs. Mahoney," Danny said politely, stepping out from behind the girl.

Cecelia had been so focused on Angela that she hadn't even noticed Danny. He looked about the same as the last time she'd met him. He was still wearing the earring and scruffy clothes, but this time he also had a black band around his arm. She realized the lecture she'd been about to give to Angela would have to wait. "Hello, Danny. I assume you were at the demonstration, too?"

"He was one of the organizers." Angela kicked off her snowy boots. "He needs some flyers I have upstairs on my desk."

Left alone with the boy, who appeared to be about Angela's age or a little older, Cecelia looked him over more carefully. He fit the classic image of a rebellious kid almost perfectly. "I understand the demonstration got a little out of hand," Cecelia commented.

"Nothing serious," Danny answered.

"But weren't the police involved?" she asked. If he was one of the organizers, he was probably also one of the troublemakers. Maybe she should have Adam talk to him...on the other hand, maybe it was better to keep them as far apart as possible.

"The police only intervened once, and that was just for a few minutes," Danny explained. "Actually it worked out just right," he added. "Nobody got hurt, and we'll still get good news coverage." He leaned down and patted Bingo, who was wagging his tail vigorously.

Cecelia wondered how to respond. As Danny talked, she kept watching his warm, brown and intelligent eyes. She didn't want to get into a debate with him, but she suspected that beneath the surface bravado lay a very interesting young man.

"Here are the flyers, Danny." Angela said as she hurried back down the stairs. "Mary Beth stacked some books on them and I thought they were gone."

Danny took the papers and stuffed them inside his worn denim jacket. "Thanks a lot, Angela. Don't forget to watch the news tonight to see what kind of coverage the demonstration got." He pushed open the storm door and headed down the walk toward his beat-up Ford.

"I'm not sure I like his attitude about demonstrations," Cecelia observed when he was gone. "He seems to think causing trouble is the way to get attention."

Angela shook her head. "You worry too much, Mom. You have to get to know Danny to understand. He's really unique."

Cecelia sighed. "Yes, I imagine he is."

"Hey, what's for dinner?" Angela asked as she hung her jacket on a hook. "I'm starved!"

"Well, the boys ate all the spaghetti...."

"But I know where you can find two perfectly good peanut butter sandwiches," Adam said, appearing behind her. "Your mother and I were just leaving."

"And I get to stay home and eat peanut butter," Angela complained.

"You could have tomato soup instead," Cecelia added without sympathy.

Adam helped Cecelia with her coat, pulled on his own and picked up his brick from the hall table. "It's kind of late to drive all the way to the inn, but there's a good barbecue place out by the base."

"That sounds fine," Cecelia replied.

"It sure does," Angela agreed.

"You've been out," Cecelia reminded her daughter. "Now it's our turn."

As Adam closed the door behind them, Cecelia drank in the chill air and with it an overpowering sense of freedom. In the darkness, the snow glistened pure white, and icicles shimmered along rooftops across the street. As they walked down the front sidewalk together, Adam took her hand, and Cecelia felt very close to him. "You can't imagine how much easier it is to have someone share the worrying," she said softly as

Adam opened the car door for her. "Sometimes it's very hard to be a mother."

He looked down and saw her eyes sparkling in the glow of the street light. "I imagine it is. But remember, being a mother is only one of your roles," he answered. With his fingertips he touched her cool, smooth cheek. "Don't forget you're also a woman."

Cecelia met his eyes. They were dark and searching, and a thousand thoughts converged as she felt him lower his mouth to hers. His lips were smooth and warm, and instinctively she moved closer to him, wrapping her arms around his neck. For a few endless moments she stopped thinking entirely, aware only of his hands in her hair, his chest broad and hard against her breasts and his mouth moving ever so slightly in rhythm with hers.

Only their lips had met and yet Cecelia's whole body quivered in the aftershock of his kiss. Even as he let her go, she sensed an almost tangible bond between them. Something more was happening than just a casual dinner with an old friend. She could feel it, and she was certain Adam could too.

THE WAITRESS in the Smoky Pit Restaurant seated them in a corner booth beneath a display of branding irons hanging on the white stucco wall. The atmosphere was rustic, with rough-hewn beams across the ceiling and deep red carpet accenting dark wood. Adam and Cecelia sank comfortably into the deeply padded seats.

Adam ordered them each a glass of wine. He was sorry to have lost the intimacy of the inn, but the casual, easy atmosphere of the Smoky Pit had its advantages. As if by unspoken agreement, they talked casually, their words punctuated with laughter, while they consumed an entire slab of barbecued ribs.

"I don't know how we found time for all the things we did when we were growing up," Cecelia said as the waitress brought a pot of coffee. "There seemed to be endless hours then, but now..."

"Now there are more responsibilities." Adam put his hands behind his head and leaned back. "I suppose there's a point in all our lives where we have to suddenly grow up, and the clock starts moving at a different rate."

Cecelia didn't answer. She knew exactly when she'd grown up. It was the moment the nurse took her first baby from her arms. But Adam wouldn't know about that. By the time she had delivered the baby, he had been gone for months. "Maybe we do all have a turning point," she finally said. "Do you remember yours, Adam?"

His eyes were dark, his jaw muscles tight, but his voice strangely normal as he answered her. "My turning point was when I punched out of my F-4 over North Viet Nam."

"I thought about you so much, Adam. We heard these stories..."

"They were probably all true." Adam leaned forward, watching her face carefully. He seldom discussed Viet Nam. He didn't even like to hear other people talk about the war because their experiences usually made him break out in a cold sweat. But somehow he had to make Cecelia understand what he wanted from her and why it was so important. Telling her what had happened to him in Viet Nam was probably where he had to begin.

Thoughtfully, he ran his fingers along the fine white scar on his cheek. "That day I was shot down began like any other day. We were all down on the flight line doing our preflight check, hot as hell and swatting at the mosquitoes. I swear those damn things were as big as buzzards. Never left us alone. Then we saw a couple of choppers coming in and knew they were loaded with beer. Walt Jankowsky—he was my weapons systems operator—and I started arguing about whose turn it was to pick up the beer when we got back. That was the kind of stuff we talked about, never about the mission until it was over."

"You weren't afraid?" Cecelia asked, watching him intently.

"Scared as hell, sometimes, but we never admitted it. That's why we focused on the beer."

Cecelia nodded. She knew what kind of fear that was, like the fear that had gripped her when she'd gone into labor the first time and she was alone. She'd never screamed or cried. All the terror had been locked inside.

"We took off out of Da Nang, flying formation like always, and at first everything was routine," Adam continued. "We took some small-arms flack, but that was normal. We were zeroing in on our first attack point south of Hanoi when we started seeing some SAM missiles. That was a little more serious, but nothing we hadn't dealt with before. Except sometimes they can sneak up on you...."

Cecelia waited silently for Adam to continue. He'd chosen to share a private part of himself with her, and she wondered why.

"Then my left wingman came on the radio. 'SAM, five o'clock.' That's the last thing I ever heard him say.

I felt the hit back in the tail and the plane pitched over. I yanked the control stick to bring the nose back up, but the damn stick was frozen solid. That's when I knew the hydraulics were gone and I was going down. My life stopped. Time stopped. That was the turning point. Afterward nothing mattered but survival.''

Adam picked up the coffeepot the waitress had left on the table and filled his cup. He seemed almost oblivious to Cecelia.

"First I looked out the cockpit window. I saw a clearing down below us. That was the worst place to go down, over a clearing, because it usually meant a village where you wouldn't have a chance of getting out alive. There were some mountains ahead of us, and that would have been a better option, but by then our whole tail section was on fire. There was no way to make it any farther, so I reached for the ejection handle.

"The next thing I remember my chute was open and I was hanging there in the sky, watching another F-4 make a final pass, getting a fix on our location. Then I looked for the other chute—Walt's chute—but it wasn't there. When I saw our plane slam into the side of a mountain in a ball of fire I knew he never got out." Adam swallowed hard. "Walt was one of the best. Had a wife and two kids waiting for him back home."

Adam leaned forward and shook his head. "You know, Cecelia, it was the craziest thing. Unreal. I felt detached, almost like I was watching one of those late night World War II flicks. I kept thinking it couldn't be happening to me. Not to Campbell, the hottest fighter pilot in the squadron." Again Adam ran his fingers over the scar on his cheek. "But it was. And there wasn't a damn thing I could do about it."

Cecelia's eyes traveled over the rows of commendation ribbons and combat decorations above the left pocket of Adam's blue uniform jacket, grim reminders of the reality of war. She waited for him to go on.

"I hit the ground right at the edge of the village and popped my chute latches. For a minute I thought if I ran fast enough I might get away into the jungle. But I hadn't taken two steps when they were all over me, screaming in Vietnamese, grabbing my supplies, tearing off my flight suit. They took my dog tags, smashed my contact radio. I never even got the lousy antenna up. The guy who grabbed my watch put it on right away. He must have been wearing half a dozen others, all gold and silver. That's when it hit me, when I saw those watches and realized they all came off guys like me, guys who weren't around anymore."

Cecelia closed her eyes.

"They'd probably have killed me if a couple of North Vietnamese soldiers hadn't shown up and heaved me into the back of an old pickup truck." He stopped to take a long drink of coffee. "I didn't know the half of it then. That truck turned out to be my own private taxi to the Hanoi Hilton."

"Prison camp?"

"Right." His tone turned sarcastic. "The accommodations weren't bad. Private room, if you didn't mind the dark and the leg irons. Wooden platform for a bed. Not very comfortable, but you got used to it. The food got kind of monotonous, though. Rice, not much of it, but on a real good day it was spiced up with some fish-head broth. The toilet didn't work too well, probably because it was nothing but a can and tended to overflow. Lots of rats and cockroaches for company, though. And after a while I learned the code so I could tap on the wall and talk to other prisoners—''

"Adam, stop!" Cecelia couldn't bear to see him reliving his agony. "You survived," she said softly. "You came home. That's all that matters."

"I survived because I was worth more to the North Vietnamese alive than dead. It was that simple. But sometimes survival isn't enough." He leaned forward, meeting her eyes. "Conditions for POW's were beyond description, Cecelia. Worse than anything you can imagine. We all came back home with problems. Not just broken bones and internal injuries, but other things, too, like parasites, malnutrition, vitamin deficiencies. You name it. We had it. The human body, even in peak condition, can only withstand so much."

Suddenly Cecelia understood there was a point to his story. "What are you trying to tell me, Adam?"

"The doctors said it was probably the vitamin deficiency that finally got to me, but hell, it doesn't matter what it was. The result was the same."

He looked at Cecelia and she saw the pain in his eyes. She held her breath.

"I'm sterile, Cecelia."

"Sterile?" The word hung between them.

He paused, watching her face until he was sure his meaning had sunk in. "Yes, Cecelia, sterile. That was my going-away present from Hanoi. I'll never father another child."

"No," Cecelia whispered hoarsely. She heard the clank of silverware as a waitress cleared a nearby table. A telephone rang somewhere in the distance. The small, mundane noises penetrated her consciousness as she fought against what Adam was telling her, while knowing deep inside that she couldn't escape the truth. Nor could he.

As Adam watched her, he knew the time had come to tell her why he had come back to Spokane. Now she would finally be able to understand what he wanted from her. "I told you all this for a reason," he explained quietly. "Now that you know, maybe you'll be willing to help me."

He took her hand and while his touch warmed her, his voice conveyed a sense of foreboding.

"The reason I came back, Cecelia, is because I want to find our son."

"You want to find our son?" Cecelia couldn't believe what he was saying.

"Yes, and I figured this would be the logical place to start."

Cecelia stared at him, feeling frightened and betrayed. "No!" she cried. The past came rushing back, overwhelming her, threatening to shatter everything. She jerked her hand away from Adam. "No," she repeated. "Dear God, no!"

"Cecelia, please listen to me. I look around at the young airmen and I realize any one of them could be my son. I see kids on the street that look a little like you or like me, and I wonder. I have only one child, Cecelia, and there won't be any more. Try to understand."

"No, Adam, *you* try to understand. I'm sorry about everything that's happened to you, but nothing we do now is going to change any of that. We made a choice— good or bad, we gave up our baby for adoption, and we can't go back. My whole life is built on that choice. Nobody knows about the baby except you and Pop and me. We're not going to change that."

Adam was silent while the waitress poured fresh coffee. He wasn't getting through to Cecelia. He tried again. "My situation is different from yours. You have five other children. I have no one. My parents are dead. I have no brothers and sisters. Can you deny me the right to know my only son?"

Cecelia leaned across the table and looked directly into Adam's eyes. "You have no idea what you're asking. In addition to what it would do to me, finding our son could be the most painful experience you've ever had. He could hate you for forcing your way into his life. Let it alone, Adam."

"Don't you think I've considered all that? Whatever the consequences, all I want is a chance to know my son. Is that asking too much?"

"Yes," Cecelia replied. "That's asking too much. I won't help you, even if I could. It's wrong, wrong for you, for me, for him, for everyone. It would be a tragic mistake." She slid out of the booth and reached for her coat. "Now please take me home. I can't talk about this anymore."

Wordlessly, Adam stood up and pulled on his topcoat. He realized that, at least for the moment, there was nothing more to be said.

The ride home was silent and uncomfortable. As he pulled the Bronco in front of Cecelia's house, Adam turned to find her staring straight ahead. "Do you wish I hadn't come back?" he asked as he switched off the engine.

Cecelia studied him for several seconds before she answered. "Yes, Adam, right now that's exactly what I wish." She opened her car door and walked alone into the darkened house. Her eyes filled with tears when she wrote in her journal that night.

Adam wants to find our son. I'm so afraid. I can't let him do it.

THE MORNING AFTER the antinuclear demonstration Danny's mother was already in the kitchen when he came down for breakfast.

"Morning, Mom." He ran his fingers through his rumpled hair.

"You really ought to get your hair cut, Danny." Bernice Mitchell took a sip of her coffee and continued reading the newspaper.

"Don't start. It's too early in the morning for an argument. All I want to do is grab some breakfast and get to my eight-o'clock class on time." He opened the refrigerator and took out the milk. Ever since his father died she had been on him constantly. His hair, his clothes, his friends. Nothing suited her. He poured himself a generous bowl of cereal, topped it with milk and sat down at the table. "Are you through with the front section of the paper?" he asked.

"If you're wondering whether your demonstration made the front page, it did." His mother handed him the paper.

Quickly Danny skimmed the story and took a look at the picture. He was right in the center of a group of protesting college students, arm raised to throw an egg. Pleased, he broke into a grin. "Hey, this ought to shake a few of those colonels off their butts, don't you think, Mom?"

"Your activities may do more than that," Bernice responded tersely. "I watched the late news on TV last night in my bedroom. I don't like all these antinuclear activities you're involved in, Danny. You're going to wind up in jail—right on your butt—if I may borrow your terminology.''

Danny shrugged. ''No big deal. A few hours locked up would be good publicity.'' He shoveled another spoonful of cereal into his mouth.

His mother watched him silently for a moment. ''Don't eat so fast. You'll get gas.''

''Geez, Mom! Can't I do anything right?'' Deliberately he gulped down several more huge bites of cereal. ''I have a right to protest something I think is wrong. Nuclear weapons stink. They're immoral. If we don't get rid of them, some imbecile is going to blow us all off the face of the earth one of these days. Is that what you want to happen?''

''Of course not, Danny, but—''

''Then get off my back and let me do the job I have to do.''

''Your father never would have allowed this to go on....''

''Dad would be proud of what I'm doing. He always stood up for what he believed was right.''

''But he was never violent in his protest. He wouldn't like these demonstrations, Danny. If he were alive—''

''Yeah, well Dad's not alive. He's dead, as dead as they come.'' Danny shoved his chair back and came to his feet.

''Please, Danny.'' Bernice put her hand on his arm. ''I know how much you miss him. I know how hard it is for you without a father. You've changed so much since he died. You're so angry all the time, and I'm worried about you. Please, won't you try—''

Danny shook off her hand and pulled on his ragged down-filled vest. ''I am trying, Mom. I'm doing the best I can.'' He grabbed his books from the kitchen counter and turned toward the back door. Then, catching a glimpse of the hurt in his mother's faded blue eyes, he paused for a moment and studied her more carefully. For the first time he realized she looked old. She didn't stand as straight as she used to, and her face was gray and drawn. Now that he thought about it, her cough was worse, too. Sometimes, when he couldn't sleep at night, he heard her rummaging in the nightstand for her heart medicine. Suddenly an awareness shot through him. One day his mother was going to die, too. He reached out and squeezed her shoulder gently. "Don't worry about me, Mom. I'm fine. Danny Mitchell can take care of himself." As he strode toward his car he tried to ignore the uneasy feeling in the pit of his stomach.

THE MARCH WIND had turned bitter, blowing away any warmth from the sun that appeared only intermittently between dense, gray clouds. Water ran steadily along the street curbs as mounds of dingy snow melted, refroze during the night and melted again the next day. The nebulous time of year, Cecelia thought as she opened the front door of The Kangaroo Pouch. The beauty of winter was gone, but the promise of spring was still too remote to seem a possibility.

"Did I get any calls?" she asked Jeannie as she hung up her coat.

"If you mean did Adam Campbell call—no, not today," Jeannie answered. She picked up Benjamin from the crib and sat down with him in the bentwood rocker. "You've had me tell him you were busy so many times that he's probably given up."

"I didn't ask about Adam." Cecelia wished her sister weren't so perceptive. She watched Benjamin squirm down into the crook of his mother's arm and nuzzle hungrily at her breast. Jeannie settled back in the chair and within moments the baby's fussing was replaced by rhythmic sucking broken only by gentle cooing sounds. She had seen Jeannie nurse the baby a hundred times, but today for some reason the scene stirred disquieting feelings about the baby she had given away. Cecelia sat down to take off her boots.

"You've been crabby and cross and preoccupied for two weeks—ever since you went out to dinner with him," Jeannie observed. "Just exactly what is your problem with Adam Campbell?"

Cecelia felt her sister's eyes on her and looked away. Jeannie deserved an answer. But how could she tell her anything without telling her all of it? She unzipped her left boot. For all those years she'd kept the secret buried so deep that sometimes months passed without her thoughts touching on the past. Everything had been just fine until Adam had talked about looking for their son. She'd begun to relive all the old feelings, all the guilt and shame and grief of giving up her baby. The burden was almost unbearable, coupled with the fear of what could happen to her life, and to all of them, if Adam succeeded in his search.

Pacing across the office Cecelia looked out the window at the gray March day. She couldn't keep her secret any longer. She had to tell someone. A delivery truck rattled past, and its wind sucked loose papers from a dumpster and scattered them across the dirty snow.

Cecelia turned back toward her sister. There was no good way to lead into what she was about to say, no way to soften what had happened. She looked directly at

Jeannie. "Twenty years ago next summer I had Adam Campbell's baby."

"You what?" Benjamin let out an angry cry as he lost his mother's breast and Jeannie automatically shifted him back, still staring at Cecelia. "How could you have had a baby and I never knew?"

"You were only twelve years old then. Besides, no one knew. No one but Mother and Pop and Adam...and Aunt Nellie, of course."

"The summer you went to Aunt Nellie's!"

Cecelia saw the flash of understanding in her sister's eyes as the puzzle pieces came together. "Except I wasn't at Aunt Nellie's," she explained. "I was in Portland at a home for unwed mothers."

"Oh, Cecelia." Jeannie's eyes filled with tears of compassion. "Why didn't you ever tell me?"

Cecelia paced back to the window, staring through the glass at an icicle dripping rhythmically onto the sash. "I didn't tell anyone. I was so ashamed and I felt so guilty."

"But why?"

Cecelia heard the confusion in Jeannie's voice. She realized her sister truly didn't understand. "I guess you are just enough younger that attitudes had begun to change by the time you grew up," she answered slowly. "When I got pregnant..." She stumbled on the word. "When I got pregnant," she repeated, "it was a shameful thing. People whispered about you if they knew."

"But the baby... What happened to the baby?"

Cecelia walked slowly back across the room and sat down. "He was put up for adoption."

Jeannie looked down at Benjamin who was cradled contentedly in her arms half-asleep, and then back at her sister. "You gave away your baby? How could you?"

Cecelia's voice dropped almost to a whisper. "I had no choice."

"But you could have kept it. We'd have all helped you raise it . . ."

"It wasn't like that then," Cecelia interrupted. "Attitudes were different. The child of an unwed mother had two strikes against him from the very beginning."

"And Adam wouldn't marry you?"

Cecelia stared at the floor. "Yes, he would have married me." She swallowed hard, feeling tears well up in her eyes as she tried to make her sister understand. "But we weren't ready, Jeannie. I was too young and he was just finishing at the academy. I'd been in love with him from a distance for years and years but we'd only dated for a little while. We went skiing one day and got snowed in at a cabin on the mountain."

"And that was the only time you had sex?"

Cecelia nodded. "The only time. Can you believe that? One time and I got pregnant." She reached for a tissue and wiped her eyes. "Do you feel differently about me now that I've told you?" she asked hesitantly. "Do you think I'm terrible?"

"Of course not!" Jeannie gave her an incredulous look. "How could you even ask? It happens. Women get pregnant when they don't mean to. That's the way life is sometimes. I only wish you'd told me a long time ago so you wouldn't have had to go through it alone."

"Do you really mean that?"

"Yes, I really mean it."

Cecelia sat quietly for a moment, while Jeannie rocked Benjamin to sleep. Watching them today, she felt alone and empty, just as she had when the nurse had taken her own baby from her. Even though she was sure she had done the right thing, even though she had five more children, sometimes she still wondered about the one she had given up. And she wondered even more now that Adam had come back into her life. "Could I hold Benjamin?" she asked.

"Sure," Jeannie answered softly.

Cecelia took the baby and cradled him next to her breast. He was warm and sweet and soft. He smiled in his sleep, and tiny milk bubbles trickled from the corner of his mouth. The sisters sat in silence for several minutes.

"I'm sorry, Cecelia." Jeannie reached over and touched her arm. "Now I know why you were so undone when Adam showed up. But you seemed to like him . . ."

"That's part of the problem," Cecelia admitted. "I do like him. He kissed me and I felt like . . ." Cecelia wasn't sure how to explain it.

Jeannie smiled. "You felt like a woman." She smiled at Cecelia. "Don't let the past spoil it for you."

"It's not the past; it's the future that frightens me," Cecelia replied. She paused and looked down at the baby sleeping in her arms. "Jeannie, Adam's sterile. Ever since Viet Nam. He can't have any more children."

Jeannie's eyes widened.

"He came back to Spokane because he wants to find his son."

"How do you feel about that?" Jeannie asked hesitantly.

"I think it's the worst thing he could do."

Jeannie nodded. "So do I." She stood up and put her hands on Cecelia's shoulders. "Sometimes people do such stupid things."

"What if he's successful? How are my kids going to feel when they find out I have an illegitimate child? How can I face them? And then I think about the child himself, except he's not a child anymore. He's a young man. Heaven knows how he might react. He may not even know he's adopted." Cecelia gently stroked Benjamin's soft, downy hair. "I understand how Adam feels." Her voice broke, and her eyes filled with tears again. "But I can't....I just can't...."

"Wait a minute." Jeannie stopped her. "You're getting way ahead of yourself. You said Adam wants to find his son. How does he propose to go about finding this boy after almost twenty years?"

Startled by the question, Cecelia looked up at her sister. "I don't have any idea."

"Does he have anything to start from? The name of the adoptive parents, the home, anything?"

Cecelia thought for a moment. "He might know the name of the home, but I don't think so. He thought I went to Aunt Nellie's just like everyone else."

"And Aunt Nellie can't correct him. She's been dead for ten years."

Cecelia took a deep breath and began to consider the situation in a different light. "Besides that, Aunt Nellie lived in Seattle, and the home for unwed mothers was in Portland. The baby wasn't even born in the same state. Adam wouldn't know where to start."

"Frankly, Cecelia, I'm not sure he's really going to pursue it. Once he has time to think it over, he'll realize it would be impossible to find his son."

Cecelia stared at her sister. "Damn," she said slowly. "I think you're right, Jeannie. There's no way Adam could trace the baby. There just isn't enough information available to put the pieces together."

"So let's quit worrying about something that isn't even a problem and get back to work." Jeannie stood up and grinned at her sister.

Slowly, Cecelia's face softened into a smile. The tension that had been paralyzing her began to subside, and for the first time in days she felt as though the sun might filter through the clouds. She laid the sleeping baby in his crib and walked to the front of the shop.

CHAPTER FIVE

JOE RILEY HAD a pretty good idea that Cecelia had seen Adam. His daughter hadn't phoned him or stopped by the house in more than a week, which wasn't like her—unless she had something on her mind she didn't want to talk about. She was just like her mother, who always got really quiet when something was bothering her. Maybe a nice lunch would loosen up Cecelia. It was a good day for it, since he had to pick up the christening gown and tell Cecelia about that woman who'd called.

The bell on the shop door jangled loudly. Too loud, Joe thought privately. No need to let everybody in the building know when somebody was coming into The Kangaroo Pouch. But he kept his opinion to himself because there were more important things to talk about—like Adam Campbell.

"Hi, Pop." Jeannie grinned at him from behind the counter as he made his way between two racks of spring jackets.

"Hello there, yourself," he answered. He never worried about Jeannie. That one never kept a thing to herself. When she had a problem everybody and his uncle knew about it. "Where's your sister?"

"In the back. She probably heard you come in." Jeannie rounded the end of the counter to give her father a hug.

"I imagine she did. That bell's loud enough to wake the dead."

"But, it's a beautiful antique." Cecelia glanced up at the gleaming brass bell as she walked out of the back room.

"Not criticizing, just commenting." Pop hugged Cecelia and then held her at arm's length to scrutinize her more carefully. "Now tell me what my favorite daughters have been up to," he said, still looking directly at Cecelia.

She knew exactly what was on his mind. "You want to know about Adam Campbell." As she busied herself folding some toddler-size T-shirts, she caught Jeannie's eye, warning her not to talk.

"You seen him yet?" Pop watched Cecelia carefully. He hadn't missed her signal to Jeannie. He was right. Something was going on.

"Yes, Adam stopped by to see me," Cecelia said. She continued folding the shirts without looking up.

"And how was he?"

"Pop! You know perfectly well that Adam is fine. You talked to him before I did."

"Guess I did." He cleared his throat, then paused. Cecelia wasn't talking and there was no point in pushing. He'd just have to try again later. "Have you got the christening gown ready?" he asked Jeannie.

"I've got it right here." With a grin at her sister, Jeannie went behind the counter and reached into one of the lower cabinets for the christening gown that had been worn by generations of Rileys.

Cecelia looked at the gown fondly as Jeannie handed it to their father. Both the fabric and the color had softened with age, leaving the heirloom antique white. No one remembered whether that had been its original color. What they saw was the handwork of their grand-mother and the warmth of tradition that included them all. All but one, Cecelia thought. All except her first son.

"Won't be too much longer till we've got another member of the family," Pop said. "Talked to Jim last night and he said he thought Cindy would only make it another two months. I'm betting she doesn't wait that long." He tucked the gown, which was carefully sealed in plastic, under his arm and turned toward Cecelia again. "How would you like your old Dad to take you out to lunch? I'll even break down and go to that fancy place you like, the one that serves the salads with those little sandwiches on the side."

Cecelia's eyes misted and she was almost tempted. She knew her father was offering to listen and help when he sensed she needed him. But after talking with Jeannie, she was convinced there was no way Adam could find their son. And after what Adam had said about letting the past alone, she wasn't sure he was even going to look. If she were alone with Pop, she'd break down and explain it all, and then he'd worry. There was no need for that. "Pop, you know how you hate the English Tearoom," she said, patting Pop's arm.

"Now, that doesn't matter. If that's the place you like, then that's where I'll take you."

Cecelia reached over and gave him a quick hug. "I'm really too busy today, and I brought a sandwich anyway."

"Well, I'm not too busy, and I'm starving. I'd love to go to lunch," Jeannie announced. "And I'll even settle for a hamburger. Do you mind watching Benjamin, Cecelia? I'm sure he'll sleep for at least another hour." As she talked she pulled on her coat and took her father's arm.

"Wait a minute. You don't have to be in such a gol-darned hurry. There was something else I needed to tell Cecelia." He fumbled in his pocket and produced a piece of paper with several items listed on it. Muttering to himself, he ran his finger down the notations. "Yep, here it is. Bernice Mitchell. I got a phone call from her the other day. Said she was an old college friend of yours."

"Bernice Mitchell?" Cecelia echoed. "I don't know anyone named Bernice."

"Maybe she was just a casual acquaintance," Jeannie suggested.

"Maybe so." Joe Riley put the list back into his pocket. "We had a nice talk, though."

"What did she want?" Cecelia asked.

"Needed your address. She said she'd lost track of you and wanted to get in touch."

Cecelia searched her memory and again came up blank. "How odd. I'm sure I would remember the name Bernice."

"Oh, just don't concentrate on it, and your subconscious will eventually remember who she is," Jeannie advised. "Come on, Pop, I'm hungry."

"All right, all right," her father grumbled good-naturedly. He stuffed the list back in his pocket and allowed his daughter to lead him out of the shop. "You seem to be in a mighty big hurry to get me away from Cecelia," he complained as he and Jeannie started down the sidewalk.

"What's the matter?" she retorted. "Aren't I good enough to take to lunch?"

"Except for being too bossy, you're fine," Pop assured her with a twinkle in his eye. "But it's your sister I want to talk to. What's the matter with her? She's been avoiding me ever since Adam Campbell showed up in town."

"Boy, you really get right to the point, don't you?" Jeannie said as she skirted around a puddle.

"Yep. Must be the Irish in me. Come on, now, what's going with Cecelia?"

"Oh, I guess she's just a little undone about seeing an old boyfriend. That can be kind of hard, you know. It stirs up a lot of feelings."

"Is Adam married? He didn't talk about his family the day he stopped to see me."

"No wife—never has been—and apparently no kids, either," Jeannie answered.

Joe Riley nodded. He wanted to press his daughter for more information, but then he remembered she didn't know about Cecelia's baby. As they turned into the deli he wondered if Adam ever thought about the boy. His only son, it seemed now. Too bad things hadn't been different back then. Adam had missed a lot by not raising a son.

ADAM LOFTED THE BASKETBALL from twenty feet out and watched it drop through the net. If only he could deal with Cecelia as well as the ball. She was obviously avoiding him. That's why he'd stopped by the house instead of phoning again. When Cecelia wasn't there, he'd let the twins talk him into coming to the gym to shoot baskets. With luck she'd be home by the time they got back.

Kevin passed him the ball and Adam shot again. He hadn't played basketball in years. He'd forgotten the smells of paste wax and sweat and the hollow echo of the balls hitting the shiny floor and ricocheting off the backboard. He wished he'd been able to play ball with his son when he was growing up. That opportunity was gone, but there would be other things they could share.

Sean grabbed the ball from under the basket and passed it to Kevin, who drove in for a lay-up. The twins were pretty good, Adam observed, especially for thirteen-year-olds. Even though they were obviously growing like weeds, their coordination was better than he would have expected. Sean rebounded again and passed the ball out to Adam. "Let's see you put in another one," he challenged.

Adam dribbled in and stuffed the ball with an easy hook.

"Hey, show me how to do that," Kevin said. "If I can get that down I'll make all-stars for sure."

"You're going to make all-stars anyway," Sean told him. "We make it every year."

Adam took up the position under the basket and passed first to Kevin and then to Sean, giving them detailed instructions each time they drove the ball in. After about twenty minutes, he could see definite improvement. He wiped the sweat off his forehead with the tail of his T-shirt. He wondered if his own son was into sports. Probably was. Adam hoped he'd had an adoptive father who shot baskets in the winter and played catch in the spring and kicked a soccer ball around with him. Those were the things that brought fathers and sons together, the protective screen that allowed them to carry on seemingly casual conversations about girls and sex and beer blasts. As he watched Sean and Kevin, he wished he could have been the one to give his own son that chance.

"Hey, Adam," Sean yelled. "You gonna stand there all day with the ball or what?"

Realizing he hadn't been paying attention, Adam motioned to Sean. "Switch places and come in from the left side."

"I can't do it left-handed," Sean complained.

"Then practice," Adam told him. "If you want to be a basketball player, you have to learn to use both hands."

Sean missed the next five shots. When he made the sixth, he broke into a grin, his braces flashing in the bright overhead lights. "Maybe I could get the hang of it," he said hopefully.

"Of course you can. Try it a couple more times and then we have to go." Adam watched him lope back across the court. All these two needed was a little direction. If they were his boys... The thought jarred Adam. He'd come back to Spokane with the specific intention of finding his own son, counting heavily on Cecelia's help. Maybe if he'd cooled his heels instead of rushing, she'd have been more receptive. As it was, she was avoiding him, and that bothered him more than he liked to admit for a whole lot of reasons. In the future, he decided, things would be different. He'd go slow. He wouldn't bring up the subject again until she'd had some time to get used to the idea.

Adam called to Sean and Kevin and the boys reluctantly left the court and picked up their jackets. Adam knew the twins would have been happy to stay much longer, but he was anxious to go home and see their mother.

"Will you come to the gym with us again?" Sean asked as they walked home three abreast, their sneakers splashing in puddles left over from the rain.

"Yeah," Kevin seconded. "You're pretty good."

"Maybe we can work something out," Adam agreed. First he was going to have to work things out with Cecelia.

"Do you play baseball, too?" Sean asked, bouncing the basketball back and forth with Kevin as they walked.

"I used to play some," Adam answered nonchalantly, thinking about the two no-hitters he'd pitched while in high school.

"Super!" Kevin exclaimed. "We can all go out to the batting cages."

"And some of the guys and their dads get together for a pickup game on Sunday afternoons," Sean added. "It'd be nice to have somebody when everybody else's dad is there." Before Adam could answer, Sean challenged Kevin to race him to the porch, and the twins instantly took off at a dead run.

Adam followed more slowly, thinking about what Sean had said. That was very much the same way he'd felt when he was growing up. He'd have latched on to any adult male who took an interest in him. With his father dead, there had been times when he didn't fit in. From his perspective now, he realized that probably hadn't mattered to anyone else. But it had mattered to him.

Cecelia was waiting for them when they walked into the kitchen. In fact, she'd been waiting for nearly an hour, ever since she'd come home and found out that Adam had gone to the gym with the boys. She barely saw the twins when they came tromping into the kitchen. Her gaze was focused on the man behind them, trim and tall in jeans and a light jacket, his face flushed from exertion and from the chill evening air. He paused in the kitchen doorway as though waiting to be invited in.

"Hey, Mom," Sean began excitedly. "You remember that hook shot Derek Hanson kept making last week when his team beat us? Adam showed us how to do it."

"And he plays baseball, too," Kevin added, heading directly for the cupboard that housed a fifty-four ounce jar of peanut butter.

"Yeah, he's going to do that with us, too." Sean took a quart jar of grape jelly out of the refrigerator. "Right, Adam?"

"We'll see what we can work out," Adam answered. He wasn't looking at Sean or Kevin. His eyes were on Cecelia, who was seated at the kitchen table with a cup of tea in her hand. She was wearing a deep pink sweater that looked as though it would be very soft to touch, and something in her eyes told him that she might not mind. "Sorry I didn't let you know I was coming," he apologized. "I tried to call several times, but I couldn't reach you."

Cecelia hesitated. She glanced at the twins who were each slathering peanut butter on thick slices of bread to make triple-decker peanut butter and jelly sandwiches. This wasn't the time to discuss anything important. "I'm sorry I wasn't here," she answered. "Have you had dinner?"

"I ate early tonight." He couldn't quite figure out her reaction. After she'd avoided him for two weeks, he'd expected a cool reception at best.

"Hey, Mom, I'm home." Angela appeared in the kitchen door. "Will you tell Mary Beth to get off the phone? Kim says she's been on for an hour."

"Tell her I said if she doesn't hang up in the next two minutes she'll be on phone restriction for the rest of the week." Cecelia turned back to Adam. "Now, you were saying—"

"I was about to suggest we go for a ride." He walked over to Cecelia and put his hand on her arm. He felt her quiver ever so slightly and realized what he wanted was time with Cecelia, without a string of interruptions. "I'd like a few minutes alone with you," he said softly, "and I don't think we're going to find them here."

Her eyes, a very deep blue, met his. "Neither do I," she agreed. He was standing very close to her and she wanted him there. None of it made any sense, but she couldn't go on feeling one way and pretending something else. "Let me tell the kids I'm going," she said, starting for the front hall to get her coat.

As they were about to leave, Mary Beth bounced down the stairs. "I don't see why Angela's phone calls are more important than mine, and I always have to be the one to get off—" She stopped abruptly when she saw Cecelia buttoning her coat. "Hey, where are you going? We're supposed to pick out the material for my prom dress tonight."

Cecelia frowned. She had told Mary Beth they'd go to the fabric store. She mentally weighed the situation. The dance wasn't for two more weeks. Tomorrow would be time enough. "There's been a change of plans," she said calmly.

"But, Mom, you promised—"

"As I recall, we were going to go as soon as I got home, but you were on the phone," Cecelia reminded her.

"But I'm off now."

"And I'm going out for a little while," Cecelia said firmly, feeling Adam's strength beside her. "We'll shop tomorrow. No arguments."

"But, Mom—"

Cecelia didn't wait to hear the rest of her sentence. The sounds of Mary Beth's voice and the stereo and Kevin bouncing his basketball faded into silence as Adam closed the front door behind them.

"You have a lot to deal with," Adam said as he pulled the car away from the curb. "But that's not why you've been avoiding me."

"No," Cecelia admitted. "It's not. You know what the problem is, Adam." She stared at her hands, which were folded in her lap.

"Yes, I know what the problem is." He resisted the temptation to try one more time to explain to her what it would mean to him to know his only son, because he knew from looking at her that she hadn't changed her mind. He'd wait, just as he'd decided to do, and in time she'd come around. "Let's leave the past alone, Cecelia, at least for now," he said finally.

"That sounds good," she answered, both surprised and relieved. Since her talk with Jeannie, she'd overcome the fear that had made her not even want to talk to Adam. Now he seemed to be saying he was willing to back off. Maybe, once they'd talked about it, he'd realized the folly of searching for their son. Adam reached over and took her hand, and Cecelia felt her whole body relax. They seemed to be on their way toward exorcising the ghosts of their past. Maybe everything really could be all right.

"Is there anywhere special you'd like to go?" he asked.

"Just so it doesn't have teenagers, rock music, or ringing phones."

Adam laughed. "You want what I want. Some place quiet where we can be alone for a little while." He squeezed her hand. "Any suggestions?"

As he touched her, Cecelia felt her body awaken in anticipation. She met his eyes as she searched in vain for an answer to his question. "I don't know, Adam. I just know my house isn't the place."

"Unfortunately neither is the BOQ—the bachelor officers' quarters where I'm staying. I'm supposed to be there temporarily, but they way they're going, temporary is looking like several months."

His eyes held hers for a long moment and suddenly he remembered. There was a place they could go, not ideal, but somewhere. He could take her to the river, where they used to park after dates. "Let's take a ride," he said, turning the corner. He checked the car clock. It was getting late, but not that late. They could be out there in ten minutes. He reached across and took Cecelia's hand again. He wanted to hold her against him and touch her.

Adam switched on the radio and they rode in comfortable silence. Cecelia kept her fingers twined in his, wanting more of him. So many years had passed since she'd felt the sensations that coursed through her. He didn't have to drive very far before she could guess their destination. She couldn't decide whether she was surprised or not, but she did know that feelings inside her were growing pleasantly intense.

"Are we going where I think we are?" she asked, as he turned onto a road that ran along a high bluff overlooking the Spokane River.

"Is it all right?"

Cecelia barely hesitated before giving in to her feelings. "For a little while," she answered softly.

As they approached the area high above the river, where they once had parked, they found it deserted. Ignoring the signs that warned against trespassing after dark, and trusting his memory, Adam turned onto a dirt road that was nearly hidden by dense underbrush. Branches from the trees hung low and brushed across the windshield as the Bronco bumped and lurched in the ruts. Finally they came to a small clearing. Adam stopped and turned off the headlights.

"I can't remember the road being this bad twenty years ago," he said.

"I don't think it was," Cecelia answered, "or your old Chevy would have never made it down here." Her eyes adjusted slowly to the darkness; the night seemed very black and very still.

She felt herself tremble as they sat quietly, watching the moon shimmer on the dark water. She was alone with him, completely alone for the first time in almost twenty years. She knew he was going to kiss her, and she knew she wanted him to. Deep inside her, reason ignited small sparks of doubt, but mostly she wanted him. She stared at amber lights glowing in the windows of a solitary house across the river, and somewhere in the distance she heard a dog bark.

Adam reached across the space between their individual seats and took Cecelia's hand. His touch was like a jolt of electric current.

"As I recall, my old Chevy had a single front seat." Adam frowned at the gear shift between them. "It was easier to get close to you."

Cecelia laughed softly. "I guess it was."

Again there was silence. Adam lightly traced a path on the back of Cecelia's hand.

"That tingles," she breathed, but it more than tingled. It sent shivers racing through her.

"I know," he answered.

Cecelia moved over in her seat, as close as she could get to the center, then stopped and looked at Adam uncertainly. "I think I'm a little nervous," she admitted. "I feel like I did when I was seventeen—not quite sure I belong here and afraid we might get caught."

This time it was Adam's turn to laugh. He brushed her hair back from her cheek and looked deeply into her eyes. "You're definitely not seventeen. You are a very beautiful and sensuous woman. We're both adults, and all we want is some time together."

He reached over and took Cecelia in his arms. "I've wanted to do this right, since that first day in your kitchen," he murmured. He lowered his head and his mouth covered hers, his lips moving slowly, softening hers and making them swell with longing for him. She reached up and buried her fingers in his hair as she pulled him closer.

Then his mouth was on her cheek, her ear, her neck, covering her with kisses. She was hungry for him, more so than she would have believed possible, almost more so than she could admit. The longing that drew her to him welled up from deep inside. She wanted to capture him and hold him and somehow make this last forever.

Sliding his hands inside her open coat, Adam pulled her still closer to his body and buried his face in her hair. He let his hand linger on the swell of her breast and felt the shiver that ran through her.

"Oh, Adam," she whispered. "It feels so good to be near you." He slipped his hands under her sweater, along the silky fabric of her slip and across the bare skin of her back as he held her close. He kissed her again and wanted her more.

She touched his cheek with the tips of her fingers, overwhelmed by sensations that had been buried inside her for so long. Everything about him—his touch, his smell, the taste of his lips—was exciting, washing over her and filling an emptiness she hadn't known was there.

"We desperately need some time together, Cecelia, and not out here in a cold car." He struggled with his anger at circumstances neither of them could control. Bringing Cecelia to the river had been fine twenty years ago but not worthy of the woman she'd become. Anyone with the logistical knowledge to command a bomber wing should be able to do better.

"But where can we go, Adam? We don't have many options."

He looked over at Cecelia. "I don't know where, but I'm sure as hell going to find someplace. And I'm going to find it soon."

Adam held her hand all the way home, and then walked her to the door and kissed her briefly.

She pulled away as quickly as he did, sensing the explosive emotion between them. Something had changed. No, that wasn't it. Something *hadn't* changed. That incredible attraction they'd felt for each other twenty years ago was still there. Slowly she walked through the house, which was blessedly quiet, and climbed the stairs to her bedroom. How could she go through five children and a marriage to a man she had loved dearly and still feel this way about Adam after not seeing him for almost twenty years? She hadn't dreamed about him. She hadn't missed him, certainly not after she'd met Tom. She had been totally committed to her marriage. And yet there was no mistaking the way she had felt about Adam tonight. Or the way he'd felt about her.

As she passed the full-length mirror in the upstairs hall, she stopped and looked at herself carefully. Her eyes were bright and her cheeks were flushed a deep pink. She looked as though she had been doing exactly what she had been doing. Making love. Adam had said she was sensuous. What would it be like with a man— with Adam—after all this time? The memory of his hand on her breast made her shiver as she removed her clothes. Would she please him now? Her curves were fuller, and her body was no longer young and firm. Would it matter?

Cecelia had just taken her nightgown from the drawer when the phone rang. She glanced at the clock. Almost midnight. Maybe just a wrong number, she thought as she reached for the receiver.

"I hope I didn't wake you," the deep voice said, and a warm glow spread through her.

She sat down on the edge of the bed, holding the soft nightgown against her bare skin. "No, Adam, I wasn't asleep."

"I forgot to ask you something. I meant to invite you to go to the wing dinner with me next Saturday."

"And that couldn't wait until morning?"

There was silence on the other end of the phone. "Well, actually," Adam said slowly, "I guess I needed an excuse to call and say good-night."

"You never need an excuse to call me, Adam."

"Cecelia?" He paused. "I meant what I said about wanting to find a place to be alone with you. Is that what you want, too?"

She hesitated, realizing what he was asking. But she knew how she felt, and she didn't want to pretend. "I . . . I think so, Adam."

She heard his deep, rich laugh. "I guess that's what you'd call a qualified affirmative," he said ironically. "All right then, I'll come up with something. Good night, Cecelia."

"Good night, Adam," she answered softly. Then she hung up the phone and reached for her journal.

Tonight I told Adam I want to make love. I can't believe I said it. I'd almost forgotten what it was like to feel like this.

CHAPTER SIX

MOUNDS OF PINK TAFFETA overflowed the table and spilled onto a white sheet that covered the floor. The sewing machine hummed steadily. But as Cecelia worked in the tiny sewing room she'd carved out of a corner of the basement, her mind wasn't on the dress she was making for Mary Beth.

She was thinking about Adam, just as she had been all week. The children had teased her unmercifully about being off in a dream world, and she had only smiled, glad they couldn't read her mind. Glancing at her watch, she snipped the threads at the end of the seam and quickly turned the dress to machine baste the waist to the bodice. She had to get down to business. Adam was picking her up in exactly two hours to go to the wing dinner, a major social event at the base. She'd been looking forward to it since he'd called so late that wonderful night the week before. She smiled, remembering that night and the heady pleasure of Adam's hands, touching, exploring. . . .

"Hey, Mom, is my prom dress ready for me to try on, yet?" At the sound of footsteps on the basement stairs, Cecelia looked up. Mary Beth had been down to check on the progress of the dress at least a dozen times.

"One more seam," she answered, and the sewing machine began humming again as she guided the slippery fabric under the needle.

"Please hurry, Mom." Mary Beth was jiggling impatiently from foot to foot. "You already said if it isn't fitted before I go to the cheerleading clinic, you can't get it finished in time. And my ride's going to be here—"

Cecelia held up the dress. "All set. Watch out for the pins." She dropped the pink taffeta over Mary Beth's head and turned her around to fasten the back seam.

"Oh, Mom, I love it!" Mary Beth beamed at her image in the old mirror that was propped up against the furnace. "It's just what I wanted, strapless and everything."

"Not strapless," Cecelia muttered, her mouth full of pins.

"Oh, don't put straps on, please. Everyone will be wearing strapless."

"And everyone will spend most of the evening in the ladies' room hiking up their dresses—except you. You will be able to dance all night without a worry. Turn around."

Mary Beth wrinkled up her nose and turned. Once again there was the sound of footsteps on the basement stairs, and Kim, with Bingo trotting behind her, appeared in the sewing room. At the sight of Mary Beth in the long pink dress, Bingo's tail started to wag, and in an instant he had scooted underneath the voluminous skirt. Only his feather black tail stuck out, thumping happily on the cement floor.

"Get Bingo out of there," squealed Mary Beth.

Kim flattened herself on the floor and lifted up the taffeta skirt. Immediately Bingo wiggled to the other side.

"He's going to tear the dress!"

"Oh, no, he isn't."

Cecelia pulled up the skirt and grabbed for the dog. She had no time for shenanigans. All she wanted was to get the dress fitted and to take her shower. By the time Adam arrived, she was going to be absolutely ravishing.

With a playful bark Bingo darted between Cecelia and Kim and raced into the laundry room, knocking over a box of powdered detergent on his way. The white footprints he left in his wake followed him across the floor where he wedged himself behind the dryer, daring someone to pursue him.

"Cecelia, are you down here?" Adam's voice called.

"No," Cecelia whispered, closing her eyes. "Not yet."

With a delighted bark, Bingo ran out from behind the dryer, and just as Adam turned the corner from the basement stairs, the dog jumped up to greet him, leaving white footprints all over his black pants.

"I'm sorry," Kim apologized, grabbing Bingo around his stomach.

"Adam!" Cecelia gasped. "What are you doing here already?" She stared at him. He was impossibly handsome in his full-dress uniform, a short black jacket with silver eagles gleaming on the shoulders and rows of miniature medals on the left side of his chest, a white tucked shirt, black bow tie and formal black trousers. A rakish grin crossed his face as he surveyed the scene before him.

Bitter disappointment welled up in Cecelia. This wasn't how it was supposed to have happened. In all her fantasies he'd first seen her walking slowly down the stairs, elegant and smiling in her deep purple moire cocktail suit. Instead she was standing in the basement wearing jeans and a grubby sweatshirt, surrounded by

sewing and children and an unruly dog that tracked
soap powder on Adam's pants.

"I thought I'd come by a little early, and maybe we
could go out for a drink." Glancing down at the footprints on his trousers, he added, "But maybe I should
have called." The corners of his mouth twitched in
amusement.

"Yes," Cecelia said firmly. "You should have
called."

"I'll take Bingo outside," Kim interjected, obviously anxious to escape.

"What about my dress?" Mary Beth asked. Even she
looked uncomfortable.

"Take it off upstairs," Cecelia told her.

"If you need to finish whatever you were doing—"
Adam began.

"No, we're finished." Cecelia sighed as both girls
disappeared in the direction of the stairs.

When a quick glance upward told him he and Cecelia were alone, Adam took her in his arms. "I'm sorry
I'm not ready," she apologized, nearly crying in frustration as she buried her head in his chest.

"Would you believe I think you are absolutely beautiful the way you are?"

Cecelia shook her head.

"Well, I do," he continued, his fingers ruffling her
hair. "Don't hurry getting dressed. We've got lots of
time."

Slowly Cecelia raised her head and stepped back. he
was half smiling, obviously amused rather than annoyed by her predicament. There was a tenderness in his
eyes that enveloped her and held her and almost made
her smile. "Thank you, Adam," she whispered. "Is
there anything I can get you while you wait?"

He glanced down at his trousers again. "Maybe a clothes brush," he suggested, grinning at her. "I know where to find the scotch."

DANNY FOCUSED HIS CAMERA lens on a dozen core members of his antinuclear group who were stuffing envelopes at his mother's old mahogany dining room table. The scene would make a great publicity shot for the campus newspaper—dedicated students working their tails off for global disarmament. A few more hours of work and every senator and representative in Washington would have antinuclear letters in his office by the middle of next week. He zoomed in on Angela Mahoney with the stacks of envelopes on one side of her, an empty pizza carton on the other and the setting sun filtering through the lace curtains behind her. Perfect, he decided. Photo editors were always pushovers for pretty girls.

At the sound of the shutter clicking, Angela looked up. "Danny Mitchell, exactly what are you planning to do with that picture?"

"Send it to every newspaper in the area," Danny answered, refocusing from a few inches to the right. "Look gorgeous. We need all the publicity we can get."

Angela grinned automatically until the shutter clicked again. Then her expression changed to a frown. "I'm not sure my mom's going to be thrilled by having my picture plastered all over." She glanced at her watch. "Speaking of my mom, I've got to go home."

"Hey, sit still, Angela. I need a few more pictures and you're the most photogenic person here." Danny raised the camera viewfinder to his eye again.

Angela shoved her chair back from the table and pulled on her jacket. "Sorry, I really can't stay. I promised Mom I'd be home to keep an eye on Sean and Michael while she's out tonight.''

Danny scowled. Angie was always tied up with her family. The twins' basketball games. Computer games with Kim. Mary Beth's birthday. Dinner with her grandfather. Once in the middle of an important meeting she'd even had to go bail the dog out of the pound. ''Can't one of your sisters watch Sean and Michael?'' He followed Angela to the front door.

She shook her head and pulled her car keys out of her coat pocket. ''Mary Beth is gone to an overnight cheerleading clinic, and Kim has a regular babysitting job on Saturday nights. I'm the only one left.''

Danny leaned against the door and tried again. ''Maybe if you call your mom and tell her how important this mail campaign is, she'd be willing to change her plans.''

''No way. She practically made me swear on a Bible that I'd be at home tonight. She's going to some big dinner out at the Officers' Club.''

''You mean out at the base? Your mother is going out with some Air Force officer? That really sucks, Angie. You're here all afternoon working on antinuclear stuff while your mother is at home getting ready to cozy up with some lousy Air Force pilot. If I were you I wouldn't go home at all.''

''What do you mean 'not go home at all'?'' Two bright spots of color rose in Angela's cheeks. ''That's not how it works at our house. Come on, Danny. Move away from the door so I can leave.''

Danny calmly folded his arms on his chest, but didn't budge an inch. ''Why do you let your mother run all over you all the time? Angela, you're eighteen years old.

You should call and tell her you're not going to babysit while she's out to dinner with some warmonger."

"Listen, Danny Mitchell. Adam's an all-right guy, even if he is in the Air Force, and besides, my mother has a right to go out with anybody she wants. It's her life. I don't have to agree with her, or anybody else in my family for that matter. We're never all going to think the same and agree on everything. But we still care about each other, and we keep our promises. That includes staying with my brothers tonight, regardless of what you think. So just get your stubborn body away from that door and let me go."

Stinging from Angela's words, Danny silently stepped aside. She had no sooner slammed the door in his face, than it opened again and she poked her head back into the hall.

"Sorry I blew up." She gave him an embarrassed smile. "I really like you, Danny, and I do believe in what we're doing. It's just that sometimes, well, family comes first. You understand."

Danny nodded, mostly because he didn't see much point in arguing. What he did understand was that she had a family to go home to, people she cared about and loved, people who loved her in return. Ever since his father died, Danny had felt as if he didn't have much of a family left. Only his mother, and she was old and sick. Yes, she loved him, and yes, she cared about him, but it was different. She probably wasn't going to be around much longer, anyway. Not that it mattered. He didn't need her. He didn't need anybody.

He watched Angela drive away, and for just a fleeting moment he wondered what it would be like to have a bunch of brothers and sisters. Always somebody around if you were trying to drum up a game of monopoly, or needed to borrow a pair of jeans. That didn't sound too bad. But on the flip side, you always had to plan around other people. He could do pretty much whatever he wanted, and nobody cared.

"Danny?" His mother came into the hall, carrying her needlepoint bag. "Was that the Mahoney girl I heard you talking to?"

"Yeah, that was one of them."

"One of them—how many Mahoneys are there?"

"Five kids, altogether. Angela is the oldest." Danny turned and started back to the dining room.

Bernice Mitchell watched her son thoughtfully for a minute and then asked, "Are they a nice family?"

"How would I know?" Danny shrugged. "I haven't even met most of them." He paused, and his gaze drifted out the window. "Except they have this dog. He's one of those stupid Heinz 57 mutts, all blotchy brown-and-black fur, with floppy ears and an ugly, feather tail. They call him Bingo..." His voice trailed off when he noticed his mother's rapt expression. Her eyes were glued on him, and she was hanging on every word, as if he was telling her some big, important news. "Why are you so interested in the Mahoneys all of a sudden?"

"No particular reason," his mother answered quickly. A shadow crossed her face, and she seemed nervous as she gripped her bag first with one hand and then the other. "Danny—" Her voice faltered. "I'm sorry we never got you a dog. It just never seemed like the right time, and puppies are so hard to house-break...."

Danny's back stiffened. "It's all right, Mom. I don't need a dog. I don't need anything. I'm just fine the way

I am." Scowling, he wheeled around and headed back into the dining room.

THE LOBBY of the Officers' Open Mess, more commonly known as the club, was dimly lit and the carpet was thick and plush. Strains of music from a swing combo floated out from the main dining room. As they circulated among the young lieutenants and captains and their wives, Adam kept Cecelia close to him. He seldom enjoyed the required social functions his job entailed, but tonight was different. With Cecelia on his arm, the delicate scent of perfume lingering in her hair, Adam's whole perspective had changed. He smiled with satisfaction as he watched her. She seemed to be enjoying herself.

"You're the most beautiful woman here," he whispered as they approached the hors d'oeuvres table. "I don't want to share you for very long."

Cecelia smiled up at him, wondering exactly what he had in mind. She had never felt so comfortable in a room filled with strangers as she did that night with Adam. She had wondered at first if she might be an outsider, but Adam deftly included her in each conversation, and she fit in easily. By the way he introduced her and stood near her, some part of their bodies always touching, she sensed he was proud of her.

Before they went in to dinner, Adam made a point of introducing her to George and Diane Lathrop, whom Cecelia could tell were his close friends. She liked them immediately.

"I understand now why Adam couldn't postpone that date a few weeks ago," Lathrop said as he took Cecelia's hand. Cecelia decided not to ask him to explain his words.

During dinner Cecelia was pleased to find that they were seated at the head table with the Lathrops. The dinner was good—prime rib with oven-roasted potatoes and French-cut greenbeans and a chocolate parfait for dessert. While they ate, the Lathrops kept them entertained with stories of their nomadic Air Force life, and Cecelia found herself laughing and enjoying the evening. She was sometimes aware of Adam watching her, and she wondered what he was thinking.

As the combo switched from background music to dance numbers, Adam guided Cecelia to the floor in the center of the room and took her in his arms, leading her expertly to a familiar song.

"I'd forgotten what a good dancer you are," Cecelia said, her body relaxed and free as she moved with him.

"It takes two," he murmured, pressing his hand against her back. She was soft and warm and smelled delicious.

The rhythm changed to a slower tune, and Cecelia moved her hand on his shoulder so that the tips of her fingers barely touched the back of his neck.

"That feels good," Adam murmured into her ear. Her fingertips rested just inside the edge of his collar. He pulled her close until he could feel the pressure of her breasts against his chest and her thigh touching his. As their bodies moved together in a slow, sensual rhythm, a pervasive warmth rippled through Cecelia. She felt what was happening between them, as insistent as a heat wave building. More than anything she wanted to be alone with him. "Adam," she murmured softly.

"Are you thinking what I'm thinking?"

"Yes." There wasn't a trace of hesitation in her voice.

The song ended and they made their way through the crowded room, picked up their coats and left the club.

Neither of them said a word until they were out on the highway, driving toward the outskirts of town.

Adam took her hand, and Cecelia inhaled sharply as shivers ran up and down her body.

"I've thought of a place where we can go. It's not ideal, but..." Adam glanced over at her.

"Anywhere. I just want—" Cecelia stopped. He knew exactly what she wanted. He wanted it, too.

Adam turned his Bronco into a dimly lit parking lot and stopped the car in front of a pink neon sign: Hideaway Motel. The word Vacancy flashed on and off at regular intervals.

"Well, what do you think?"

"I guess the name is appropriate." Cecelia looked beyond the sign, through some pine trees, to the small, brick motel.

"I don't imagine this place takes credit cards." Adam peered skeptically through the windshield.

"No, I don't think so."

Both of them were quiet for a moment. Then Adam opened the door of the Bronco. "Why don't you wait here while I get a room key?"

Cecelia nodded in agreement and watched while Adam walked into the office. She couldn't quite believe she was going into a motel room with a man who was not her husband for the express purpose of making love. What would they do first? Undress? Talk? She wasn't sure. It was easier when everything happened spontaneously. Maybe she'd just take off her suit. She had once read that a woman was very sexy wearing only a slip. Yes, that's exactly what she'd do. She'd go into the bathroom and take off her suit and come out in her slip. Where was Adam, anyway? Why was he talking so long just to pay and get a key?

The door to the office opened and a couple came out, heading in the direction of one of the end units. Cecelia studied them, wondering if they were married. The man was middle-aged, portly and bald. The woman was much younger, blond, and wearing high-heeled red shoes. She was carrying a six-pack of beer. They probably weren't married, Cecelia decided, but they looked as though they belonged here, especially the woman. They unlocked the door of a room and disappeared inside. Cecelia swallowed hard. Somehow she was sure that the blond woman knew absolutely what to do first.

As she waited, Cecelia felt her desire switch to apprehension, until she was no longer sure she could go through with the plan. Yet, there really was nowhere else to go. Once they were inside the room and they were together, everything would be all right again, she told herself. But as she stared at the flashing pink neon, she grew more and more uncomfortable.

"Cecelia?" Adam opened the car door.

"Did you get the key?"

Adam slid into his seat. "No."

"Why not?" A sense of relief swept through her.

Adam took her hand. "Did you notice the couple that came out of the office?"

"Yes."

"They bothered me. They were so . . . so . . ."

"Cheap?" She finished for him.

"Yes, cheap. We're not like that, Cecelia. I can't take you into a trashy motel." He took her in his arms. "Do you understand?"

Cecelia laid her head on his chest. "I don't think I could have gone through with it, Adam. I want to make love with you and I would have tried, but I don't think it would have been good."

"No, not the way we want it to be." He kissed her gently. "The time and place will come."

Cecelia traced the edge of his jaw with her fingertip. "I certainly don't see how."

Adam kissed her again, this time with passion. "When we want something enough, we can make it happen," he replied in a husky voice. "One way or another."

ADAM'S WORDS ECHOED in Cecelia's mind the following Friday morning while she sat at the kitchen table drinking a cup of coffee. As she watched fat raindrops splatter on the window, she found herself playing with a mental image of the motel out on the highway, its neon sign flashing. At the time, she had been relieved they hadn't gone inside, but now she wasn't so sure. Adam was away on a short assignment, and she missed him terribly.

She picked up the flowing yards of Mary Beth's pink taffeta dress from the dining room table and sat down in a chair by the window, still lost in her thoughts. Maybe one day Adam could come for lunch—a long lunch that didn't necessarily include a sandwich. She shivered. She could almost feel herself in Adam's arms, her bare skin next to his.... She certainly wasn't wary of him anymore, Cecelia realized, laughing quietly at herself. Then she sobered, wondering what had changed. Gradually the answer came to her. Adam hadn't mentioned their son ever since that night he'd agreed to put the past behind them.

Cecelia adjusted the zipper opening so that the edges of the dress lined up perfectly, and anchored the zipper in place with a pin. She too had locked the memories of their baby back in that dusty closet of her mind where she'd kept them for so long. Now she and Adam were free to focus on each other. What a lovely thought. Carefully she pinned the zipper on top of the opening and basted it in place with long running stitches. Just as she finished, the doorbell rang and Bingo streaked into the hallway barking loudly. Cecelia frowned. All she had left to do were the hem and the hooks and eyes. She was in no mood to be interrupted, especially on the only day she had taken off from work in months.

After banishing Bingo to the kitchen, she opened the door to find herself face-to-face with an older woman wearing a gray wool coat and carrying a large, black umbrella. "May I help you?" Cecelia asked.

The woman took a step backward. "Are you Cecelia Riley...No—" she faltered "—I mean, are you Cecelia Mahoney?"

Cecelia looked at the stranger carefully. Her hair was salt-and-pepper gray and her face deeply lined. She was obviously nervous. Cecelia was virtually certain she had never seen the woman before.

"I'm Cecelia Mahoney," she answered. "Should I know you?"

The woman lowered her umbrella. "No, not really. I stopped by your shop, and the woman there told me you were at home today." She looked up at Cecelia uncertainly. "I...I'd like to talk to you for a few minutes. We have something in common."

Cecelia hesitated, struggling with a growing urge to close the door. What could she and this person possibly have in common? The woman's eyes were pleading with her. Reluctantly she opened the door wider, and the woman followed her into the living room.

"My name is Bernice Mitchell," she began. Without unbuttoning her coat, she sat down on the edge of the sofa and folded her gloved hands in her lap.

Bernice Mitchell. The name was familiar. Cecelia sat down on the wing chair across from her, and then she remembered. "Aren't you the woman who called my father?" She studied the woman carefully. Bernice Mitchell had to be twenty years older than she was. "You said you knew me from college?"

The woman's eyes clouded. "I didn't know what else to tell him and I had to find you."

"You had to find me?" Cecelia asked, increasingly uneasy. "Why? Why did you have to find me?"

"I'm Danny Mitchell's mother." She looked at Cecelia as though waiting for a response.

"Danny Mitchell," Cecelia repeated, thinking hard. She knew that name, too.

"I believe he knows your daughter, Angela."

"Oh, yes," Cecelia remembered. Danny Mitchell was the boy who was the antinuclear leader. Sandy-brown hair, scruffy, a real individualist. Apparently Bernice Mitchell thought her son had some problem that involved Angela.

"I'm not here because Danny knows Angela," Bernice continued slowly, as though she had read Cecelia's thoughts. "I've come because of Danny."

She paused, leaving Cecelia even more confused. Thinking about the unfinished dress, Cecelia tried not to be impatient.

"Danny's father died several months ago, and since then I've learned that I am ill," Bernice Mitchell continued. "We really have no other family..."

Cecelia looked at the sad brown eyes set in a face etched with worry and grief. Whatever this woman had come to talk about was obviously very hard for her, and Cecelia was quickly coming to the conclusion that she didn't want to get involved.

"Mrs. Mitchell, are you sure you want to be telling me this?" she asked gently. "It doesn't seem to have anything to do with me. Perhaps if you spoke with your minister or a close friend," she suggested kindly.

Bernice Mitchell shifted uncomfortably. "No, Mrs. Mahoney, this has a great deal to do with you. I haven't been quite sure how to tell you, so I guess I'll just do it directly. Mrs. Mahoney, Danny is your son."

Cecelia's mouth went dry. Her lips opened but no words came out. She sank back in her chair and stared at the woman across from her. Her meaning was unmistakable, but it couldn't be true.

"There must be some mistake," she said in a hoarse whisper.

Bernice Mitchell looked at her compassionately. "I'm terribly sorry, Mrs. Mahoney. I was afraid it might come as a blow after all this time."

"No, you don't understand," Cecelia insisted. "You've made a mistake."

Wordlessly Bernice Mitchell opened her purse, took out a plain, sealed envelope and handed it to Cecelia. "We adopted Danny when he was only two days old," she explained. "When I undressed him that first afternoon, this was caught down inside his blankets."

Her hands shaking, Cecelia opened the envelope. A tiny blue and white beaded hospital identification bracelet fell into her lap. She picked it up, examining it carefully, knowing even before she looked at it what she was going to find. As she turned it over in the palm of her hand, she gasped softly. Neat block letters spelled out "Riley."

Cecelia's breath emerged in a shudder and she very nearly burst into tears. She had watched the nurse put that bracelet on the baby's ankle just before she had been allowed to hold him for those few moments. She gripped the bracelet tightly in her fist and closed her eyes, remembering how the baby had cried as the nurse pulled him away. Then she remembered her own tears. It had seemed they would never stop. Her breathing ragged, Cecelia raised her eyes to the woman across from her. "Why have you come?" Her voice was defeated, accusing. "What are you trying to do to me?"

"I'm sorry, Mrs. Mahoney, really sorry. I didn't come to hurt you. I came to help Danny." She looked directly at Cecelia, her eyes pleading, her voice firm. "Mrs. Mahoney, I came to ask your permission to tell Danny that you're his birth mother."

Cecelia stared at the stranger in disbelief. "Danny is nearly twenty years old. How can it possibly help him to tear open my past?" Her voice rose in anger. "I gave up my baby, Mrs. Mitchell. I've hated myself for it every day of my life. And now you're telling me I have to go through the agony all over again?" Cecelia buried her face in her hands. "Go away, Mrs. Mitchell. Go away and leave me alone."

Bernice Mitchell didn't move. Several minutes passed before Cecelia became aware of her again, sitting ramrod straight on the edge of the couch cushion, waiting. Slowly Cecelia raised her head. "Don't you understand?" she pleaded. "I have another life now. I have five teenage children. None of them know. This is my secret, Mrs. Mitchell."

After a moment, the woman answered softly. "It's *our* secret, Mrs. Mahoney."

"Are you threatening me?" Cecelia sat up straighter.

The stranger's eyes were sad. "I want you to hear me out. You're a mother protecting your children. So am I. The only difference is that my child is also yours."

Cecelia was quiet as she sensed her inward acceptance of what the woman had just said.

"I'm old, Mrs. Mahoney, not objectively old, but in a few months or maybe another year or two my heart is going to wear out."

Her statement was matter-of-fact. Cecelia said nothing.

"When I die, Danny will have no one. We were older when we adopted him, and our families were small. All of them are gone." Bernice Mitchell waited for several moments. When no response came, she went on. "Danny came to us at a time when we had almost given up ever having a child. Sometimes I think we were too old. We were so far away from the things he cared about. He and his father were close, and I know Danny misses him terribly."

Again she hesitated, then leaned forward and spoke in a voice so low that Cecelia had to strain to hear her.

"We loved him so much, Mrs. Mahoney, more than anything else in the world. We wanted everything for him. And maybe, maybe if we'd had a little more time..." Her voice wavered and she didn't finish the thought. "Danny is struggling. He needs love and support to find himself." Her eyes met Cecelia's. "When Danny was a baby I took him as my own and I loved him and I gave him everything. But I won't be here to finish what I started. That's what I want you to do. I beg you, Mrs. Mahoney, please help Danny. I have nowhere else to turn."

Silently Cecelia turned the hospital bracelet over and over in her hand, touching the tiny blue and white beads one by one. She had no answer. To say yes would be to risk her whole life caving in around her. To say no...how could she say no?

And then there was Adam to consider. His questions came rushing back: *"Do you know anything about the people who adopted him? Do you suppose there's any way to find out?"* Adam would want the child told. This was his son, his only son. But that didn't make it right. There wasn't any right.

"I don't know what to say to you," Cecelia answered slowly. "How can we be sure that telling Danny wouldn't just confuse him more? I can't believe a nineteen-year-old could accept a new family."

"It wouldn't be easy," Mrs. Mitchell admitted. "I have no illusions about that. But it's the only option I have."

Cecelia understood. She debated whether to tell Bernice Mitchell about Adam. Finally, she decided. "There's something else you should know." She paused. "Danny's father is back in Spokane."

"His father?" Bernice Mitchell's eyes lighted up. "Does he know about Danny?"

"Yes." Cecelia didn't elaborate. "I'd like to talk to him before we make any decisions. Is there a hurry—?" Cecelia stopped, not knowing how to ask the question.

Bernice Mitchell seemed to understand. "If you mean because of my heart condition, there's no hurry. I came to you now because I was afraid I would lose my courage." The visitor stared awkwardly at her hands. "No mother gives up her baby because she wants to. I know that. After I found the bracelet, Bill checked the hospital records and traced you. He said we should know where Danny came from, just in case. I didn't agree with him, and I vowed from the beginning I would respect your privacy." She looked at Cecelia, her eyes brimming with tears. "I didn't want to come here, Mrs. Mahoney. I hope you understand. I did it for Danny."

Compassion welled up in Cecelia as she saw love strong enough to make a mother go to any length for her child. "Thank you, Mrs. Mitchell. Thank you for everything you've done for Danny. I need to think about what you've said and I need to talk to—" she hesitated "—to his father."

"Of course," the woman replied. Taking a slip of paper from her purse, she stood up. "I've written down my address and telephone number in case you should want to contact me." She handed the paper to Cecelia and turned to go. "I won't do anything until I hear from you, Mrs. Mahoney," she said as she reached the front door.

Cecelia held out her hand. "Please, call me Cecelia."

After a moment's hesitation, Bernice Mitchell clasped the outstretched hand in both of hers. "Whatever you decide, I want you to know I do understand," she said softly. "But you could be so good for Danny."

She turned and left abruptly, picking up her umbrella from the porch and opening it as she started down the steps into the steady rain. Cecelia looked up at the dismal, gray sky. The day's magic was gone.

Somehow, through a blur of tears, Cecelia finished Mary Beth's dress, her fingers numb and her heart breaking. A moment she had dreaded for nearly two decades had come and it was far worse than she'd ever imagined. All the guilt at giving away her baby came rushing back, and now her whole life was about to be destroyed. She was going to pay for what she had done, and then the sins of the mother would fall upon the children.

That night Cecelia stared at the blank page in her journal for a long time before she finally wrote:

> I know who adopted my baby. His widowed mother came here this afternoon. She is ill and wants me to finish raising her son—my son—after she dies. I feel like my whole life is about to be destroyed.

Tears streamed down her cheeks as Cecelia dropped the journal and her pen and turned out the light. Her sleep that night was tormented.

TWO DAYS PASSED before Cecelia began to think rationally. It was Sunday afternoon. Kim was doing homework, Mary Beth was giggling into the phone, Angela was polishing her nails at the kitchen table, and Sean and Kevin were watching a ball game on television. Cecelia fixed a cup of tea and picked up her jacket. She needed to be alone. Her shoes sank into the soft ground as she walked across the backyard to the gazebo, which looked dingy and sad, its white paint cracked and faded and one of its posts rotted away. She dusted the winter dirt off one of the benches with the palm of her hand and sat down.

For the first time since Bernice Mitchell's impassioned visit, Cecelia mentally reviewed their conversation without breaking down. The questions she asked herself were logical and methodical: how would a nineteen-year-old—who was no doubt by his thinking already a man—respond to having a new family thrust on him?

And what about Adam? Cecelia took a sip of tea. Although her encounter with Danny had been brief, what she did remember about him struck a dissonant chord when she thought about Adam. Danny was a protestor, a rebel struggling to find himself, as his mother had said. He was nothing like Adam's idealized vision of his son. The only positive note about the whole situation was Adam's two-week trip to Atlanta. At least she would have some time to think.

The next afternoon, Jeannie blanched when Cecelia told her about Bernice Mitchell. Jeannie's reaction was much the same as Cecelia's had been when she finally came to her senses: there were no easy answers and for the moment the best thing to do was nothing at all. After they spent the entire afternoon discussing the problem, Cecelia agreed with Jeannie that sooner or later Adam should be told. But not right away. In the days that followed Cecelia silently repeated Jeannie's advice a hundred times: "The important thing is your relationship with Adam. Spend time with him. Enjoy him. When the time is right to talk about Danny, you'll know."

As Adam's return to Spokane drew closer, Cecelia grew more apprehensive. How would she feel when she actually saw Adam? When he took her in his arms, would Danny be there between them like a ghost driving them apart? "No," she whispered to herself, "I won't let that happen."

CHAPTER SEVEN

ADAM SET HIS SUITCASE under the coat rack just inside the door to the Officers' Club bar, letting his eyes adjust to the dim light as he scanned the room for George Lathrop. He spotted his friend near the end of the curved black bar talking to two other colonels from wing headquarters. Adam had agreed to meet Lathrop and give him an informal rundown on the Atlanta business as soon as he got back, but he was dead tired, and now he regretted his promise. As Adam started toward the group of men, Lathrop caught his eye and excused himself.

"You look like it was a long two weeks," Lathrop said, shaking Adam's hand. "How about a drink?" He led the way to a small table on the far side of the bar.

Adam sank into the padded arm chair and placed his hat on the corner of the table. "You're right. I could use a drink. A drink and a hot shower and about twelve hours in the sack."

"With or without company?" Lathrop chuckled.

"I'm living in the BOQ," Adam reminded him. "Do I have a choice?"

"Depends on how ingenious you are." Lathrop raised his hand, and a waiter hurried over to their table. They gave their drink orders and Lathrop sat back in his chair. "Now," he said, "tell me about Atlanta."

Slowly sipping his scotch and water, Adam tried to keep his mind on business as he briefed Lathrop. Thoughts about Cecelia kept intruding. Before he'd left Spokane, he had promised to come up with some place where they could be alone. That had been two weeks ago, and he wasn't any closer to a solution now than he had been then. He'd had brief hopes for the motel, but it wouldn't have worked. She hadn't been comfortable with it and, frankly, neither had he. Damn! You want to make love to a woman. She's willing. And you can't find a place to go.

"You tired, Campbell?"

"What?" Adam was suddenly aware that he had completely forgotten the conversation. He glanced at his watch. "I am a little tired. It's midnight, Atlanta time."

"That the only thing wrong? You seem preoccupied."

"Yeah, I guess I am. I've got a problem I can't solve." He took the last swallow of his drink and nodded toward the waiter. Then he looked at Lathrop. "If you wanted to be alone with a woman, where would you take her?"

Lathrop eyed him thoughtfully, taking the question in stride as though the subject hadn't changed. "I suppose you've been over the obvious choices."

"Like what?"

"Her place?"

Adam shook his head. "Too many kids."

"The BOQ's out. How about a motel?"

"That's not quite right. I want to be alone with her, really alone. I need some time."

The waiter set a fresh drink in front of each man. Lathrop picked up a plastic swizzle stick and methodically swirled the ice cubes in a Wild Turkey and water. His face creased into the same frown as when he was preoccupied with his work. Adam had seen that expression a hundred times. He didn't interrupt. Lathrop was excellent at strategic maneuvers.

Several minutes passed before Lathrop laid the stirrer on the table and sipped his drink. He looked up, his eyes intense. "As far as I can remember," Lathrop began slowly, "the time in my life I felt most alone was when I was out in the wilderness at survival school."

Adam tried to cover his disappointment. "That doesn't sound like what I had in mind."

A half smile crossed Lathrop's face. "No, I imagine not. But let me finish. Around here you can drive twenty or thirty miles and be in the middle of nowhere with nothing but trees and mountains and sky. Eastern Washington and Idaho are about as beautiful as any place in the world. If you stay away from established camp grounds, you can be out for days and not meet a living soul."

"I'm beginning to follow you." Adam's mind raced. "Another week and we'll be well into May. The nights will still be cold, but the daytime should be all right."

Lathrop nodded. "The nights could be a problem, but I might be able to work something out for you. There's a little cabin over in the hills near Coeur d'Alene, away from the lake. It might be available. Lathrop looked curiously at Adam. "This woman, is she the one you brought to the wing dinner?"

"Yep."

"She didn't look like the wilderness type. Has she ever backpacked?"

Adam shrugged. "Beats me. But there's always a first time."

"In that case, you want the cabin. You can get all the gear you'll need in rec services, but the packs are heavy. You'll be in better shape if you don't have to haul food, and with the cabin you can get most of what you need up there ahead of time."

"You're all right, George," Adam said gratefully.

"Somebody else's problems are always easier to solve than your own." Lathrop picked up the bar check and signed it. "Now go home and get your beauty sleep. If you're going to take up the life of a rugged outdoorsman, you'll need it."

ADAM WAS WHISTLING as he walked up the sidewalk to Cecelia's house the next afternoon. New green shoots had sprouted through the winter brown of the lawn, and the bushes were beginning to look alive again. Warmth from the sun soaked into Adam's bare arms. Perfect weather for a camping trip, he decided. And in another week or so it should be even better.

He noted that the station wagon wasn't in the driveway. He hoped that didn't mean Cecelia was gone. He'd come to play baseball with the twins, some of their friends and their friends' fathers, but what he really wanted was to see Cecelia. He had missed her far more than he had ever anticipated while he was in Atlanta, and he was excited about the plan he and Lathrop had come up with. He hoped she'd be as enthusiastic about backpacking together as he was.

He rang the doorbell twice, and a moment later heard feet pounding down the stairs. Mary Beth opened the door, her ponytail clutched in one hand and a hair clip between her teeth. "Come in," she said, removing the clip and fastening it around her hair. "Mom made Sean and Kevin go over to Mrs. Burke's to trim her bushes before they could play ball but they should be back any minute.''

Adam followed her into the kitchen. "Where's your mother?" he asked.

"She took Kim over to some friend's house to work on a computer program."

"Is she coming back?"

"I suppose. Want a Coke?"

Adam shook his head, disappointed by Cecelia's absence.

"She'll be gone for a while because it's all the way across town." Mary Beth opened a Coke and reached into the cabinet for a glass. "Sure you don't want something to drink?"

"All right. I guess I will have a Coke." Adam wasn't particularly thirsty, but he figured if he was going to have to wait he might as well be sociable. He watched Mary Beth bounce across the kitchen to put ice in the glasses. She didn't look a bit like Cecelia, but of course she wouldn't. Funny thing, though. Sometimes kids did look like their adoptive parents. Maybe when they were on the camping trip, if there was any opportunity, he would try again to talk to Cecelia about finding their son. Once upon a time that would have been the primary reason for the trip, but things had changed. Now what he wanted most in the world was to be with her.

Mary Beth brought his Coke to the table and went back to the cabinet for a bag of potato chips. "Sean and Kevin are really psyched about this baseball game," she volunteered. "It was so mean of Mom to make them go cut Mrs. Burke's bushes first. They could have done it next weekend, instead."

"Oh, I don't know. They'll probably be through pretty soon." Adam wasn't about to get in the middle between Mary Beth and her mother.

"Hey, do you know anything about finding people?" Mary Beth asked as she opened the bag of chips and dropped it on the table.

"Not much. Are you looking for someone particular?"

"My mother." Mary Beth munched on a chip. "My *real* mother," she clarified. "I'm adopted, you know."

Adam scooped out a handful of chips and put them in his mouth. He wasn't sure how to answer.

"Do you think that's wrong? To want to find my mother, I mean." Mary Beth sat down across from Adam.

The question was loaded, and Adam knew it. Yet he couldn't help but equate her feelings with his own desire to find his son. "I don't see that it's wrong," he said carefully. "It sounds like a natural desire."

Mary Beth looked relieved. "That's what I think, but Mom is a real pain about it. She says I don't have any right to intrude on someone's life. But it's my *mother* we're talking about."

"Well, she does have a point," Adam said diplomatically. He didn't want to undermine Cecelia, and he didn't want Mary Beth to throw his words up to her mother.

"She's just trying to run me," Mary Beth continued. "She's afraid if I find my real mother she won't be in control anymore."

The front door slammed and Adam breathed easier. He needed an escape.

"You ready to go?" Sean appeared in the kitchen doorway.

Adam stood up. "Sure am." He wished it had been Cecelia, but the boys were next best. "See you later," he said to Mary Beth, who was glaring at her brother, obviously irritated that the conversation had been cut short.

Mary Beth was still sitting at the kitchen table eating potato chips and reading a magazine when Cecelia arrived home twenty minutes later.

"Have Adam and the boys left already?" she asked Mary Beth, as she put the milk in the refrigerator.

"Uh-huh." Mary Beth didn't look up from her magazine.

Cecelia was relieved. She'd hoped they were already gone. She hadn't seen Adam since Bernice Mitchell's visit and she felt unsure of herself. "Did they leave very long ago?" she asked her daughter.

"Not too long," Mary Beth mumbled, still reading.

"Did Sean and Kevin finish cutting Mrs. Burke's bushes?"

Mary Beth smacked the palm of her hand on the magazine page and glared at her mother. "How am I supposed to know?"

"I thought maybe they mentioned it when they came home," Cecelia said patiently.

"They didn't mention anything. Adam had to wait for them because they weren't back yet when he got here. At least he's reasonable, more reasonable than you'll ever be."

"What brought that on?" Cecelia sighed. "Never mind," she added quickly. "I don't want to know. If anyone's looking for me, I've gone over to the park to watch the baseball game."

She grabbed a light jacket off the hook in the hall and walked outside, letting the storm door slam behind her.

Time to put in the screen, she decided. The lilac bush at the corner of the porch was beginning to bloom, and the grass was growing. Spring had definitely arrived. The season had a freedom about it, a sense of newness and hope that was inescapable, she thought as she admired a clump of brilliant yellow daffodils along the edge of the path leading to the ball park.

She rounded the closed concession stand and climbed to about midpoint in the bleachers before she spotted Adam. She stopped, her heart pounding. For that moment all the fears and doubts disappeared in a rush of happiness. Whatever else they had to deal with, she was glad he was home.

Realizing he hadn't yet seen her, she watched him as he stood near the fence swinging a bat. He picked up a second bat and swung, his movements fluid with strength and grace. His whole body was firm. His arm muscles rippled below the sleeves of his navy-blue T-shirt as he continued warming up. Cecelia saw him glance over at the dugout, but knew he still hadn't spotted her.

She walked up two more steps and sat down on the empty bleachers, still intent on Adam. Jeannie's advice came back again: *"Enjoy him. Spend time with him."* That was exactly what she intended to do. She knew she would eventually tell him about Danny. But she also knew there was no hurry. She wasn't being dishonest by waiting, and it would be better to choose the right time and the right place.

Adam shifted his stance so that she saw him almost in profile. His hair was barely visible beneath one of the twins' baseball hats he'd pulled low on his forehead to block the afternoon sun. The expression on his face was sober as he concentrated on his swing. He was obviously giving it everything he had. He'd always been that way, she remembered, from the time he was a kid coming over to play with her brother.

When Adam stepped down into the dugout, Cecelia scanned the rest of the field. She counted about seven or eight boys and an equal number of men, none of them, she noted, in as good physical shape as Adam. She knew the twins were probably in heaven right now. They'd talked about these father-son games all last year but had refused to go because their dad was dead. She needed to thank Adam for serving as surrogate, although she suspected he was enjoying it as much as the twins.

"Okay, play ball," shouted someone's older brother, who had apparently been designated umpire.

Adam reappeared, and on his way to the plate, glanced up toward the bleachers. A broad smile lighted his face when he saw Cecelia. She smiled back, and for one telling moment their eyes locked. She was there, and that, Adam realized, was what he'd been hoping for.

"Play ball," the umpire yelled again, and Adam turned his attention back to the game. He took the first pitch and, with a magnificent swing, blasted it over the fence.

Cecelia watched the twins run toward home plate to congratulate him after he trotted around the bases, all of them grinning with pride. She could see already that it was going to be a good afternoon.

An hour later, with the twins' team leading ten to two, the fathers decided to call it quits and go home to finish their yard work. Several of them shook hands with Adam, and as Cecelia walked down from the bleachers, she heard them asking if he would come to play again. Still beaming, the twins thanked him and took off with a group of boys to ride bikes.

Adam met Cecelia at the opening in the fence and only with enormous effort did he resist taking her in his arms. "I missed you," he whispered, taking both of her hands in his and brushing her cheek with his lips.

"Me, too." Cecelia looked up at him. "I never knew two weeks could be such a long time." Relief flooded through her. The secret hadn't built a wall between them, at least not yet. And when it did, that would be when she had to tell him. Maybe by then they'd be able to work out some reasonable plan of action.

"Did you walk or drive?" he asked her.

"On a day like this? I walked, of course."

"Good." He took her hand and they started down the gravel path. "We can walk back together. And how about a stop on the way?"

"Where?" She remembered Adam's promise to find a place where they could be alone. Surely not this afternoon..."

"Olson's ice-cream parlor."

Cecelia laughed and felt her cheeks flush. "Spectacular idea," she agreed.

They turned down a street completely overhung with huge oak trees, their branches full of fat buds. Everywhere the grass was turning green around winter-brown patches, and near the porch of one old house a huge bed of early red tulips was in bloom. "It's my favorite time of year," she said happily as two squirrels dashed in front of them in a mad chase toward a nearby tree.

"Mine, too," he agreed, opening the ice-cream parlor door.

They walked past white wire-backed chairs arranged in groups of two and three around small glass tables on their way to the counter. After studying every one of the thirty-seven flavors of ice cream in the case and carrying on a heated debate on the virtues of pralines and cream versus strawberry cheesecake, they finally ordered two banana splits and two cups of coffee which they carried to a table in the corner. Cecelia dug her spoon into the giant dish of ice cream, liberally coated with chocolate, caramel and strawberry sauce and heaped with a mound of whipped cream. She took a huge bite and sighed happily. She couldn't even remember the last time she'd eaten a banana split.

Adam watched Cecelia with satisfaction. Just being with her made his life seem more complete. "I think I've solved our problem," he said casually.

"What problem?" Her spoon was poised with fudge sauce dripping back into the bowl.

"I've finally figured out how we can be alone."

Cecelia's stomach did an odd little flip-flop and she put the spoon back in her dish.

"It just came to me last night," he continued, seeing no need to mention Lathrop. "The most secluded place around is out in the woods. We can take off for a weekend, and there will be no people and no noise, nothing but the sun and the sky and the trees—and us," he added with emphasis. He noticed Cecelia's puzzled expression. "Don't you think that sounds good?"

"It sounds wonderful but I'm not sure exactly what you're getting at."

"We can go backpacking, just the two of us."

"Backpacking?"

"Sure. Over by Coeur d'Alene there are some great trails. What do you say?"

"I...I don't know what to say. I haven't been camping for years and I've never gone backpacking.

Besides, I can't just leave. What about the kids? The shop?" She hesitated. "Adam, I don't think so."

Adam took a large bite of ice cream. The backpacking idea was the only one he'd been able to come up with. He wasn't going to give up that easily. "You're not totally indispensable, you know." He grinned. "Close maybe, but not totally. You need to get away from your kids once in a while. It will teach them to appreciate you."

"But, Adam, I don't have any equipment. I don't know how to backpack."

"Just leave all that to me," he answered authoritatively. "All you need is something to sleep in. And some boots. Do you have any boots?"

"Only my snow boots."

He frowned. "Those won't do. You'll need to buy a pair of good hiking boots and be sure to break them in. I'll take care of everything else."

Cecelia was overwhelmed. Somehow the conversation had turned from whether they were going at all to how they would make the preparations for the trip. She couldn't imagine just dropping everything and going backpacking. She looked carefully at Adam to make certain he was serious. He obviously was.

With a grin, he leaned against the wire back of his chair. "We'll have a wonderful time next weekend, Cecelia."

"Wait a minute. We can't possibly be ready to do this by next weekend! I'm not even sure about doing it at all."

"All you have to do is buy some boots, let Jeannie know you can't work Saturday and make arrangements for the children. That shouldn't take more than a week."

"I suppose not...."

"Good, then it's settled," he said with finality. "You'd better finish your ice cream before it melts."

Cecelia looked at the spreading puddle before her and then back at Adam. "I think I'm full," she replied. She didn't tell him that if the butterflies in her stomach didn't go away, she might never eat again.

FIRST THING MONDAY morning, Cecelia bought her hiking boots. She still hadn't come to terms with making the trip. But she bought the boots anyway, just in case. The salesman warned her, just as Adam had, that she needed to break them in. When she told him she might be backpacking the following weekend, he urged her to wear the boots for several hours every day until then. On a whim, she had him box her shoes, and she walked awkwardly to work wearing the new boots.

"You look as if you're going on a mountain climbing expedition," Jeannie observed when Cecelia clomped into the shop. "But in your yellow linen dress?" she asked.

As Cecelia explained that she was breaking in the boots and why, she could tell Jeannie was working very hard not to laugh. When she finished, Jeannie shook her head.

"Cecelia," she said finally, "you've never backpacked in your life. You don't know the first thing about it."

"Adam said he would take care of everything," Cecelia answered. "All I needed to do was buy boots and make arrangements for the children." She hesitated, looking at Jeannie. "Do you think I'm making a mistake going backpacking with Adam?"

"Going with Adam? No, definitely not. It's a wonderful idea. But backpacking? And what about Danny? Can you handle an entire weekend with Adam and not tell him?" Leaving her question unanswered, Jeannie disappeared into the front of the shop.

Her sister's words sent a chill through Cecelia. She'd tried not to think about Danny, but Jeannie was right. This weekend might be the time to tell Adam. And, Cecelia reasoned silently, it might not. She'd just have to wait and see. Sometimes if you put things off long enough, they worked themselves out.

That afternoon, when Cecelia made it clear that she was serious about backpacking, Jeannie suggested that Pop might be willing to spend the weekend with the children while Cecelia was gone. When Cecelia phoned him, he was enthusiastic.

"Don't get to see enough of those youngsters," he answered. "They're going to grow up and get away from me before I know it." There was a pause. "How long did you say you'd be gone?"

"Just over the weekend, Pop," she assured him. "If that's a problem..."

"No problem at all. Just take enough warm clothes. It gets cold out there at night, you know."

After she hung up, Cecelia felt the flush rise in her cheeks as she realized what she'd done. She'd just called her father and essentially told him she was going to spend the weekend sleeping with a man. Maybe he hadn't picked up that part, she thought hopefully. She closed her eyes. No, Pop was too sharp for that. At least he had chosen not to discuss it.

Cecelia knew her next hurdle would be telling her children. Alone in her bedroom after dinner, she practiced several approaches: "The spring weather is so beautiful that..." "I think it's time I went away for a day or two..." "Adam and I are going backpacking...."

She phoned Adam in despair. "This isn't going to work," she said. "There is simply no way to explain to five teenagers, whom I am trying to raise as morally responsible young adults, that I am going backpacking for a weekend with you." When Adam laughed, she almost hung up the phone.

He patiently pointed out that she was a mature adult and to be held hostage by fears for her children's moral character was ridiculous. Especially when all she was doing was going on a backpacking trip with an old friend. "Tell them we're taking two tents," he said chuckling.

"Are we?"

He laughed again and didn't answer. He almost told Cecelia about the cabin which Lathrop had arranged for them, but he decided he'd rather surprise her.

The next morning Cecelia was up early. She dressed quickly. With her high-heeled pumps in her hand, she clumped downstairs in her hiking boots to fix pancakes. Breakfast was the most hectic time of day at their house, and so it seemed the obvious opportunity to slip something by without a major reaction.

Bingo pounced on her as soon as she entered the kitchen, attacking the rawhide laces on her boots as if she had bought him a new toy. "Cut it out, Bingo," Cecelia ordered. Bingo stopped chewing briefly and looked up at her, his tail wagging happily. Then he resumed his game, yelping loudly when Cecelia scooped him up and deposited him outside the back door.

"What's the matter with Bingo?" Angela asked, dropping her books on a chair. Before Cecelia could

explain, Angela stopped dead still and stared down a
her mother's feet. "What are those awful brown thing
you're wearing?"

"Hiking boots," Cecelia answered. She checked th
temperature of the griddle and began pouring pancak
batter.

"Oh," said Angela.

Cecelia could tell that her daughter had been ren
dered temporarily speechless, but Kim and Mary Bet
were not.

"Hiking boots?" Mary Beth wrinkled up her nose i
disgust. "Mom, they're gross."

"Does this mean you're starting some sort of ne
exercise program?" Kim inquired.

"Something like that," Cecelia answered, putting
plate of pancakes on the table.

She saw the look her daughters exchanged. Just wait
she thought.

Sean and Kevin appeared simultaneously, both hov
ering over their mother with outstretched plates. "Wh
are you wearing those weird shoes?" Kevin asked as sh
filled his plate with pancakes.

"They're hiking boots," Cecelia explained again
giving the rest of the pancakes to Sean. Behind her sh
heard the girls whispering at the table.

"When are you going to begin hiking?" Angel
asked.

"This weekend," Cecelia answered, bracing hersel
as she poured more batter on the griddle.

"You and Aunt Jeannie aren't going to start a walk
ing program like some of those other ladies aroun
town?" Mary Beth demanded. "I'd be *so* embar
rassed."

Cecelia decided the moment of truth had come. "Actually, I'm going to go over to Coeur d'Alene to do some hiking this weekend."

"With Aunt Jeannie?" Kim asked.

"No," Cecelia said. "With Adam."

Silence. Cecelia didn't turn around.

"Are you going Saturday or Sunday?" Mary Beth asked. "I wanted you to take me shopping for spring clothes—"

"I'll be gone both days," Cecelia answered calmly. "We're leaving Friday morning."

Behind her, even the sounds of chewing had stopped. She scooped the last of the pancakes on a plate and turned around in time to see puzzled expressions on the girls' faces. Sean and Kevin were still focused on their breakfast and the sports section of the morning paper.

"The only way you can hike for three days is if you camp overnight," Kim said slowly. "You never go camping."

"We're going to be backpacking," Cecelia said.

This time all five children stared at her.

"With Adam?" Kim asked.

"Overnight in a tent?" Mary Beth's eyes were wide.

Sean looked up from the sports section. "Nah, they'll need two tents. Adam's too big to fit in one backpacking tent with anybody else."

Mary Beth almost choked on her pancakes.

"Are you sure you know what you're doing, Mom?" Angela asked in a carefully controlled voice.

"I think it's going to be a marvelous weekend," Cecelia proclaimed. "The wildflowers are in bloom, and the trees are just beginning to leaf out, and the weather should be absolutely glorious. Besides, it's time I took a vacation." Cecelia held her breath hoping Angela would accept her answer. The girls looked at each other, and no one said a word.

"Hey, does that mean we get to stay alone?" Kevin asked, showing an interest in the conversation for the first time.

"Absolutely not," Cecelia told him. "Pop will be here with you for the entire weekend."

"Oh, no," Sean groaned. "He'll make us do all the yard work."

"And he insists we all be in by eleven o'clock," Mary Beth wailed.

"And he's good for you," Cecelia said firmly. "If I hear one word of complaint from him about anyone, you're grounded for a month. Now hurry up or you'll all be late for school."

They left in a chorus of grumbling, the boys going out the door first followed almost immediately by Mary Beth and Kim. Only Angela hung back. "Mom, you really should think this over," she said in confidential tones.

"I've thought it over," she assured Angela. "Now hurry up or you'll be late for psychology."

Giving her mother a very knowing look, Angela finally left. Heaven save us from overprotective eighteen-year-old daughters, Cecelia thought as the screen door slammed.

That night and the next day Cecelia good-naturedly ignored several pointed comments. The children seemed to have decided that the idea of their mother going backpacking with a man was very funny. But on Wednesday night, when Adam brought over a pack for Cecelia to try, they were uncharacteristically quiet. Only Angela ventured a question.

"You're really going to do this?" she asked.

"Yep," Adam said. "You have some problem with that?" His gaze was quite direct.

Angela looked away. "None at all," she replied and disappeared up the stairs.

When she was gone, Adam checked to make sure they were alone and, finding that they were, gave Cecelia a hug. "Are they giving you a hard time?" he whispered.

"Off and on," she murmured, pressing her head against his chest. As he held her, some of her doubts subsided.

Adam checked the pack carefully and adjusted it to Cecelia's size. "What's in here only weighs ten pounds and about all you need to add is an extra pair of jeans, something to sleep in, and any personal items. You won't need much." He secured the pack on her shoulders. "Think you can carry it?"

Cecelia was surprised at how light the pack seemed with the weight resting totally on her hips. "This is really easy," she told him.

"Just don't take too much," he warned again. He promised to pick her up at eight o'clock Friday morning.

The next day at lunchtime she took a long hike through downtown Spokane, pleased that walking in the boots seemed to be getting easier. She wasn't quite sure the left one fit properly, but there wasn't much to be done about that now.

On the way back to The Kangaroo Pouch, she passed the display window of Illusions and stopped to admire the exquisite lingerie. As she stood there, she remembered Adam had mentioned twice that she would need something to sleep in. She knew he probably meant sweats or flannel pajamas. It was cold in the mountains at night.

She smiled and walked into Illusions, her hiking boots thumping on the hardwood floor. Twenty minutes later she emerged carrying a small gold-colored bag. Inside was a wispy black teddy with a wide panel of lace down the front and narrow ribbons that tied at the shoulders. It wasn't at all the thing someone would take on a camping trip, which was exactly the reason she'd bought it. She wondered whether she would have the courage to wear it.

That night, before she went to bed, Cecelia looked at the teddy again. She stroked the black satin ribbons, which felt cool to the touch and realized that never, in thirty-nine years, had she owned anything so sexy. She almost put the garment away in her lingerie drawer, but at the last moment she tucked it into the very bottom of her pack. Taking the teddy didn't mean she'd have to wear it.

As she slipped between the sheets, Cecelia realized that in twenty-four hours, she and Adam would be somewhere alone in the woods. She shivered slightly. The prospect was frightening and exciting and overwhelming all at once. Before she turned off her light, she took out her journal and wrote a swift notation:

I am going backpacking with Adam for the weekend. Everything is ready—I hope.

CHAPTER EIGHT

CECELIA TOOK ADAM'S HAND as they entered the cool shade beneath the towering pines. She felt a sense of exhilaration as the forest swallowed them up, blocking out the rest of their lives and leaving them completely alone. One glance at Adam told her he felt the same way. "You realize it's just you and me and that chipmunk over there?"

Adam looked at the chipmunk. "Scat!" He grinned at her. "Now it's just you and me."

She laughed, and they set out at a brisk pace. Cecelia drank in every detail, the sound of their boots scraping against the rocks, the shrill cadence of a bird's song, the smell of pines, and with every step she was aware of Adam just ahead of her on the narrow trail. The more they hiked, following the gentle grade of the trail steadily upward, the more wild and free Cecelia felt, as though she and Adam were embarking on a magnificent adventure.

As the trees opened and Adam offered his hand to help her climb to the top of a ridge, the thrill of discovery raced through Cecelia. Beneath them she could see a deep blue river slashing through a canyon, crashing white against the rocks, frothing and boiling in whirlpools and then rushing on to pound the rocky bed downstream. The pines stretched thick and green on either side of the water. Far beyond, snowcapped mountain peaks rose majestically against the sky.

"Oh, Adam, it's magnificent!" Cecelia exclaimed, enchanted by the raw beauty of the land. "Look at the waterfall." Standing close beside him on a massive rock that hung out over the raging river, she pointed to the side of the ridge. The spring runoff, full of melting snow, poured down the mountainside, cascading over a shelf of rock before disappearing below. "Let's climb down and see where the water ends." Cecelia's eyes sparkled with excitement.

Adam smiled at her. He had never seen her so alive, so open and vibrant. And he, too, felt totally free for the first time in months. Somehow his life gained perspective out here, and much of what ordinarily seemed important was reduced to insignificance. "All right, if you're game to climb to the bottom of the waterfall, then so am I," he replied, taking her hand.

They made their way down a steep incline, slowed by the weight of their packs. When they finally reached the bottom of the falls, they discovered a small, bubbling pool, banked by sandy soil and hidden by the dense forest surrounding it.

Adam unbuckled his waist strap and let his pack ease slowly to the ground. "I think this must be the place we reserved for lunch. What do you think?"

"Sure looks like it to me," Cecelia agreed. She dropped her pack next to his. Feeling strangely light with the weight off her back, she stretched high and threw her head back to catch the full heat of the sun on her face.

Adam caught her in his arms and whirled her around, then pulled her to him and kissed her. His light and playful gesture stirred Cecelia's emotions with a dizzying force. Pressing against him, she reached up around his neck and pulled his mouth back to hers. She kissed him with lips soft and sweet and demanding, wanting more and more of him.

"Cecelia, do you know what you're doing to me?" Adam's voice was husky and rough as he struggled for control.

"I don't care as long as you make me feel like this."

When Cecelia kissed him again, Adam groaned and slid his hands under her sweatshirt. She gasped as he caressed her and pressed her body still closer to his. "You don't know how many times I've wanted to hold you like this, Cecelia," he murmured. He wanted to take her right there under the pines by the bubbling pool but convention held him back. A bed of pine needles was no place to make love to a woman for the first time. Cecelia hadn't been with a man for years and he wanted it to be good. No, he corrected himself, not just good. He wanted everything to be perfect. Summoning all his determination, he started to pull away.

"Adam, what is it?" she whispered, her fingers stroking his soft flannel shirt.

"I want you, Cecelia." His voice strained with desire.

"Then why did you stop?"

He saw the anxiety in her face and knew he had to explain. Her fingers were inside his collar, stroking his neck. He found it very hard to think. "Not here," he said more brusquely than he meant to. "Not like this."

"Why not?" He followed her gaze to the waterfall that shimmered in the sunlight as it poured over rocks that rose rough and hard out of the earth, and then to the towering pines that whispered in the afternoon breeze. "I think this is a perfect place," she said softly. "Why not here?"

He met her eyes, a deeper blue than he'd ever seen them, and suddenly, all his reservations were gone. "When you put it that way, I can't think of a reason in the world," he answered, as he stripped off his down vest and began to unbutton his shirt. Taking it off quickly, he laid the shirt out flat on the mossy ground and sat on it, bringing Cecelia down with him.

"Adam, we've waited so long," she whispered as she buried her fingers in the crisp dark hair on his chest. "I thought we'd never be alone."

Heat spiraled through her as his hands moved across her bare back and inside the waistband of her jeans. She caressed him, her fingers guided by the movements of his body and his low moans of pleasure. All at once she was burning inside and she wanted to be part of him.

She felt her clothes falling away, and then his were gone as well. They came together quickly, and Cecelia cried out once and after that she couldn't remember. All she knew was that she was free, like the water spilling down the mountainside in the burning heat of the sun.

ADAM'S ARMS CRADLED HER as Cecelia opened her eyes. The sunlight slanting through the pines warmed her as Adam's hands gently stroked her winter-white skin. "You took me to this wonderful place," she murmured dreamily, "and I didn't ever want to come back." She snuggled her head against him and heard the muffled beating of his heart.

Adam stroked her cheek. Lying there with her body molded against his, he let his thoughts wander back across the years and wondered again what their lives might have been like if circumstances had been different. He heard a rustle of leaves. A twig snapped. Their bodies tensed but they didn't move.

As they watched, a young buck emerged from the forest and walked almost soundlessly to the edge of the pool to drink. Cecelia knew he must have seen them and then apparently decided that they belonged to the quiet, peaceful setting and posed no threat to him. The animal was so close that she could see his tongue lapping into the cold water and the droplets spray in the sunshine as he shook his head. Cecelia held her breath until he walked slowly away, leaving only his footprints in the soft sand near the waterfall.

"I feel like he accepted us," Cecelia said softly as he disappeared into the trees.

"Maybe he did," Adam answered, propping his head on his elbow and smiling down at Cecelia. "Maybe he's been watching us."

"Oh, Adam, I don't think so."

"Why not? What we were doing is pretty universal, you know. Only humans hide it away."

Cecelia glanced down at their bodies, Adam's lean and firm beneath dark curls of hair on his chest and abdomen, hers so soft and white next to his. She felt no embarrassment. She touched his chest, brushing her fingers across the wiry hair as she traced it downward.

He tensed and drew in a sharp breath. "Keep doing that and we'll start all over," he promised.

A little shiver ran through Cecelia. "Maybe we could stay here all weekend," she murmured, "and never get dressed. We'd just be part of the natural order of things."

Adam touched her breast playfully with his lips, nuzzling and biting, and Cecelia dropped onto her back with a gasp. "Oh, that feels so...so—"

"So wonderfully arousing," he finished for her, drawing back and glancing up at the sun which was dropping toward the tops of the trees. "That's why I'm going to stop right now. We've got a ways to go before dark." He crouched on his knees and held out his hands to her. "Besides, we haven't had lunch. That's also part of the natural order of things."

Cecelia laughed, realizing suddenly that she was ravenously hungry. They dressed quickly and Adam dug in his pack for their lunch. As she mixed lemonade in their sierra cups, he unwrapped two fat submarine sandwiches, pears and cookies.

She looked at the sumptuous meal. "If you had all that in your pack, I don't see how there was room for a tent and sleeping bags and your clothes..."

"Trust me," Adam mumbled around a large bite of pear.

Cecelia's expression grew serious. "I do trust you, Adam. I didn't realize how much."

He studied her as she sat leaning against a fallen tree, the sunlight glinting off the water and playing in her hair, and he knew he was in love with her. Maybe he'd always loved her and maybe that was part of the reason no one else had ever been right for him. "You are one hell of a woman, Cecelia Mahoney," he whispered, "and I guess you already know I've fallen in love with you."

"Because the sex was good?" she asked bluntly.

He shook his head. "No, you've got it backward. That's why the sex was good."

Cecelia sat back on her heels and smiled at him. "You know, Adam, I think you're right."

"Of course I'm right," he answered. Her smile made her whole face glow. All he wanted was to hold her and sit there with her under the big cedar while they watched the evening come. But with no tent and no sleeping bags, he knew that wasn't feasible. They had to get moving. "It's time to go," he said. "If we don't pack up and get out of here in the next five minutes, we're never going to make it by dark."

Perplexed, Cecelia stood up. "You make it sound as though someone is expecting us."

"Not on your life," he assured her. "This whole weekend belongs to us." He picked up her pack and held it while she slid her arms through the shoulder straps and then knelt down to put on his own pack.

Cecelia decided not to question him further. Adam obviously had this trip all mapped out and he wasn't about to change his plans. Or to discuss them. She had been the one in charge for so long that having someone else make the decisions was nice for a change, she decided as she followed him into the woods.

By the time Cecelia and Adam emerged from the trail to a gravel road in a clear area of the forest, the sky had turned dusky purple streaked with pink. The sun had disappeared behind the mountains. Ahead of them a small cabin was nestled in the trees. After sliding his map and compass into an outside pocket of his pack, Adam turned and took Cecelia's hand. "That's home for the weekend. What do you think?"

Cecelia blinked to make sure the cabin with its gray weathered siding and curtained windows wasn't a mirage. Her legs ached from walking and one shoulder was sore where the strap on her pack had rubbed it. In spite of her heavy parka, the evening chill had crept through her. "It looks like a dream come true," she said, squeezing Adam's hand. "But I thought we were sleeping in a tent."

"A cabin has certain advantages." He smiled down at her. "Including a bed."

"That's a big advantage."

They dropped their packs on the small front porch and walked inside. Cecelia was charmed by the rustic simplicity of the one-room cabin. The furnishings were simple: red-checked gingham curtains at the windows; a wooden table and chairs near the potbellied stove; and a high, rough-hewn bed covered with a patchwork feather quilt.

Remembering the sandy earth by the waterfall, Cecelia looked at the bed and then at Adam. "Now I understand why you wanted to wait until we got here."

"Are you sorry?"

"What do you think?"

Adam's eyes told her he already knew the answer. "I've got another surprise," he said, his lips buried in her hair. "That ice chest in the corner has two very thick steaks and a bottle of wine inside. All I have to do is start the grill."

Cecelia smiled. He'd thought of everything, planned the weekend perfectly. And he'd done it all for her. "I love you, Adam," she said softly.

"Because I brought the steaks?"

She grinned, remembering her own response when he'd told her he loved her. "No, silly, not because you brought the steaks. Just because I do."

Adam hugged her, laughing.

"I don't suppose this establishment has a bathroom," Cecelia said hopefully as she looked around.

"Nope. No plumbing or electricity. But I suspect there are facilities out back." Adam chuckled to himself. He had never really thought about it before, but backpacking was more convenient for men than women.

"I get the picture," Cecelia muttered, heading for the door. "At least it beats the bushes."

By the time Cecelia returned, Adam had started the coals, lighted a kerosene lantern and taken their packs inside. He was sitting on the porch steps drinking wine from a sierra cup. Cecelia sat down beside him and accepted the cup of wine he handed to her. The crisp air and the exercise had left her physically exhausted, and yet it was a pleasant kind of exhaustion. Her body was completely relaxed with all the strain and tension wrung out of it. Her mind, totally unencumbered, absorbed the sounds of the forest and the strength and security of Adam's arm around her shoulders.

"Shall we drink a toast?" He raised his cup to hers. "A toast to us, Cecelia, and to our future together."

She paused, realizing the significance of what he was saying. A racoon chirped somewhere off in the gathering darkness, and a bird called to its mate. Only one uncertain note disturbed the otherwise perfect evening. Adam still didn't know about Danny. Could she toast the future without telling him? If she discussed it now, Cecelia reasoned, the world would intrude on the cocoon they had spun around themselves. It was too soon, she decided. The night belonged to them.

She met his eyes, dark and tender in the deepening shadows. "I'll drink to that, Adam, to us and our future." The mellow wine warmed her, and she laid her head on Adam's shoulder. She realized that if she was looking for a definition of happiness, she'd have to look no further.

They ate dinner inside by lantern light, and afterward Adam built a fire in the pot-bellied stove and put on a pan of water to heat. "I'm going to make sure the charcoal is out and take care of a few other things," he told Cecelia. "If you mix some of that hot water with some cold from the pump in the sink, you can take a bath.

"All the comforts of home," Cecelia observed, thinking that a bath in any fashion would feel very good. She watched Adam's flashlight fade and then fixed the water, undressed, and bathed, all the time humming to herself. Shivering with cold, she dug down into the corner of her pack until she felt the seductive silk and lacy teddy. Adam had planned surprises for her. Now she had one for him.

"WHAT DO YOU SUPPOSE Mom and Adam are doing right now?" Kevin yawned as he moved his Monopoly piece six spaces to Baltic Avenue. He and his brothers and sisters, along with Pop, had been engrossed in a Monopoly game since just after dinner.

Ignoring his question, Kim held out her hand. "You landed on my property. I want my rent money." With a grimace, Kevin reluctantly counted out the required amount.

"It's almost ten o'clock, and it's a lot darker in the woods than it is here," Sean answered. "I bet Mom and Adam are already in bed."

"Yeah, they were probably tired after walking all day," Kevin agreed.

Mary Beth rolled her eyes at Angela. "They may be in bed, but they're not sleeping."

"Mary Beth!" Kim glanced uncomfortably at her grandfather.

"Well, it's true." Mary Beth defended herself. "They didn't go backpacking to look at the spring flowers.

They wanted to be all alone, with nobody to bother them, so they could—"

"Shut up!" Angela warned her sister.

"So they could what?" Kevin asked.

"You know." Sean gave his brother a meaningful look as he rolled the dice.

"Oh, that. You think our mom's out in the woods doing that?"

Both boys coughed loudly.

"You two are disgusting," Kim told her brothers.

Pop had been sitting quietly, sizing up the situation and wondering what he should say, if anything, to his grandchildren. He wasn't sure what to tell them. A few years back, when his own brood was growing up, he would have taken a very moralistic approach. But times had changed, and so had kids. They were exposed to a lot these days, what with movies and television, and they had a pretty fair idea of what was going on in the world. Probably no point in beating around the bush. He relit his pipe. "Yep, I imagine Mary Beth is right," he began. "I suspect Adam and your Ma wanted to spend some time alone with each other."

The silence that followed Pop's statement was deafening. All action at the Monopoly board ceased, and five pairs of eyes were suddenly riveted on him. Even Bingo stopped scratching his ear and cocked his head. Pop cleared his throat. Well, now he had opened the can of worms. What next? His gaze moved slowly around the table, meeting each pair of eyes in turn. "I think your Ma and Adam kinda like each other. How do you feel about that?"

Several bodies squirmed uncomfortably until Angela finally answered. "Mom has a perfect right to like anyone she pleases and do anything she wants," she said.

"Oh no she doesn't," Mary Beth countered. "She's out there in the woods, alone with a man, doing things she'd pulverize *us* for doing."

Angela glanced helplessly at her grandfather, and Kim busied herself sorting the Monopoly money into tidy piles.

"What's Mom doing that's so awful?" Kevin asked.

Again Pop looked around the table. "Your mother isn't doing anything awful. She and Adam are getting to know each other again after a long time, and they're probably doing some loving, too."

"Oh." Kevin lowered his eyes.

"Nothing wrong with that," Pop continued. "Perfectly natural for two adults—" he emphasized the word adult and looked directly at Mary Beth "—who care a lot about each other."

"Are Adam and Mom going to get married?" Sean asked.

"Too soon to tell about that." Pop drew in on his pipe again. "But your Ma's been a widow for a long time now, and Adam's never been married at all. He's a fine man. If they decide they love each other enough, it might be a good thing for both of them." Pop had spent a considerable amount of time one afternoon, mulling over that very question, and had come to exactly the conclusion he had just shared with his grandchildren. More than that, he'd heard the excitement in his daughter's voice when she had told him about this weekend with Adam. She had sounded more alive, more vibrant, than she had in years. If she and Adam could unsnarl the past enough to make a future together, then they had his blessing.

"I like Adam," Kim said softly. "I like the way he treats Mom, like she's really special, or something." Blushing slightly, she went back to sorting the money.

"Yeah, he's okay," Kevin said. Sean nodded in agreement.

"I suppose he's all right," Mary Beth added. "But if you ask me, they act like two people who know each other pretty well, considering they haven't been together for twenty years." She gave Pop a suspicious look. "Were they in love with each other back then?"

"Could be," Pop answered slowly.

"Then why did Adam go away?" Why did Mom marry Dad, instead?" Angela frowned, and Pop could tell she was trying to put some pieces of the puzzle together.

"Well...." He began slowly, knowing he had to be careful of what he said. "Your Ma was pretty young, just finishing high school, when Adam graduated from the Air Force Academy. Then he went on to pilot training and Viet Nam. By the time all that was over your Ma was married to your Dad and most of you were underfoot—"

"But if Mom loved Adam, why didn't she wait for him until he came back from Viet Nam?" Angela persisted.

"That was a long time," Pop replied. "Adam was shot down and listed as missing in action for quite some time, as I recall. When we finally found out he was alive and a prisoner, a lot of years had passed, and even then we didn't know if he'd ever get home alive. After a while, we kind of lost track of him, until just this winter when he showed up again."

"But—" Angela began again.

"Nope, no more stories tonight." Pop stood up and stretched. "My old bones are getting weary, and I'm going up to bed in a few minutes. But first I'm going to have a dish of ice cream. Anybody care to join me?"

BY THE TIME ADAM returned to the cabin, Cecelia was snuggled between the cool, white sheets with the feather quilt pulled up to her chin.

"I see it didn't take you long to get into bed," he observed as he latched the door behind him. "Are you warm enough?"

Her only response was a soft laugh.

"Just wait till I get there and you'll be warmer," Adam promised.

"I'm counting on that."

Adam banked the fire in the stove. "If I'd thought ahead, I'd have brought you some long underwear."

Cecelia snuggled a little deeper in the feather bed. "What a nice thought, Adam, but that really wasn't necessary. I took care of things myself."

As he set the lantern on the table by the bed, Adam saw her eyes sparkling mischievously. With a sudden swift motion he pulled back the quilt, exposing her whole body. In the flickering light, her skin was milky white against the black lace teddy. The sheer fabric lay across the fullness of her breasts, tapering in at her slender waist, emphasizing her every curve. Adam cleared his throat. "You took care of things all right," he said in a husky voice.

Cecelia held out her arms. "I already told you, I'm counting on you to keep me warm."

Wordlessly Adam stripped off his long underwear. For an instant he stood above her, naked in the lanternlight, and Cecelia felt her whole body tremble. Then he was beside her, coarse hair against smooth skin, hard strength against feminine softness, and Cecelia felt she would never be cold again. Their lovemaking was slow and sensual, their hands and lips exploring what their eyes couldn't see. They luxuriated in the exquisite sensations of skin on silk, traveling through the peaks and valleys of desire even before Adam untied the ribbons on her teddy and slowly pulled it down.

When Cecelia awoke the next morning in Adam's arms, the night before seemed like a dream. Adam's eyes were gentle, his hair tousled as he lay beside her watching her awaken. As soon as his lips found hers, she knew he had been waiting for her, and to her amazement her body seemed to have been waiting for him. In the innocence of morning they came together again.

"I can't seem to get enough of you," Adam said, stroking her cheek with one finger.

Cecelia smiled lazily. "You'd be more accurate if you said we can't get enough of each other."

She squeezed Adam's hand, and he continued stroking her cheek without saying a word. He was thinking about how good life was. When he'd come back to Spokane, he'd been searching for answers from the past. Instead he'd found a future. Although his career was on track, and he should soon make brigadier general, the restlessness that often precedes middle age caused him to want more than that. Cecelia filled his emptiness, and now there was only one thing missing. Today, he decided, was the time to talk to Cecelia again about trying to find their son.

After a leisurely breakfast of bacon and eggs and biscuits, they left the cabin to take a walk through the cool, damp forest. Cecelia wished she'd worn an extra sock on her left foot. She'd taped the sore spot on the back of her heel, but even laced tightly, her left boot felt unsteady.

"Does your foot hurt?" Adam asked when he saw she was favoring it.

"Not really. The boot doesn't fit too well, but I don't think it's going to matter." She smiled up at him. "And if that's my biggest problem, I'd say I'm in pretty good shape." She felt enormously happy and totally complete. She hadn't been with a man for a very long time and sometimes she'd felt as though she had closed a door on her own sexuality and shut it forever. Now she knew better.

The forest was silent as they walked along, except for occasional cries of birds and a light breeze rustling the trees. Pines with long, bare trunks rose straight and tall, their deep-green branches reaching for the sunlight. A chipmunk scurried across the trail and disappeared behind a moss-covered rock. Ahead of them the trees parted, and they found a craggy cliff where they could look out across the wilderness and see the mountains meet the sky.

Adam led Cecelia up the rocks above a quiet stream that meandered along until it disappeared into the trees. "There's something I want to talk to you about," he said as they sat down on a broad, flat rock.

"Just make sure it's something lovely and happy and whimsical," she answered, closing her eyes and tipping her face toward the sun.

"I'm afraid not."

Not only his words but the tone of his voice told Cecelia he was about to break the magic spell their lovemaking had cast. She'd known they would eventually have to deal with reality, but she was sorry the time had come so soon. "Whatever it is, Adam, I'm listening," she said quietly.

"Cecelia," he began, "you know how much I love you. I want to be a part of you in every way I can," he continued slowly, "and there's a bond between us we haven't acknowledged."

She tensed.

"You can't keep denying it, Cecelia. We have a son who is part of us both."

Their son. So that was what this discussion was to be about. Cecelia reached out and touched Adam's arm. "I understand what you're trying to tell me, really I do."

"No, you don't, at least not all of it," he interrupted. Adam's eyes darkened and his face grew taut. "You can't possibly understand the rage inside of me. Try to imagine having a son you've never seen and then think about not being able to have another child." He jammed his hands in his jacket pocket and looked directly at her. "Damn it, Cecelia, why can't you be pregnant with my baby now when I love you so much, instead of twenty years ago when neither of us was ready?"

"I don't know, Adam," she replied softly.

He took her hand, and she could feel the intensity surging through him. "I want to find our son. Except for you, he's all I have, or ever will have." His voice grew softer. "He's part of us, created from our love—however immature that emotion might have been—and I want him in our lives."

Cecelia swallowed hard, knowing that now she had to tell him about Danny. She also knew she held the ticket to what Adam wanted so much. How could she ever persuade him not to use it? "There's something I have to tell you, Adam," she said haltingly. "But please promise me you won't rush into anything."

He nodded, puzzled.

Her words came slowly at first. She watched his expression change as he listened and then started to truly understand. By the time she had finished her story, beginning with Bernice Mitchell's visit and ending with a description of Danny, Adam was grinning broadly.

"I can't believe this," he kept saying over and over. "I thought it would take months, or even years to find him. Don't you understand what this means, Cecelia?"

"It doesn't have to mean anything." She saw a shadow cross his face, and she looked away. "I know how much you want this, Adam, but I think you're about to make a big mistake. There are lots of people involved, lots of people who are going to get hurt."

"You're wrong, Cecelia." The determination in his voice left no doubt about where he stood. "You think your children won't understand, but you underestimate them. And who else is there to get hurt?"

"Danny."

"You just told me his adopted father is dead. Now you're saying that finding his natural father will hurt him?"

"Not hurt him, exactly, but . . ." Cecelia looked out at the clouds that shrouded the mountaintop beyond a vast expanse of earth and sky. The serenity was a harsh contrast to the turmoil inside her. Somehow she had to make Adam realize he was pursuing a dangerous fantasy. "I think Danny is going to see you as an intruder," she told him bluntly. "I know that sounds unfair, but he's so very different from you. His hair is long and unkempt, his clothes are even worse than most college kids, he wears an earring—one earring. I doubt if he's ever held a baseball bat or a ball in his hands.''

Adam leaned forward. ''Don't you see? That's all the more reason—''

''No, let me finish,'' Cecelia interrupted. ''Danny was one of the leaders of that antinuclear demonstration out at the base a few months ago.''

Frowning, Adam thought about the sandy-haired boy with the black bandana and an egg in his hand. Then he rejected the image. There'd been hundreds of kids out there. Surely that one hadn't been his son.

Realizing that she was beginning to get through to him, Cecelia plunged ahead. ''And in addition to Danny, think about everyone else. No one knows about the baby except Pop and Jeannie. Even if my children could accept Danny, I'm not anxious to discuss my illegitimate child—''

''Illegitimate? I haven't heard that word in years. You make it sound as though having Danny was wrong, somehow.''

''It was wrong, Adam. I've never stopped feeling ashamed—'' Her voice broke and she couldn't go on.

Adam took her in his arms. ''I'm sorry,'' he said softly. ''Society is so accepting of single mothers now that I almost forget how bad it was for you back then. But, for Pete's sake, Cecelia, you did nothing to be ashamed of. It just happened. If anyone is to blame, it's me. I'm older than you. I knew what could happen, and I did nothing to prevent it. I've never forgiven myself for getting you pregnant.''

''I wanted to make love just as much as you did,'' Cecelia reminded him.

''I remember.'' Adam smoothed her hair back from her face and smiled. ''That hasn't changed, has it?''

She shook her head.

"And if you love me enough to give yourself to me, then you have to trust me. At least go partway. Come with me to visit Bernice Mitchell and let me find out about Danny. At least let me know what my son is like."

His plea was so moving. If Danny were her only son, the only child she would ever have, she would feel the same way Adam did. Maybe there wouldn't be any harm in his talking to Bernice. "All right," she finally said. "One visit with his mother if you promise not to contact him." But she knew she was deceiving herself. Meeting Danny's mother wouldn't satisfy Adam for long.

"I won't do anything without telling you first, Cecelia," Adam replied. "And until we get home, we won't even think about it anymore. The rest of the weekend is ours."

He reached out to help her up and she quickly ended up in his arms. He kissed her with a joyful abandon that she knew reflected his excitement about Danny. But then he kissed her again and she felt his focus change.

"I think we have an appointment back at the cabin," he whispered.

"Race you," she answered playfully and took off down the trail.

"Are you sure you know where you're going?" he called out, loping easily behind her.

"Of course," she shouted over her shoulder. "It's just back the same way we came." Ahead of her the trail forked but she didn't hesitate, certain she should go to the right.

"Cecelia, wait!"

As she heard him shout, she saw the precipice ahead of her and tried to stop. Grabbing for a scrub pine to steady herself, she felt her left boot catch in a crevice between two rocks. One rock gave way and then another. Her ankle caught and twisted, and for an endless moment she balanced precariously.

Then with a cracking sound another rock gave way. Her boot wrenched free and she was falling, tumbling down. As she plummeted over the embankment, with rocks gouging into her body and brambles tearing at her face, she tried frantically to grab at anything that might stop her fall.

"Help, please help me," she screamed.

"Cecelia!" Adam shouted. He saw her falling and hurled himself down the incline after her, skidding on the rocks, finally stopping against a large bush beside her. He put one hand under her head and felt the pulse in her neck with the other. Her heartbeat was steady and her breathing was strong, but from the way her foot was twisted he knew before he even tried to move her that bones were broken. He'd have to get help quickly—he had to get her out of there by dark.

Cecelia's eyelids fluttered. Adam was kneeling above her, cradling her head in his hands and saying her name again and again. She closed her eyes.

CHAPTER NINE

CECELIA TRIED TO FOCUS, but glaring white lights bore down on her. She tried to move, but a sharp pain laced through her back. Her body felt like lead. There were other sounds, clanking, clattering sounds and muffled voices in the distance. She felt pressure on her hand.

"Cecelia?"

The voice again. She forced her eyelids open, squinting in the light. Slowly she saw the person above her— the shape of the head, the shock of sandy hair across his forehead, the wonderful, gentle eyes, agonized now and dark with worry.

"Adam," she said softly, seeing him as though in a dream.

"Thank God, Cecelia, you're finally awake."

She had been sleeping, maybe for a long time. She wondered why. She tried to sit up but this time the pain knifed through her right leg and she cried out, falling back against the pillows.

"Lie still, Cecelia," Adam ordered. "Everything's going to be all right."

But it wasn't all right. She sensed that. She tried to move again, to see where she was but instantly the pain came back. "What's happened, Adam? Where am I?" She was fully awake now.

"You're in the hospital, Cecelia. Don't you remember at all?"

"We were backpacking," she said slowly. "We were going back to the cabin. I was running and then..." Her voice faded and she looked up at Adam.

"And then you lost your footing and slid down the embankment." He tried to banish the image of her lying there pale and still. Fear had driven him at a dead run down the trails toward the isolated ranger's cabin where he could call for help. Now as he looked at her, she seemed so fragile beneath the stark white hospital sheets.

"Am I hurt?" she asked in a small voice.

"You broke your ankle and you have some bruises and scrapes that are going to hurt for a while, but otherwise you're all right."

She shifted her weight and moaned. "I feel awful."

His eyes clouded. "Cecelia, I'm so sorry." He pressed her hand between both of his.

"You sound like you think it's your fault."

"I told you I'd take care of everything. Fine job I did."

He looked as miserable as if he had pushed her down the hill himself. "I was the one who tripped over my own feet and fell. You were the one who had to take care of me." Cecelia wanted to sit up and take him in her arms and assure him he wasn't responsible, but everything was such an effort. "How did I get here, anyway?" she asked him.

"I called for help from the ranger's cabin and they flew us out by helicopter. There's a clear spot not too far from where you fell." His voice was shaky as he briefly recounted the rescue. "You were only half-conscious most of the time. The paramedics said you were in shock."

Cecelia tried to imagine Adam's ordeal. "I'm the one who's sorry, Adam," she said weakly. "I ruined everything."

"You? If I hadn't insisted on going backpacking—"

"Adam . . ." Cecelia managed a smile. She squeezed his hand again and her eyes sought his. "I wouldn't trade this weekend with you for anything in the world."

"Even after what happened?"

"Even after what happened," she said firmly.

He watched her eyelids grow heavy as she struggled to stay awake. The doctor had told him she would probably be groggy for several more hours, and as much as he hated to leave her, he knew the best thing for Cecelia was sleep.

"I'm going to stop by your house and make sure everything's under control there," he said. "I'll come back in the morning."

"You mean I have to stay in the hospital?" Cecelia asked sleepily.

"Just for a day or two," Adam assured her. "Then I'll take you home."

"Mmm. If you promise. . . ." Her eyes closed, and Adam watched her drift away. Reluctantly he let go of her hand and turned away, taking with him the image of the fragile beauty, who had become a part of him in a way no other woman had before.

BY THE TIME ADAM RETURNED the next day, Cecelia's mood had changed considerably. She was propped up against the pillows, staring intently out the window although the view offered nothing but sky with an occasional cloud floating by. When she saw Adam, she managed a smile, but not a very enthusiastic one.

"How do you feel this morning?" he asked cheerfully. He wished he'd brought flowers. The room was stark and institutional. Although it was a semi-private, the other bed was empty.

Cecelia grimaced. "Frustrated. Mad. Like a prisoner in this stupid cast." She awkwardly shifted her weight and, with great effort, pushed her body a few inches upward against the pillows. "If all I broke was my ankle, I don't see why I'm in plaster almost up to my fanny."

Adam tried not to laugh. She looked so appealing swathed in white, her dark curls spread out against the pillow. Her pallor was gone and her cheeks had a pink, healthy glow from the weekend outdoors. "Casts always seem bigger than necessary, especially when you have to haul them around." He sat down on a chair near the bed. "Have you been up yet?"

"Three times." Cecelia winced, just thinking about it. "And on top of everything else, the doctor says I strained my wrist when I fell, so I'm terrible with crutches. That means I either hop or don't move for at least a week." She lapsed into silence, staring out the window again. It all seemed so unfair.

"A week isn't very long." Adam tried hard to be encouraging. "And you'll have help. Pop and the kids were really sympathetic, and Jeannie said not to worry about a thing. She'll take care of the shop."

"I know," Cecelia answered darkly. "They called me. All of them. I've done nothing but talk on the telephone." She glowered at Adam. "I hate it here," she said vehemently. "Please take me home."

Adam nodded his head. "First thing in the morning," he promised. "I brought you some clothes." He showed her the bag Angela had painstakingly packed after much discussion of what her mother would be able to comfortably wear.

"But I want to go home now," Cecelia protested. She looked as though she might cry.

Adam didn't answer. He pulled his chair closer to the edge of the bed and took Cecelia's hand. It lay limp and unresponsive in his. For the next hour he tried to talk to her, but without much success. Although she said she wasn't in pain, she obviously felt helpless and depressed and nothing he said seemed to make things any better. Finally he left, agreeing to relay to her family that she didn't want any visitors or any phone calls.

Cecelia was convinced she would never be happy again. She spent all day in a blue funk. She rejected lunch, except for a cup of tea, and left the newspaper, delivered by a cheery volunteer, unopened on the table beside her bed. She wanted nothing except to be left alone. But after several hours passed and no one came or called, she felt deserted and angry. When a motherly, white-haired nurse brought her dinner, Cecelia told her to take it away.

The nurse removed the cover from the tray and placed it in front of Cecelia. "You're not going to get well unless you eat."

"I don't want to eat," Cecelia sulked.

"You think that over," the nurse said firmly. "You don't know how lucky you are. In a few weeks you'll be just fine. I have a dozen other patients who would give anything to be able to say that." She squared her shoulders and walked away quickly.

The emotion in the woman's voice jarred Cecelia. She looked down at the cast on her leg and then thought about Adam and her children and all the people who loved her. Slowly her anger and resentment ebbed

Tears flowed silently down her cheeks as she realized how lucky she was. Tomorrow she was going home.

WHEN ADAM ARRIVED to pick her up, Cecelia was dressed and ready. Balancing awkwardly on her left foot, she reached up and hugged him and he held her tightly for several moments, wondering at the metamorphosis.

"I'm sorry I acted like a two-year-old," she whispered.

"Never mind," he answered. "Let's go home."

The house was quiet when they arrived, except for Bingo, who barked furiously and danced around Adam's feet as soon as he opened the door. The children were all at school, and on his way to the hospital, Adam had dropped Joe Riley at the airport to catch a plane to Fresno. When Jim had called the night before to say Cindy was in labor, Adam had been secretly glad. He wanted to take care of Cecelia himself.

"Out, dog!" he ordered, giving Bingo a shove with his foot. Then he swept Cecelia in his arms and carried her grandly up the stairs, ignoring her laughing protests.

"I really don't need to go to bed, you know," she said as he placed her gently on the quilt. "I just have a broken ankle. I'm not sick."

Adam looked confused. "I guess I just thought after you came from the hospital—"

"But as long as we're here . . ." She smiled up at him and held out her arms.

He sat carefully on the edge of the bed and let her pull him down to her, terribly afraid he might hurt her. When she kissed him, his body tightened. Her mouth was inviting, her lips warm and wet.

"Come to me, Adam," she said softly, smiling as she ran her fingers slowly along the inside of his thigh. "We're all alone."

The offer was irresistible. A shudder ran through him. "I'll hurt you, Cecelia."

"No, you won't." She playfully pulled him down again but as he bumped against her leg, she cried out in pain.

Quickly Adam drew back. "Are you all right?"

"I'm fine." She looked up with a rueful smile. " guess I was a little overoptimistic. The doctor said wouldn't feel any pain after a few days and so thought—"

"You thought you'd just hurry things along a little."

"But Adam, we're never alone—"

"We will be. I've already arranged to take some extra-long lunch hours."

"Really?" Cecelia answered. The prospect of having her leg in a cast for a few weeks was looking decidedly better.

"Now we're going to get out of the bedroom while still have any willpower left." Adam carried Cecelia downstairs as easily as he'd taken her up and settled her on one kitchen chair with her injured leg in its bulky white cast propped up on another. Over a lunch of ham sandwiches, potato chips and iced tea, he broached the idea of visiting Bernice Mitchell.

Cecelia's expression grew sober. "I know I agreed that we see her," Cecelia admitted, "but I'm still not sure it's for the best. Danny is nearly grown, Adam, and he's very different from what you expect. I've tried to explain that to you—" The image of Danny standing in ıer hallway with his long hair, black armband and the ːarring in his ear came back to Cecelia.

"Why don't you let me find out for myself?" Adam ısked quietly. "That's the only way I'm going to really ⸤now."

Cecelia lowered her eyes, realizing she had no valid ırgument. She told Adam that she didn't feel up to the ⸤isit, and they agreed that she could call Bernice Mitchell to make the arrangements, but he would go ılone.

"Thank you, Cecelia," he whispered as he left her ate that afternoon in the oversolicitous care of Kim and ⸤ngela. "Thank you for understanding about Danny. t's something I have to do."

Cecelia had a sudden rush of panic, wondering if ⸤he'd misunderstood his intentions. "But you're only ⸤oing to talk to his mother, aren't you?"

"Yes," he promised. "Until you and I agree other-⸤ise, that's all I'm going to do."

THE ONE-STORY HOUSE where Danny and his mother ⸤ved was a combination brick and frame structure, ⸤mall and not too well kept. The bushes were badly in ıeed of trimming, Adam noted as he walked briskly up ⸤he front sidewalk. Patches of brown crabgrass dotted ⸤he lawn, giving it an untidy look in a neighborhood ⸤here other yards were immaculately tended. Adam ⸤emembered that Danny's father had died last fall, and ıis mother had been ill.

As he rang the doorbell, Adam checked his watch. He ⸤as only a few minutes late, despite the last-minute ⸤neeting with Lathrop. Too bad he hadn't had time to ⸤hange out of his uniform, but he supposed that didn't ⸤natter. It was more important that he complete his visit

and leave before Danny came home. Bernice Mitchell
had told Cecelia that Danny had classes until four. That
gave them almost two hours. Would that be enough—
or too much, he wondered.

The latch clicked, and with a combination of cur-
osity and apprehension he watched the white wooden
door open. After nearly twenty years of wondering
about the child he'd fathered, he was about to find out.

The woman in the doorway was sixtyish, with a
deeply lined face. She looked as if she'd experienced
more grief than joy. Her graying hair was combed
neatly back from her face. She wore no makeup.
"Come in, Colonel Campbell," she replied when he
introduced himself.

Adam followed Bernice Mitchell into a casual, comfortably furnished living room with a large, green-
striped sofa, two overstuffed green chairs and a wood-
frame rocker. She motioned for him to sit down and
after setting aside a needlepoint canvas, she seated herself in the rocker. He felt her studying him, and when
he glanced up, she quickly looked away.

"I have to apologize for staring at you," she said
nervously. "It's just that Danny looks like you. Not so
much right now, maybe, but I can see the resemblance
in your eyes. He is obviously your son."

"Yes, Danny is my son," Adam assured her quietly.
He was intrigued by the idea of a physical resemblance. Cecelia hadn't mentioned that. "Do you have
a picture of him?"

"I got out all the photograph albums from when he
was little." She gestured toward a stack of large, vinyl-
covered books on the coffee table in front of them.
"Maybe you'd like to look at them."

Adam opened the first album and found photos of a tiny baby sleeping in a white crib, lying on a blanket, drinking from a bottle, holding a rattle. The pictures went on, page after page, a testimony to new parents totally immersed in their baby boy. Adam felt little kinship for the child who looked like a hundred other babies. He flipped the pages faster, moving quickly into a second album and then a third.

Bernice Mitchell watched him go through the albums. "His father took so many pictures." She hesitated. "I mean, my husband. . . ."

Adam looked up to see the uncertainty in her face. "No," he said. "You were right the first time. He *was* Danny's father."

Bernice Mitchell looked away. "I have a picture of Danny that was taken two years ago. It's in my bedroom," she said, standing up. "That's the one you should see."

After she left to get the picture, Adam looked around the room again. He saw no sign of anything that belonged to Danny—except possibly some of the books in the bookcase that stretched across an entire wall at the end of the room. A picture on an end table between the green chairs caught his attention, and he stood up to look at it more closely. It was an enlarged snapshot of a slight, balding man carrying a bag of some kind.

"That was the only recent photograph I had of my husband," Bernice Mitchell said from behind him. "I had it enlarged after . . . after he passed away."

"Had he been ill for some time?" Adam asked sympathetically.

"Several years."

Adam sat back on the sofa without questioning her further. She obviously still had difficulty talking about her husband's death.

"I always thought it was too bad that Danny and my husband, Bill, didn't look anything alike," Bernice Mitchell continued. "That can be an important bond." She handed Adam the picture she'd brought from the bedroom. "I'm sure you can see his resemblance to you."

Adam stared down into a pair of brown eyes very much like his own. He did see the resemblance immediately, and although he knew he should have expected it, he was startled just the same. This was truly his son, he thought, still somewhat in awe of the fact. They were as close biologically as if he'd raised the boy. No matter what had happened since, the boy carried his genes, his and Cecelia's. He was a blend of both of then, and when Adam looked more carefully, he could see that Danny's mouth and the shape of his face were very much like hers. Adam studied the picture, memorizing every detail.

The boy in the portrait was half smiling, as though someone had said something to amuse him just before the photographer snapped the shutter. He seemed fully grown and yet young, with a gentleness about him. He was, Adam decided, not handsome in the classic sense although one day he might be. In the photo he was more what a girl might consider "cute," and what her mother would call appealing. "How old was he here?" Adam asked.

"Seventeen." Bernice Mitchell hesitated before she added, "Of course, he looks much different now."

Adam glanced at her. "Why's that? It's only been two years and he doesn't look as if he's got much more growing to do."

"No," Bernice Mitchell answered slowly, "Danny hasn't grown much physically since that photo. But he's changed. He's changed in appearance and he's changed inside."

Adam frowned, not sure what she meant. Cecelia had told him Danny was a commuter student at Eastern Washington State University, which was how he knew Angela. He knew college sometimes had a real impact on kids. "Maybe he's reacting to school," Adam suggested.

"No doubt that's part of it," Bernice Mitchell replied. "But ever since Bill's death, he's been different—angry and hostile toward the world in general. I've tried to talk to him about it, but I never get very far. Besides, he isn't home much anymore."

"Where does he go?" Adam didn't like what he was hearing.

"He's very involved in a singing group..." She looked down at her hands. "And for the past several months he's been caught up with nuclear protest demonstrations. I've warned him he's likely to be arrested, but he doesn't seem to care."

"You're right, I don't care."

Their heads turned sharply. The angry voice had come from the hallway, splitting the silence of the afternoon with an electrifying tension. Danny stood with his hands on his hips, his feet planted firmly.

"Danny!" Bernice Mitchell half rose from her chair.

Adam stared at the youth who bore virtually no resemblance to the picture he held in his hand. The young man in front of him was shabby and unkempt, wearing an old T-shirt over jeans that were torn at the knee. Beneath his shaggy haircut, an earring flashed in one earlobe. Cecelia's words came back: "He's not like you, Adam—" How long Danny had been standing there, Adam asked himself, and how much had he heard?

"Who is this guy?" Danny demanded. He walked into the room with his eyes fixed on Adam in a hostile glare.

"He's..." Bernice Mitchell groped for an explanation. "He's a friend."

"Those are my baby pictures." He pointed at the albums spread out across the coffee table. "And that's my graduation picture." Danny stared at his mother. "What's going on here, anyway?"

Bernice Mitchell turned frightened eyes toward Adam. She obviously had no idea how to answer.

Adam made an instant decision. He was cornered. He had no choice. "Danny," he said, standing up, "I'm Adam Campbell." He extended his hand. At first, he thought Danny was going to shun him entirely. But, after a moment's hesitation, Danny took his hand in a brief, perfunctory handshake.

"Who are you?" Danny asked, obviously still wary.

"Well—"

"Are you a friend of my father?"

"Not exactly," Adam answered, stalling for time. What was he going to say? What reason could he give for sitting in Danny's living room, looking at his baby pictures, discussing him with his mother?

Danny stared at his uniform, eyeing the commendation ribbons and the silver wings. "Then what are you doing here? Is it because of the demonstration? Are you here to arrest me?"

"No, of course not, Danny." Adam answered quickly. "The fact is . . ." He took a deep breath. There seemed no room for anything but the truth. "The fact is, Danny, a long time ago—" He glanced over at Bernice Mitchell and saw immediately that she would be no help.

Danny's eyes smoldered as he looked Adam over. "Why don't you quit stalling and spit it out?"

"All right," Adam agreed. "The reason I'm here, Danny, is because I'm your natural father."

Danny looked as though Adam had slapped him across the face. He lurched backward one step and then another, never taking his eyes off Adam. "I don't believe you." He hissed out the words. "I don't believe you."

"It's true, Danny." Adam took a step toward him.

Danny's hands flew in front of his face. "Don't come near me," he shouted. "Don't touch me. I don't want any part of you and your medals and your nuclear bombs."

"Danny, if you'll just listen to me for a minute—"

"I'm not going to listen to you. I'm never going to listen to you." Danny's voice rose. "You had no right coming here. I hate you—do you hear me?" he demanded, his voice between a scream and a sob. "I hate all of you."

He turned and ran, slamming the front door behind him with such fury that the entire house shuddered. Adam stared after him. Bernice Mitchell buried her face in her hands, crying softly. The air in the room, which had been so highly charged with emotion, grew flat and empty in the silence. After several moments passed, Adam picked up his hat from the corner of the table.

"I'm sorry," he said in a tight voice. "I'll go now. There's no need to see me out."

Bernice Mitchell didn't answer. Adam could still hear her crying when he closed the front door.

DANNY SLUNG HIS BACKPACK and his sleeping bag into the back of the old Ford and screeched out of the garage. His tires left hot, black tread marks on the driveway. He didn't care. Seething with anger, his hands clamped tightly on the steering wheel, he simply drove. His only purpose was to get as far away as fast as he could. His head was pounding with words he couldn't accept. *"I'm your natural father. I'm your natural father. I'm your natural father."* Over and over again, like an unrelenting drumbeat.

It wasn't true. It couldn't be true. He already had a father and his father was dead. That Air Force bastard, in his uniform with all the ribbons across his chest, couldn't be his father. There was no way. Cold, clammy perspiration began to trickle down Danny's back. His stomach tightened, fighting churning nausea. Ignoring the climbing needle on the speedometer, he pressed the accelerator harder. Sixty. Sixty-five. Seventy. He had to get away. The highway was nearly empty, endless and straight. He could drive forever. Never go back. Never again face that bastard who claimed to be his father. Seventy-five. Eighty.

Behind him a siren shrieked and lights flashed in his rearview mirror. "Damn!" If he just drove a little faster, maybe he could get away. He floored the accelerator and careened around a curve, skidding into the loose gravel on the shoulder of the road. He checked his mirror again. The police car was still right behind him, matching every maneuver. He skidded on the gravel again, this time nearly losing control of the car. His whole body was trembling now. He had never felt so helpless, so trapped. With a guttural, almost primitive, sob of defeat, he took his foot from the accelerator and began to apply the brakes.

"Hey, what's the matter with you, kid? Are you trying to kill yourself?"

Danny tried hard to focus on the policeman's face, but everything was so fuzzy. Silently he handed over his driver's license and the car registration.

The policeman scrutinized the license. "Daniel Mitchell. Is this you, kid? Is this your name?"

Danny opened his mouth to answer, but no words came out. Daniel Mitchell. Was he Danny Mitchell? Or was he really someone else? He caught a reflection of his face in the sideview mirror of the car. His eyes. Dark brown. His eyes were the same, exactly the same as Adam Campbell's. Horrified, he looked up at the policeman. "I'm sorry," he whispered in a hoarse voice. "I don't know my name. I don't even know who I am, anymore." Then he laid his head on the steering wheel and sobbed.

BY THE TIME ADAM RANG the Mahoneys' doorbell, he was numb. He'd destroyed any chance he might have had with Danny. The boy hated him. He didn't even know him, and he hated him. Cecelia's words kept coming back: "I don't know if it's for the best.... he isn't like you, Adam...." She'd been right all along, and he'd refused to listen to her. And he'd promised to do nothing more than talk to Danny's mother. Now he had screwed up the whole thing. Damn! He never should have come back to Spokane. Clenching his fists, he forced himself into an outward calm to mask his anger.

Mary Beth answered the door, lighting up when she saw him. "Mom's upstairs," she told him, "but I guess you know that. I think she's on the phone with Aunt Jeannie."

"I'll go on up." Adam started toward the stairs.

"Wait!" Mary Beth stopped him. "There's something I want to show you." She led him into the kitchen and pointed to a magazine open on the table. "I found this really great article that's going to be a big help."

Adam stared down at the headline: "Adopted girl finds 'Real' Mother—joy overflows." Below the words was a photo of a tearful woman embracing a teenage girl.

"It tells all about how the girl searched all these records and followed up on clues—"

Adam turned toward Mary Beth, his eyes hard. "Let it alone. Don't mess with the past. Just leave it alone."

Shocked, Mary Beth drew back. "But when I talked to you before, you seemed to understand. You said finding my real mother was a natural desire."

"And now I'm telling you it's a lousy idea." Adam turned on his heel and headed toward the front hall, leaving Mary Beth with her mouth open. He took the stairs two at a time, not stopping until he reached the open door of Cecelia's bedroom.

When she saw him, she mumbled something into the phone and hung up quickly. "Adam, you're back." She held out her arms.

Closing the bedroom door behind him, he walked to the foot of the bed. Now that he saw her, he was again staggered by what he had done. She seemed so fragile lying there beneath the blue and white quilt, so trusting as she reached out to him, so happy that he'd come to her. But all that would change. In a few more seconds, it wouldn't be like that at all.

As soon as she saw his face, Cecelia knew something was terribly wrong. Her arms dropped to her sides. "What's happened, Adam?" A note of fear crept into her voice. "What is it? What's the matter?"

"He knows, Cecelia." Adam's voice was dead quiet. "Danny knows."

"Oh, no." She seemed to grow visibly smaller, shrinking into the pillows. "No," she whispered again.

"I didn't mean for it to happen." The pain he felt inside made his voice hollow. "We didn't hear him come in and—"

"Start at the beginning, Adam. Tell me all of it."

She listened mutely as he struggled through the entire story from beginning to end, trying to leave nothing out, figuring she had a right to know everything just as it had occurred. At the end he said, "You were right, Cecelia. I shouldn't have gone."

She stared into space, slowly absorbing what he had told her. Everything she had feared had happened, and there would be no turning back. When she finally looked up at him, her eyes were sad. "You're right, Adam. You shouldn't have gone."

He couldn't think of anything else to say. All he wanted was to get away where he couldn't make her life any worse. He'd done enough already.

For hours after he left, Cecelia lay in bed listening to the birds sing and watching the sun sink slowly beyond the oak tree outside her bedroom window. Long past midnight she took out her journal and began to write:

Adam went to see Bernice Mitchell today. Danny now knows he is Adam's son. Our lives can never again be the same, but somehow we have to go on.

CHAPTER TEN

CECELIA TRIED TO CALL Adam every day for the next week. When she asked for him, it was always the same. The young airman who answered his phone put her on hold, and then, after about two minutes, came back on the line to tell her that Adam was in a meeting. By the end of the week the airman sounded terribly apologetic.

Every time Adam was told Cecelia was on the phone, he struggled with an overwhelming sense of guilt. But he wasn't ready to talk to her. He had spent every waking hour thinking of her and Danny and trying to decide what to do next. George Lathrop had told him about a job opening up at the Pentagon, and the more he considered it, the more he thought taking the job would be best all around. He couldn't escape the feeling that Cecelia would be better off without him, but he wasn't ready to tell her. Not just yet.

For her part, short of going to the base and camping outside Adam's office, Cecelia wasn't sure what to do. She had checked daily with Bernice Mitchell after learning that Danny hadn't been home since the encounter with Adam. Bernice didn't seem very concerned. She said Danny had taken off before when he was upset. But the boy's absence worried Cecelia, and she wanted to discuss it with Adam.

She grew increasingly annoyed as it became more and more obvious Adam was avoiding her. When Jeannie admitted that Adam had called her several times to make sure Cecelia was getting along all right, Cecelia was irate. She wondered what he'd have done if Jeannie had said that Cecelia had a problem.

But Jeannie was circumspect. "He's a man," she told Cecelia, who was hobbling on crutches through the shop on her first day back at work. "His ego was hurt and he feels responsible for everything that's happened. Besides, he's disappointed about his son."

"That's not my fault," Cecelia snapped. "I warned him finding Danny would be a mistake."

Jeannie grimaced. "That probably didn't help, either. Have you talked to Pop about Danny?"

Cecelia shook her head. "Not yet."

"He'd probably like to know he has another grandson," Jeannie observed. "He keeps count, you know."

Cecelia knew, and Jeannie's comment stayed with her all afternoon. She left the shop early, and on her way home from work drove out to Pop's.

"Didn't expect to see you this afternoon," Pop said, opening the door.

"I know." Cecelia unbuttoned her coat. "I didn't expect to come. But I've got to talk to you." She followed him into the kitchen and sat down at the table. Now she wished she'd talked to Pop earlier.

Joe Riley slowly poured two cups of coffee, giving his daughter time to compose her thoughts. There wasn't a doubt in his mind why she was here on a weekday, near dinnertime, when she usually made it a point to be home with her own family. Something was up with Adam Campbell.

"So what brings you all the way out here?" Pop said, sitting down across from his daughter.

"It's a really long story, Pop."

"I've got lots of time." He reached into his sweater pocket for his pipe.

Cecelia started at the very beginning, recounting Adam's visit, and once she got started, the whole story spilled out. Pop nodded and puffed on his pipe, not interrupting, although he had trouble containing himself when Cecelia got to the part about Danny walking in on Adam and Bernice Mitchell. Terrible thing to have happen to the boy. No wonder they were all so upset.

"Pop, what am I going to do?" Cecelia finally asked.

The look on her face and the tone of her voice reminded him very much of that day twenty years before when she'd told him she was pregnant. He didn't have any good answers for her then, either. "Sounds to me like it's mostly been done, for right now," he answered slowly. "You need time to let everything settle."

"But Adam won't even take my phone calls."

Joe Riley reached over and patted her hand. "He's had a bad beginning with the boy and he knows it. Adam will come around, if he's the man I think he is." He puffed on his pipe, considering the situation. "I'm more concerned about the boy. His mother says he's taken off before?"

"That's what she told me. She says he goes off camping when he's really upset."

"Folks have all sorts of ways of dealing with bad times. That's better than most."

Cecelia smiled at him. "It always makes me feel so much better to talk to you, Pop."

"Then maybe you should do it more often."

Hearing his gentle reprimand, Cecelia lowered her eyes. "I'm sorry."

"No need to be sorry." He patted her again. "Getting things out in the open is part of loving people. You need to think about that with your family. Now that Danny knows who his father is, maybe he deserves the whole story. Maybe your other kids do, too."

Cecelia shook her head vigorously. "Oh, Pop, I don't know—"

"You give it some thought. When the time comes, you'll do what's right."

ON SATURDAY AFTERNOON Cecelia sat on a chaise longue in the backyard with her leg propped out in front of her as she listened to the hollow tapping of a woodpecker and mulled over her life. Hearing a car door slam, she decided that Angela must be home from the grocery store, or wherever she was. She'd been rather vague about her destination.

"Mom, I brought someone to talk to you," Angela said.

Cecelia gripped the arms of her chair as she watched Danny Mitchell follow Angela across the backyard. He'd come back. Thank God he was all right. She watched him as he approached, feeling differently about him now that she knew he was her son. He was taller than Cecelia remembered and very thin. Nothing about him was either imposing or frightening. He was simply an older version of Sean or Kevin, a little more finished, but not quite a man. As he drew closer, she saw his eyes. He did look like Adam. She hadn't noticed that before, but she hadn't been looking. Not until he was a few steps away did it occur to her that he probably didn't yet know that she was his mother.

"Mom, you remember Danny?" Angela asked.

"Of course. How are you, Danny?" Cecelia tried to keep her tone casual.

"Just fine, Mrs. Mahoney." Not looking at her, he helped Angela unfold two more lawn chairs. He was sorry he'd let Angela talk him into coming.

Cecelia sensed the tension in both of them. She waited, letting them take the lead.

"I assume you know about Adam and Danny." Angela looked directly at her mother.

"What do you mean?" Cecelia decided it was best to let them spell it out.

"Adam says he's Danny's father."

Danny stared at his feet, not saying a word. Cecelia wondered how Angela had persuaded the boy to come, and why. She met her daughter's eyes. "Yes, Angela," she answered, "I know about that."

"I told you she would," Angela said to Danny. He looked up, showing an interest in Cecelia for the first time. Questions had started bugging him during those days alone in the woods. Maybe she could give him some answers.

Angela turned back to her mother. "I thought that since you knew Adam about the time Danny was born, you might be able to tell Danny some of the background..."

Angela's voice faded and her eyes widened. Cecelia had always thought of her oldest daughter as the most transparent of all her children, and today was no exception. She could almost watch Angela's mind work as she put together the time sequence and what little she knew of Adam and Cecelia. Angela looked at Danny, at Cecelia, and back at Danny again.

Bracing herself, Cecelia asked, "What would you like to know, Danny?"

"Did you really know him back when . . . when I was born?" Danny asked hesitantly.

"Yes, Danny. Adam was a good friend of my brother. I've known him since I can remember."

"What did he—"

"Wait a minute!" Angela interrupted. She'd been staring at Cecelia. Her eyes were wide in disbelief. "Mom, are you—" She tripped on the words. "Are you Danny's mother?"

Cecelia took a deep breath and looked Angela in the eye. "Yes, Angela," she answered quietly. "I am Danny's birth mother."

The silence among them stretched into the far reaches of the late-spring afternoon, broken only by the growl of a lawn mower down the street. Cecelia had half expected Danny to bolt and run, but he appeared to be rooted to his chair. Angela stared at her mother and then at Danny, speechless and bewildered now that her suspicions were confirmed.

Finally Cecelia struggled to as close to an upright sitting position as possible. She wished she could reach out and touch them both, but she knew that was neither possible nor probably the right thing to do. "I'm sorry you had to find out this way," she said, filled with compassion for both her children. "It would have been better, I think, if you hadn't had to find out at all. But now that you know, I'll try to explain as best I can."

They listened without comment as Cecelia told them about her dilemma after she learned she was pregnant and explained the reasons why the decision was made to give Danny up for adoption. As she told the story, Cecelia had the same feeling inside that she always had when she talked seriously with a child about sex. They understood, and yet they didn't understand, because what she was saying was too intensely intimate for them to grasp.

"Are you angry, Danny?" she asked when he offered no response.

For the first time he looked directly at her. He had no idea what to say. Ever since he had confronted Adam Campbell, he'd been on an emotional roller coaster. One day he was angry beyond belief, and the next day he didn't give a damn about anything. In between he felt beaten and defeated, out of control of his own life. And now, on top of everything else, he was supposed to absorb meeting his birth mother, too. "I don't know how I feel," he told Cecelia in a flat voice.

"Betrayed, maybe?"

"Maybe." His gaze wavered. "I mean, for almost twenty years I've lived with my mother and father and always thought of them as my parents, and all of a sudden I'm supposed to be jumping for joy because my biological mother and father have shown up on the scene." He shook his head. "I don't know what to think anymore."

Cecelia's heart ached for her son. What they were doing to him was wrong. Perhaps it was better that he'd been told about his birth parents. She still wasn't sure. But he never should have found out the way he had. "I'm sorry, Danny." She swallowed hard to hold back her tears. "I'm sorrier than you'll ever know." She didn't know what else to say. She had never felt so helpless in her life. Slowly she turned toward her daughter. "How do you feel about all of this?" she asked. Angela's face was pallid despite her makeup, and yet she appeared more confused than upset. Funny,

Cecelia thought, for all these years her greatest fear had been her children's reactions if they found out she'd had another child. Now she was far more concerned about how Danny felt—and about Adam.

"I'm like Danny," Angela said slowly. "I don't know how I feel, either, except it just blows my mind that he's my brother."

"Half brother," Cecelia corrected.

"Half brother, brother, it's almost the same thing. Maybe that's why I've always liked him."

"Even when I bug you?"

Angela nodded. "But better when you don't."

Danny smiled. It was weird to actually be related to Angela. He'd liked her, too, from the first time they had met in their eight o'clock psychology class. Mahoney and Mitchell, seated alphabetically next to each other. He enjoyed talking to her after class, and hearing about her brothers and sisters. He reached down to pat Bingo, who had wandered across the yard and settled down for a nap on the patio.

Cecelia watched Danny, realizing she'd never seen him smile. When he did, he was really quite handsome, and he looked even more like Adam. He was a part of them, a part of her that had been absent for too long. What had been begun would have to be finished. There would be no turning back now. "Maybe you would like to get to know the rest of the family," she ventured.

Angela brightened. "I've got it! Danny can come to our Memorial Day barbecue."

"Well..." Cecelia hesitated, realizing she hadn't even thought about the barbecue this year. She hoped such a mass introduction wouldn't be more than Danny could handle.

"Will you come, Danny?" Angela asked.

"I don't know..." He was getting in really deep, really fast. Angela and her mother—his mother—were one thing, but all the rest of them, all at once—that was something else.

"I could call your mother and invite her," Cecelia offered.

"You want her here?"

"If she'd like to come," Cecelia answered gently. "Memorial Day is a family day and she's your family. And now I suppose we're a second family, Danny, a new kind of relationship."

"Will you come?" Angela asked again.

"Well, I guess." He looked uncomfortable. "Adam Campbell won't be here, will he?"

Cecelia frowned. The situation between Adam and Danny was going to be a major problem for all of them. "Yes, Danny," she answered firmly, "Adam probably will be here." She raised her hand to stop him from speaking. "And before you say anything, I have something to say to you. Adam had no intention of confronting you last week. It was a very unfortunate accident. However you feel about the military, or nuclear war, or anything else, you need to realize that Adam is a person as well as an Air Force officer. Before you decide you hate him, you need to get to know him."

Danny didn't respond, and his face was inscrutable. Cecelia had no idea whether anything she'd said registered. "I hope you'll decide to come, Danny," she continued, holding out her hand. "We'd like very much to have you."

"I need to think about it," he answered. But he took her hand and held it for a moment, the pressure of his fingers firm on hers.

After Angela and Danny had left, Cecelia picked up her crutches and struggled to her feet, heading for the house and a cold drink of iced tea. Her mouth was dry, her throat scratchy and her entire body limp. But a major part of the scene she'd dreaded for years was behind her, and as emotionally draining as it had been, it wasn't nearly the ordeal she'd feared. She liked Danny, and she sensed that if he and Adam would give each other a chance, there might be hope for them, too.

That would be her next step, to call Adam. Again. She'd say it was a dire emergency, if necessary, but somehow she would get hold of him. And once that was done, she'd tell the rest of the children.

First Cecelia tried Adam at the number he'd given her for his quarters at the BOQ. Then she tried his office. She had intended to offer an impassioned plea to the young airman she had talked to so many times during the week, but he apparently didn't work on Saturday. The person who answered was cold and impersonal. When she asked for Adam, she was immediately told he was unavailable.

"Does that mean he's there?" she asked.

"Sorry, ma'am; he's unavailable."

"Can you get a message to him?"

"He's unavailable now, ma'am."

"Can't he be reached by radio?" Cecelia thought of the small black box Adam always carried.

"Only with authorization, ma'am."

Cecelia was growing increasingly annoyed. "Then let me speak to whoever gives authorization," she demanded.

"Sorry, ma'am. He's also unavailable at this time."

Cecelia was convinced the Air Force was the most frustrating organization she'd ever tried to deal with.

"What if I wanted to tell them somebody was about to drop a bomb on us?" she asked flippantly.

"Is that your message, ma'am?"

"No." Cecelia didn't even attempt to hide her irritation. "Just tell Colonel Campbell to call Cecelia Mahoney immediately. It's an emergency." She banged the telephone hard into its cradle, realizing it might be hours before Adam even got the message, and then she couldn't be certain he'd call. She knew she couldn't wait past dinner to tell the other children about Danny, whether or not she'd heard from Adam. Angela already knew, and while she wouldn't mean to say anything, she could come home and inadvertently tell everything. Cecelia didn't want any more sudden revelations. This time she was determined to tell the story in a calm, controlled atmosphere.

DANNY COULD HEAR HIS MOTHER coughing as soon as he opened the front door. With a deep sigh of resignation, he straightened his shoulders and walked down the hall to her bedroom. "How are you feeling, Mom?"

Bernice Mitchell answered weakly from the bed. "I'm all right, Danny. I think this new medicine the doctor gave me is helping some. I just thought I'd take a little rest before I got dinner started."

Danny watched her struggle to sit up. He knew she wasn't telling the truth. She was paler and thinner every day. "You don't have to cook tonight, Mom. I'll fix some hamburgers on the grill. Why don't you stay in here and rest for a while longer?"

"No, really, I'm fine." Bernice coughed again and leaned back against the pillows. Her face was drawn with pain. "Well, all right. If you don't mind, maybe I will rest for a few more minutes," she said hoarsely.

"Where were you all day, son? It's getting late, and I was starting to worry."

Danny hesitated. After his afternoon at the Mahoneys, he was wiped out. The last thing he wanted to do was talk about this whole mess. Then he remembered the Memorial Day barbeque, and he knew Angela's mother—his mother—was going to be on the phone about it this week. "I was with Angela, Mom. We spent the afternoon talking to her mother."

Startled, Bernice Mitchell studied her son. "Oh..."

"You knew, didn't you? You knew all along that Angela's mother was my mother, too." He felt the knot forming in his stomach again, hard and tight.

"Not exactly—" His mother's gaze wavered. "I knew your mother was Cecelia Riley, her maiden name, but it was only recently that I made the connection with Angela. After your father died—"

"You can't substitute that bastard for my dad," Danny flared. "He's not my father. My father is dead. And I don't want another mother. I have you. I don't need anybody else."

"Danny!" his mother said sharply. "You do need other people, a family to love you. Someone to care about you...when I'm gone...." Her voice broke, and she buried her face in her hands.

"So that's it." Danny ran his fingers through his hair and paced back and forth in the tiny bedroom. "You think you're going to die and you're trying to set me up with a ready-made family." He stopped pacing and took his mother by the shoulders, forcing her to look up at him. "Well, let me tell you something, Mom. You're not going to die anytime soon. I'm not going to let you. I'm taking good care of you, aren't I?"

Bernice nodded, tears streaming down her face. "You're a good boy, Danny...I love you...I just want you to be happy." Choking on her sobs, she fell back against the pillows in a spasm of coughing.

Danny helped her take a sip of water, and when her coughing had subsided, he pulled the afghan over her legs. "Just rest, Mom, everything is going to be okay."

"Please, try to get to know Cecelia Mahoney. She's a good person, a good mother. She cares about you, Danny. And Colonel Campbell—"

"No! I'll deal with Angela's mother, but I don't want anything to do with that Air Force bastard."

"He's your natural father, Danny. Like it or not, you can't change what happened." Bernice touched his arm gently.

Danny stared out the window at the bird feeder he and his father had built. He remembered his father helping him to hold the hammer, guiding his hand so the nails would be pounded in straight and the bird feeder would be sound. They'd made a good bird feeder together, and over the years they'd done a lot of good things together. But that was all over now. And no one, including his biological father, could ever replace his dad. "It's time to start the grill for dinner," he said, shrugging away his mother's hand. "And I think I'll practice my guitar while I wait for the coals to get hot."

Danny went out to the backyard and filled the grill with charcoal. After it was burning well, he settled down under the big willow tree and began playing a haunting folk tune on his guitar. From where he sat he could see the birds fly down to the feeder and eat.

SITTING ALONE in the living room, Cecelia watched the clock anxiously. She could smell the spaghetti Kim was cooking in the kitchen. She heard the back door slam and the twins' voices as they talked to their sister. Then Kevin yelled up the stairs, "Mary Beth, get off the phone and get down here. You're supposed to be helping Kim fix dinner."

Cecelia's stomach knotted. If Mary Beth was on the phone, that meant Adam couldn't get through even if he tried. Maybe now... But when Sean came to call her to dinner twenty minutes later, the phone was still silent. Reluctantly she followed her son into the kitchen where she sat down at the table, propping her cast carefully on another chair.

One by one the children joined her: first Sean and Kevin who were arguing over who had committed an error in the baseball game; then Kim, carrying hot bread from the oven; and finally Mary Beth, looking strangely domestic in one of Cecelia's old aprons she'd put on over her white warm-up suit. They were no different from the way they'd always been, talking, laughing, jostling each other, but tonight they touched her heart. She loved them all so much. If only she would be able to make them understand.

Cecelia sprinkled grated Parmesan cheese on her spaghetti and noted that the twins' plates were already more than half-empty. "Where's Angela?" she asked, realizing she'd been waiting for her oldest daughter, perhaps unconsciously hoping for her support.

"Beats me," Mary Beth answered. "If *I* were this late for dinner, you'd jump all over me."

"Don't bug Mom," Kim told her. "She doesn't feel good."

"I'm not bugging her. It's true." She looked at her watch. "I can't understand why Roger hasn't called. I don't even know what time we're going out."

"I know why." Sean gloated around a mouthful of spaghetti.

"Why?" Mary Beth glared at him.

"'Cause I took the phone off the hook," he replied smugly.

"Sean!" Mary Beth jumped to her feet and started out of the kitchen. "You just wait!"

"No, Mary Beth." Cecelia stopped her. "You wait."

"I'm going to put the phone back on the hook."

"No!" her voice silenced them all. No wonder she hadn't heard from Adam, but it was too late now. And she'd waited for Angela long enough. "Come back and sit down, Mary Beth," Cecelia said quietly. "I want to talk to all of you. We don't need any interruptions."

With a sulky pout on her lips, Mary Beth sat down. The others looked at their mother expectantly. Cecelia glanced around the table, meeting their eyes one by one, wondering how to begin.

"What I have to tell you is going to require maturity from every one of you, but I think you're all old enough to handle it."

Sean glanced sideways at Mary Beth and coughed loudly. Cecelia ignored him.

"Sometimes people do things and have to make decisions that are hard to understand later, because times change and attitudes change and it's difficult to explain the circumstances behind those decisions."

Mary Beth fidgeted. "Can't you just come to the point, whatever it is? I need to go call Roger."

Cecelia glanced around the table. The others looked equally impatient. But where should she begin? With Bernice? With Adam? With Danny himself?

The back screen door slammed loudly, and the matter was taken out of her hands. "Did you tell them about Danny?" Angela blurted out.

Cecelia watched unhappily as Angela slid into her chair.

"Tell us what?" Mary Beth demanded. "Danny who?"

Angela looked around the table, horrified. "You *haven't* told them."

"I was just about to." Cecelia took a deep breath that emerged as a shuddering sigh in the thick silence. "A long time ago, before any of you were born, I had another baby, a son, that I was forced to give up for adoption. Until very recently, I didn't know anything about him. I didn't know who he was or where he was. Now I do. His name is Danny Mitchell. He's a student at Eastern Washington State. I talked to him this afternoon."

The children stared at Cecelia with uncomprehending eyes. She didn't know what else to say to them. There was so much more they needed to know if they were to have any real understanding. Cecelia waited, bracing herself for the questions that would ultimately come.

She expected a barb from Mary Beth, or perhaps a comment from one of the boys, but it was Kim's voice, usually so soft and sweet, that grated in the quiet room. "You gave away your baby?"

Cecelia saw the anguish in her eyes. "I was very young when the baby was born, Kim," Cecelia explained gently, "and things were different then. I had no choice."

"You mean you had a baby before you got married?" Mary Beth's eyes widened as the scope of what Cecelia was saying began to sink in.

"Yes, Mary Beth, that's right." Cecelia didn't elaborate. Adam's role would come into the discussion soon enough. Right now she knew that Mary Beth was about to begin thinking of Danny in relation to her own adoption.

She saw Sean and Kevin exchange a look. "Angela, you know this kid?" Kevin asked his sister. Cecelia realized Angela had been strangely quiet ever since her initial outburst.

"Sure, I know Danny," Angela answered. "He's real nice."

"Does he play baseball?" Sean asked.

Cecelia quickly wiped her mouth with her napkin to hide her smile. She'd been worried about the effect on their psyches, while Sean was focused on finding someone to play baseball with him.

"I don't think Danny does much with sports," Angela told Sean. "He's into singing and he's really good on the guitar."

Sean glanced back at his brother and then finished his milk.

"Actually you'll all have a chance to get to know Danny," Cecelia said, seizing her opportunity. "Angela and I have invited him to come to the Memorial Day barbecue."

If she had expected enthusiasm, she didn't get it. Everyone but Angela stared at her again.

"You mean he's coming here on Memorial Day?" Mary Beth challenged. "You always said the barbecue was only for the family."

"Danny is part of the family," Cecelia pointed out.

Mary Beth's eyes widened. Cecelia could see anger and outrage building like a rumbling volcano about to erupt. "You mean you're bringing *him* here into our family and at the same time you are telling me I can't find my own real mother?" She sprang to her feet, sending her chair crashing to the floor behind her.

"Mary Beth—" Cecelia began.

"Don't talk to me. Don't you start in on me ever again. You tell me what I want is wrong and then you go off and do the same thing yourself. That's not fair. Nothing about you is fair. I'm never going to listen to you again." Mary Beth stormed out of the kitchen and up the stairs. Her bedroom door slammed with a crash that resounded through the house.

Cecelia rested her head in her hands. As often as she told herself that adolescent explosions were never as much of a crisis as they seemed, the emotion they generated drained her.

She heard Adam's voice and looked up, startled, to see him standing by the back door. He looked like a pillar of strength and she needed him so much.

"What's happened, Cecelia?" His eyes moved from one sober face to the next around the table and then back to her. "I got your message—they said it was an emergency and I tried to call—"

"It's not an emergency anymore, Adam. In one sense it's all over, and in another it's only begun." Without further explanation, she awkwardly stood up, picked up her crutches and hobbled over to him. "Adam and I are going outside," she told the children. "I want you all to help clean up the kitchen."

Adam opened the back door for her, but she realized she couldn't go quite yet. Her cards were all on the table but one. She wished she could talk to Adam first, but he'd simply have to understand.

"There's one more thing I need to tell you," she said to the group still assembled around the kitchen table. Sean and Kevin stopped bickering about who would load the dishwasher, and all four children looked up at their mother.

"You know part of the story, but not quite all of it, except for Angela who came to me this afternoon." Cecelia felt Adam tense, but she went on, suddenly anxious to have no more secrets. "What the rest of you don't know—" She swallowed hard. "What I haven't told you yet is that Adam is Danny's father."

Cecelia's final revelation hung in the silence. Adam's fingers, which had rested lightly on her elbow, pressed into her flesh. For several moments no one spoke, and then Cecelia turned and went outside, wanting nothing so much as to be with Adam. Now the children knew the whole story, and Angela would no doubt embellish it with the details Cecelia had shared with her and Danny. Everything else could wait, except for Adam. The screen door banged behind them, and she stopped at the porch steps, turning slightly, expecting to find a refuge in his arms.

Instead he towered over her, his face taut in the sliver of light from the window. "What have you done?" he demanded.

She'd expected love and support, not this. Cecelia met his eyes, her own flashing. "Don't you dare yell at me!"

"Then we'll go out to the gazebo where they can't hear us."

Cecelia jerked away from him, almost tumbling headlong down the steps. "I'll do it myself."

The rubber tips on her crutches pressed into the so
ground as she slowly made her way across the back
yard. The brilliant white outline of the gazebo shim
mered in the moonlight. The blooms on the lilacs ha
faded but she could smell their sweet perfume on th
still air like a contradiction to her anger. Adam had n
right to question her judgment without even knowing
what had happened.

"I think I deserve an explanation," he asserted, a
they approached the three wooden steps leading into th
gazebo.

Cecelia didn't answer until she had painstakingl
made her way up the steps and lowered herself onto on
of the benches inside the gazebo. She propped her leg o
a small table in front of her.

"Well?" he prodded impatiently.

"Well, what?" she shot back. "It's not easy to giv
someone an explanation when he refuses to take m
phone calls. Did it ever occur to you that it's humilia
ing to keep calling someone and find out he's effe
tively blotted you out of his life?"

"So you decided to get back at me? Is that it?"

"Adam, don't be ridiculous."

"That's certainly how it looks. We agreed not to dis
cuss Danny with anyone, and now you've told your e
tire family. That was a stupid move, Cecelia."

The fear and the tension and the guilt that had sim
mered inside Cecelia all day boiled over. "So it wa
stupid, was it? You didn't even bother to find out wha
happened or to ask about why I told them. There hav
been some stupid moves all right, but this wasn't one o
them." Cecelia's voice was rising, and she didn't care
"You're the one who went to Danny. You're the on
who told him. And you accuse me of being stupid?"

Adam didn't answer. He was hidden deep in the shadows where she couldn't see his face. She found herself wondering what he was thinking and then not caring.

"I guess I deserved that, Cecelia," Adam said haltingly. "I made a mess. I suppose you deserve to make one, too."

"But I didn't," she replied, irritated by his half-hearted apology. "I warned you from the beginning that once you started the wheels in motion there would be problems. Angela brought Danny to see me this afternoon. He's angry, Adam, angry and confused. What was I supposed to do when Angela asked me if I was his mother? Lie to her?"

"No, of course not. But you didn't have to make a general announcement."

"Oh, Adam, don't be naive. How long do you think Angela could have kept quiet, even if she tried? And some day when she blurted it out without thinking, we'd have had another confrontation—like the one with Danny. We don't need that."

He was silent again, and this time Cecelia wished she could go to him. The situation with Danny was like a wall between them, a barrier that might never come down. And the real reason for the wall was how she felt about Danny. Now that everything was out in the open, she wanted to build a bond with her son.

"After we've come this far, we can't just ignore Danny," Cecelia began tentatively. "We can't put things back the way they were."

Adam leaned forward, and she saw his face in the moonlight. The anger was gone, but his eyes were clouded. "I wish we could go back, Cecelia, because I don't see much advantage in going forward. Danny hates me. He made that very clear. And I can't say I'm exactly drawn to him even if he is biologically my son.''

"Our son, Adam," Cecelia corrected gently. "He even looks like you. And if you'd give him a chance—''

"Give him a chance? You've got to be kidding. I can't imagine him voluntarily spending more than thirty seconds in the same room with me.''

"You're his father, Adam.''

"Just exactly what is that supposed to mean?''

Cecelia rubbed her fingertips across the new white paint on the bench, feeling the roughness of the weathered wood beneath. She took her time as she thought about Adam's question, because she knew her answer could open a door or could slam it shut forever. When she began talking, her tone was low and thoughtful. "We gave Danny up and let somebody else raise him because that suited our needs at the time. Now Danny needs us, and to be honest, Adam, I think he needs you most of all.''

"He sure doesn't act like it.''

"That's the whole point.''

"What do you expect me to do, Cecelia? I don't even know how to begin.''

She heard the defeat in his voice and realized how deeply his initial failure had shaken him. "I know how you can begin, Adam, or at least where. I've invited Danny to come to the Memorial Day family picnic. I've already told him you'll be there.''

"And he's coming?''

Cecelia nodded. "I'm pretty sure he will." She didn't add that Adam was the one reason Danny might not show up. She reached toward Adam until he gave her his hand. "Will you come, Adam? Will you try?"

"I'll think about it."

Cecelia smiled. "You sound just like Danny."

CHAPTER ELEVEN

PLATTERS OF FRIED CHICKEN, a giant bowl of potato salad, beans baking in the oven, coolers of beer and sodas packed in ice, two cakes decorated with tiny American flags. Everything was ready.

And yet Cecelia didn't feel right about the picnic. She hadn't felt right about it all week. She limped out of the kitchen, using only one crutch, and stood on the back porch to survey the tables covered with festive blue and white paper cloths and the charcoal grills, their fires laid and waiting to be started for the steaks. She'd never been so well prepared, and she'd never had such an ominous feeling about a family gathering.

Bingo barked fiercely as a car pulled into the driveway. It could be the children who had ridden downtown together. Or maybe it was Danny, or Pop, or Jeannie with Bill and Benjamin. Or maybe, just maybe, it was Adam. More than any of the others, Cecelia wanted to see him alone for a few minutes. They hadn't had any time together since that one perfect weekend and she missed him desperately. Nothing was right between them, and although she knew Danny was the cause, she didn't know how to rectify things.

"Cecelia? Cecelia, where are you?" Jeannie's voice echoed through the empty house.

Cecelia answered quickly, trying to cover her disappointment. Following the sound of her sister's voice,

Jeannie quickly appeared on the porch with Bingo at her heels. She was dressed for the occasion in a red-striped blouse and red shorts which complemented Cecelia's royal-blue cotton skirt and blue-and-white plaid blouse.

"Benjamin's still asleep so Bill's going to bring him later," Jeannie explained. "I thought I'd come ahead and see if I could help you." She paused and gazed around the yard. "But you look really together."

"I may look it but I don't feel it," Cecelia replied. She needed reassurance from Jeannie. "Do you think it was a mistake to invite Danny?"

"Of course not. I already told you I think it was a perfect way to include him in the family. Besides, I can't wait to meet him." She studied Cecelia carefully. "You really do have the jitters. Go sit down and I'll get us some iced tea."

Cecelia settled herself carefully in a lawn chair, scowling at her leg, which no longer hurt but was a growing source of frustration because of the awkward cast. "It's not really Danny I'm worried about," she said when Jeannie returned with two frosty glasses. "It's Adam. He's convinced Danny hates him—and for the moment he may be right. He doesn't like Danny, either..."

"And there's more, isn't there?"

Cecelia nodded.

"Let me guess. Adam's disappointment about Danny is spilling over into your relationship."

Cecelia nodded again, realizing how perceptive her sister was. "I haven't been alone with Adam since that one weekend, not really alone. Suddenly it's as if we just can't connect."

"Have you tried talking to him?"

"For the first ten minutes it's like talking to a wall, and then we get into an argument. I don't know what to do, Jeannie. Adam was so anxious to find his son, and I was so much against it. But now that it's happened I'm really glad. I wish Adam could feel the same way."

"Maybe things will be better after today," Jeannie said hopefully.

"Maybe." Cecelia wasn't optimistic. Car doors slammed, and she heard Angela's high lilting voice punctuated by Sean's deeper one. Quiet time was over.

The children were still milling around when Pop came a few minutes later. Then Bill arrived with Benjamin, who screamed lustily until his grandfather sat down with him in the rocking chair. As Cecelia watched from the porch, smiling at the picture of age and youth, Bingo curled up at Pop's feet and made the scene complete.

"I hope the oldest grandchild is as easy to get along with as this little one," Pop said, patting Benjamin. "Danny is still coming, isn't he?"

"As far as I know he'll be here," Cecelia told her father as she hobbled down the steps. "I invited his mother, too, but she decided not to come."

"That boy must have a lot of guts, walking in on all of us at once," Pop observed.

"Was it a mistake to invite Danny?" Cecelia asked.

"I wouldn't say it was a mistake," her father answered diplomatically. "But it might be a little disconcerting for the boy, especially considering he didn't take too well to Adam."

"That's the understatement of the year." Cecelia sighed. "What am I going to do?"

"Just give it some time."

"That's your answer for everything."

"Yep." Pop retrieved the comb Benjamin had pulled ut of his shirt pocket. "How about a little iced tea?"

"Coming right up," Jeannie promised from the orch.

For the next hour the chaos built. Benjamin inter-ittently threw toys off the blanket that Jeannie had aid under a tree and then cried for his grandfather to ick them up. Bill joined Sean, Kim and Mary Beth for badminton game, and Kevin paced around, swiping hicken legs and potato chips whenever he thought no ne was watching.

The activities were going ahead as always, building oward the moment when the steaks went on the grill nd the rest of the food was spread tantalizingly over the icnic table. Yet food wasn't the topic on everyone's ind.

"I thought Danny was coming," she heard Kevin say Angela.

"He is," Angela answered. "But if you were Danny nd had to face this instant family, you wouldn't be in ny big hurry, either."

Kevin shrugged and disappeared into the kitchen.

Cecelia sensed that everyone was waiting, and she was aiting, too, not only for Danny, but also for Adam, ho was nearly an hour late. He was seldom late for nything. She couldn't help but wonder if his misgiv-gs were very much the same as Danny's.

When Adam finally did arrive, it was Pop who saw im first. "Welcome, Adam. Come look at my next-to-oungest grandson," he said, bouncing a now laugh-g Benjamin on his knee.

Cecelia watched Adam cross the yard, taking careful ock of the group, no doubt looking for Danny. He was ressed in jeans and a blue chambray shirt with the sleeves rolled up to his elbows. His face and arm looked tanned, as though he'd spent much of the las week outside. Cecelia wanted to run to him and throw her arms around him and, in that one impulsive move ment, banish all the awkwardness that seemed to hav grown up between them. But the cast on her leg was lik an anchor, and even without it she knew her desire wa nothing but a fantasy. There had been a time whe Adam would have swept her up and spun her around i a moment of pure joy. But that was before Danny cam into the picture. She couldn't be sure anymore ho Adam would react.

Adam leaned down to admire Benjamin, who gu gled appreciatively, and talked quietly to Pop for a fe moments. Not until he started up the porch steps to ward her did Cecelia sense his uneasiness.

"Sorry I'm late. Something came up at the last min ute," he said in greeting.

"I was beginning to get concerned," Cecelia ar swered, hating the polite excuse, the polite response, th distance between them she couldn't seem to bridge. Sh wished he would bend down and kiss her, but he didn't

"I take it Danny's not here yet? Or did he decide n to come?"

"Angela says he's coming," Cecelia answered. Ther on impulse, she asked Adam the same question she' posed twice before. "Did I make a mistake by invitin Danny?"

Adam's face tensed, and his eyes met Cecelia's for th first time that afternoon. "It would be a hell of a l easier if you hadn't."

"Hey, Adam, how about badminton?" Sean called waving a racquet toward Adam.

"Sure thing," Adam called back, looking distinctly relieved. "You don't mind, do you?" he asked Cecelia.

"Of course not. But Adam—" She hesitated, not sure how to say what she felt had to be said. She needed to know that the day wasn't going to turn into a disaster. "Adam," she began carefully, "when Danny does come, you will try, won't you?"

"I'll do what I can, Cecelia, but I'm not sure how much that's going to be," he answered.

She watched him spring down the steps and lope easily across the yard. A flash of irritation at his seeming indifference toward Danny quickly gave way to fear. Somehow the problem between Adam and his son had to be solved or Adam was going to withdraw from her, too. She'd fight any battle to keep from losing Adam, except she didn't know how to fight this one. Slowly she turned and walked back into the kitchen, the shouts and laughter of her family echoing behind her.

Cecelia delayed dinner until the chicken legs had disappeared entirely and the children were pacing restlessly in and out of the house. Mary Beth brought her boom box outside, and she and Angela practiced several versions of shimmy dancing while Bill and Jeannie cheered them on.

Finally Kevin cornered Cecelia. "Look, Mom, if Danny was going to show, he'd be here by now," he said impatiently. "And even if he does still come, you don't want him to find us all on the ground because we've passed out from hunger."

"I suppose," Cecelia reluctantly agreed.

"You mean we can eat? Quick, I'll take out the steaks before you change your mind."

DANNY HOVERED JUST OUTSIDE the gate to the yard. At the last minute he had decided to bring his guitar, but now he wished he hadn't. From the sound of things, the Mahoneys were a sports-minded family. He could hear the whack of the badminton birdie as someone hit it with a racquet, and over in the corner, in front of the gazebo, he saw several baseballs, two bats and a glove lying on the ground. Rock music blared, a baby cried, someone yelled over both the music and the baby, and the music was turned down. The baby continued to cry. Danny wondered whose baby it was. Angela had talked a lot about various aunts and uncles. Maybe the baby was her cousin—his cousin, or half cousin, or whatever you would call it.

Nervously Danny shifted his guitar to his other shoulder. This barbeque was a big mistake. He shouldn't have come. It would have been better to meet these people one at a time. Maybe it would be better not to meet them at all. He watched an old man bounce a baby on his lap. That would be Pop. Angela liked her grandfather a lot, and Danny could see why. He looked like a pretty laid-back guy. A sudden realization swept over Danny. That man was his grandfather, too, just as much as he was Angela's. The idea gave him a funny feeling inside. He'd never had a grandfather before. He wondered what you talked to a grandfather about.

The mouth-watering smell of steaks on the grill permeated the air. Danny was hungry. Tentatively he put his hand on the gate latch. That Campbell guy was over there supervising the cooking operation, which was exactly what he would have expected of an Air Force colonel. Always running the show. Danny stepped back and slid the guitar from his shoulder. He'd just leave it right there, behind the bushes, until the party was over.

He had an idea the colonel wouldn't be too thrilled with a kid who was into folk music. Not that it mattered, anyway.

ADAM WAS TAKING THE STEAKS off the grills while Sean and Kevin hovered over him. The girls were carrying the food outside under Jeannie's direction. Just then, Cecelia spotted Danny standing in the shadow of a bush at the corner of the house. A sense of anticipation mixed with foreboding swept through her. He'd come! That was the first step, but only a first step. She wondered how long he'd been there, just watching, and she tried to imagine how the happy, busy jumble of people must look to him. He looked more curious than frightened. Cecelia realized how odd the situation must seem to him as he stood on the edge of a solitary childhood staring at these people he was now being asked to accept as his family. Slowly, so that she wouldn't attract attention, she walked across the patio toward Danny.

"I'm sorry I'm so late, Mrs. Mahoney," he said apologetically as she approached him.

"You're not late. You're just in time for dinner. And, Danny," she added, taking his hand, "I'm so glad you're here."

He shuffled uncomfortably, obviously not sure whether he was glad or not.

"Come with me," she directed, turning back toward the porch. "I want you to meet everyone." As much as he had hoped Danny's arrival could be low-key, Cecelia quickly realized that wasn't possible.

Angela saw them first. "Danny, you're finally here. I'd almost given up on you."

Every head turned toward them, and only the steady rock beat from the boom box saved an awkward silence.

"I want you all to meet Danny," Cecelia said, praying that her voice didn't betray her nervousness. The twins adopted a sudden maturity and soberly shook Danny's hand. Mary Beth and Kim nodded and said hello, both of them apparently suffering from a sudden attack of shyness. Danny and Adam nodded to each other but didn't speak. Cecelia glared at Adam, but he didn't look at her. Bill clapped Danny on the shoulder in welcome, and Jeannie threw her arms around him in a big hug that, judging from the flush in Danny's cheeks, embarrassed him.

Pop was the one who saved the day. He shook Danny's hand, encasing it in both of his, and fixed his clear blue eyes on his eldest grandson. "Glad to have you with us," he pronounced. "How about getting something to eat? You like your steaks rare, or more on the done side like I do?"

Pop guided Danny toward the food as if he'd known the boy for years, engaging him in conversation about the best way to cook steak and which type of potato salad he liked. Cecelia could have hugged her father.

With Danny occupied, the rest of the family began to relax, and even Cecelia found herself eating a big dinner. When Adam came to sit by her, his plate overflowing, she smiled at him. "I think it's going to be okay," she said in a low voice.

"I wish I were as certain as you are," Adam murmured.

"Things were bound to be a little tense at first, but look at them. Pop and Danny obviously like each other—he's even got Danny holding Benjamin. And

Mary Beth's been over there talking to Danny. He already knows Angela."

"It's better than I expected," Adam admitted. "I wish I knew what to say to him." He took a large bite of potato salad and washed it down with a swallow of beer. He had trouble admitting that he couldn't think of a single thing to say to his own son. Objectively he knew it wasn't fair to judge Danny by appearance or even by how the boy had acted toward him. But that didn't change how Adam felt, nor did it make him any less certain that Danny would reject him, no matter how hard he tried.

"Maybe you don't need to say much of anything," Cecelia suggested.

"What do you mean?" He gave Cecelia a probing look.

"I just mean that maybe Pop's approach is the best one," she explained. "All he asked Danny was how he likes his steaks."

Adam looked thoughtful. "I see what you mean. Something nonthreatening."

"When I asked Pop what to do about all this, he said, 'Just give it time.' I always thought that was his remedy because he couldn't think of anything else, but maybe there's more to it."

Draining his can of beer, Adam stood up. "It's worth a try." He stopped by the picnic table for another helping of potato salad and then walked slowly toward where Pop was talking to Danny and Angela.

Cecelia watched as he pulled up a chair and sat on the edge of the group, eating calmly. Feeling a surge of hope, she closed her eyes, reminding herself that she would have to be content with small beginnings. At least Adam was trying.

"Danny's talking to him," Jeannie whispered triumphantly in her ear a few minutes later.

"Probably all of six words," Cecelia noted, seeing that Danny had turned toward Mary Beth, leaving Adam to converse with Pop.

"Six words is better than none. And he wasn't shouting."

"No," Cecelia agreed, "he wasn't shouting." By the time she joined the group, Adam had wandered off to play catch with Sean and Kevin, Benjamin was asleep on his blanket, and Bingo lay a few feet away with his head on his paws guarding the baby.

"I just found out that Danny plays the guitar," her father said, pulling a chair around for her.

"Mr. Riley says he has a really neat antique guitar he's going to show me," Danny added, more animated than Cecelia had ever seen him.

"I'm going to do better than that," Pop said. "My old guitar has been gathering dust in the attic for more years than I can count. I never did quite have the hang of playing it. If Danny here can get the thing back together and make music on it, then it's his."

Danny's face broke into an excited smile. "Thank you, Mr. Riley."

"Just one thing, boy. If you're going to be playing my guitar, you need to be calling me something other than Mr. Riley. A lot of people around here, whether they're family or not, call me Pop."

Cecelia saw the hesitation in Danny's eyes and then the acceptance. "All right...Pop. I'll try to remember."

"Good for you, boy. Now let's get us some of that chocolate cake."

The afternoon passed quickly, and as the sun sank into a round, red ball behind the trees, Cecelia walked slowly across the yard, realizing she'd quit worrying about Danny, and so had everyone else. Bill had joined Adam and the twins in a game of catch, Jeannie was upstairs nursing Benjamin, Pop was snoozing in his chair, Kim and Mary Beth were huddled around the boom box and Danny was sitting under a tree talking to Angela.

The day had finally settled into the comfortable familiarity of a family picnic, and Cecelia permitted herself a brief feeling of euphoria before turning her attention to the picnic table, which looked like a hoard of locusts had gone through. She commandeered Kim and Mary Beth to clear what little remained of the food, and soon Danny was helping them carry dishes into the kitchen. After a few minutes Cecelia started in to make sure the perishables were all in the refrigerator, but the sound of voices from inside stopped her at the screen door.

"You probably feel differently about Mom than I do because she's your birth mother," Mary Beth was saying. "And she'll probably treat you differently."

"She seems nice, but I don't really know her," Danny answered.

"I was really mad about you at first."

Cecelia noted that Mary Beth didn't sound a bit apologetic.

"Nothing personal," her daughter continued. "It's just that Mom seemed to think it was fine to bring you into the family, but she has always yelled at me when I wanted to find my birth mother. She can be really unfair sometimes."

"I get the feeling I wasn't supposed to be found," Danny answered. "It was sort of an accident."

"Are you glad?"

Cecelia strained to hear Danny's answer, but his voice was too soft. She reached for the door handle, feeling a pang of guilt for eavesdropping. Then Mary Beth began talking again and Cecelia stood still.

"For a while I thought Adam was going to help me find my birth mother, but he suddenly changed his entire attitude. Do you think you could help me?"

"I don't know," Danny answered. "I could try."

"I've got some ideas and a real good magazine article that talks about how to search records and everything, but I need some help getting it all together."

"I've read a little about it," Danny admitted. "We'll see what we can do, if you're sure that's what you want."

"I'm sure," Mary Beth answered without hesitation.

Cecelia rattled the screen door loudly as she opened it and joined Mary Beth and Danny in the kitchen. They looked up, obviously surprised to see her, and Mary Beth immediately asked what kind of container she should use for the potato salad. Cecelia decided that at some point she'd have a private talk with Danny about the problems Mary Beth could face if she succeeded in finding her mother. For the moment, however, the fragile beginnings of a new relationship between brother and sister were more important.

Danny and Mary Beth went back outside while Cecelia wrapped half a dozen remaining deviled eggs in foil. She thought about Adam, who had spent nearly all of his time with Kevin and Sean. If only he could form the same kind of bond with his own son, everything would be perfect, Cecelia decided. The screen door banged, and she looked up to see the twins, followed by Bill and Adam.

"This group plays a mean game of ball," Bill observed, rubbing his arm. "I'm going to be sore for a week."

"You'd better get in shape," Adam warned. "Benjamin will have you pitching before you know it."

Cecelia frowned. It was too bad Danny didn't like sports. That seemed to be the ticket for getting men together. But it wasn't fair to make him an outsider just because he had different interests.

"Hey, Mom, what's there to drink?" Sean asked.

"The cooler's in the corner," Cecelia answered. "And, Kevin, get out of the refrigerator. You can't possibly be hungry."

The ice in the cooler rattled as they dug for the few remaining sodas. Bill wandered upstairs to find Jeannie, and Cecelia hoped the twins would take off, too, and leave her alone with Adam.

Instead Sean flopped down on one of the kitchen chairs. "Hey, Mom," he announced, "Adam's going to take me and Kevin to see the Thunderbirds next Saturday."

"He is?" Cecelia looked questioningly at Adam.

"If it's all right," Adam said quickly, realizing he probably should have mentioned the air show to Cecelia before he told the boys. "The Thunderbirds are coming to Fairchild. It should be an impressive air show."

Cecelia looked at Adam sitting with her two boys around the table, all of them relaxed and sweaty, their noses red from the sun. They were a unit, comfortable together, enjoying each other, accepting the closeness that had evolved so naturally over the last few months. Danny had a right to be part of that. After all, he was Adam's son.

"I have an idea," she began. "Why don't you invite Danny to go with you? He's probably never seen the Thunderbirds."

Sean and Kevin looked up curiously. "He wouldn't go," Adam said flatly.

"I don't know why not," Kevin countered. "I can't imagine anyone not wanting to see the Thunderbirds."

"None of you will know unless you ask him," Cecelia observed.

Adam didn't answer. Cecelia couldn't tell whether he was considering the possibility or whether he had rejected it. Pop came into the kitchen to say good-night, and as he left Jeannie and Bill came downstairs carrying Benjamin in his infant seat and two bags full of blankets, diapers, and assorted baby paraphernalia.

A few minutes later the screen door banged again as Danny came into the kitchen to say goodbye. "It was a really nice picnic, Mrs. Mahoney. I liked meeting everybody."

Cecelia could tell by his face that he meant it. "We're very glad you could be here, Danny. We want you to come back anytime, whenever you feel like it. Don't wait to be invited."

When Danny turned toward the table to say goodbye to Adam and the twins, Cecelia looked expectantly at Adam. Kevin spoke first.

"Hey, Danny, we're going to see the Thunderbirds Saturday. Want to come with us?"

"I don't know, maybe," Danny answered noncommittally.

Cecelia wanted to step in and urge him to accept, but she bit her lip and held back. Her gaze shifted to Adam. He was watching Danny, his expression guarded.

"Should be a great show," Sean said. "This is the first time the Thunderbirds have come to Fairchild in a long time."

"We'd like to have you come with us if you aren't busy that day," Adam added stiffly.

Cecelia saw Danny's eyes meet his father's and hold for one brief, tense moment. What were they thinking? she wondered. What emotion passed between them as they faced each other across the kitchen? The distance between them seemed a giant chasm, too wide to cross, and yet each step that either of them took could bring them a little bit closer together.

"What time?" Danny asked.

"Two o'clock."

"I'll meet you at the front gate by the guard house."

"That's good. The base will be crowded that day."

Danny turned back to Cecelia and said goodbye again. Then he left quickly by the back door.

"So, I win," Kevin said. "He's going. We should have bet money."

"You're so broke you don't have any money to bet," Sean retorted.

"Yeah, but if we'd bet, I would have money because I'd have won." He stood up and walked toward the family room.

"He's a pea brain sometimes," Sean said and followed his brother.

Adam and Cecelia stared at each other for a moment, and then Cecelia smiled. "Just like that," she said, shaking her head.

"Just like that," Adam repeated. "I'd have given ten to one against Danny saying yes."

"Which goes to prove—"

"Unfortunately it doesn't prove anything," Adam interrupted her. "At least not yet. We've got no guarantees that Saturday will go well."

"And no guarantees that it won't," Cecelia countered. "Don't be such a pessimist."

"You're right."

Adam smiled, erasing the worry lines that creased his forehead so often lately, and Cecelia hobbled across the kitchen to put her hands on his shoulders. He pulled her body against him and neither of them could mistake the look that passed between them.

Adam looked around impatiently. "There's no place we can be alone, is there?"

"I don't think so."

He stood up and took Cecelia's hand. "Then let's go out to the gazebo for a few minutes. At least we can see anyone coming."

They walked together slowly across the yard, away from the house lights that shone through curtained windows. Once inside the gazebo, they moved into the shadows and, enclosed in almost total darkness, Adam took Cecelia in his arms. The distant sounds of voices and of muted rock music from inside the house all faded away. Adam's mouth found Cecelia's as his hands searched the soft curves of her body.

He didn't have any idea how long he held her. He was so hungry for her that he wanted to make love to her until the sun came up. He knew her body now. He'd buried himself in her softness and shared the tremors of ecstasy that bind a man and woman together. He knew she shared the feelings that raced through him, and so when she drew gently away, he let her go and pulled her down beside him on the hard, wooden bench.

"I've missed you so, Adam," she whispered.

"I know," he answered.

"What's happened to us, Adam?" she asked, tipping her face upward but barely able to see him in the darkness. "Is it because of Danny?"

Adam knew he should tell her about the job in Washington. He should tell her that if he couldn't resolve things with Danny he'd been thinking it would be better for all of them if he went away for a while. But he couldn't do it, not tonight, not the way he felt.

"I thought finding our son would bring us even closer together." His voice was so low it was barely audible. "But he's like a wedge between us, Cecelia."

"It doesn't have to be that way."

"I hope not."

He kissed her again, but she immediately realized it was different. The hunger they'd shared so openly just a few minutes before was gone. Cecelia remembered her irrational fears of twenty years ago, when she was pregnant and alone, that one day she would pay dearly for what she had done. She pressed her head against Adam's chest, her eyes wet with tears, silently praying that the ultimate price would not be losing what they'd found together.

That night she wrote in her journal:

Danny came to the Memorial Day picnic. Everything went better than I'd expected. He's agreed to go to an air show with Adam and the twins. I pray that Danny and Adam can work things out, because if they don't I'm afraid I'm going to lose the man I love so much.

CHAPTER TWELVE

THE MORNING of the Thunderbird air show dawned clear and still. The azure sky stretched to the horizon without a cloud in sight. *Perfect flying weather*, thought Adam as he pulled his Bronco into Cecelia's driveway. He had barely cut the ignition when the front door of the house burst open and Sean and Kevin came bounding down the porch stairs. Despite her crutches, Cecelia was right behind them, waving a bottle of sunscreen.

"Don't leave yet, Adam," she called. "The boys have to put lotion on their faces or they'll be burned to a crisp."

Adam took a close look at the twins' fair, freckled skin and, ignoring their vociferous protests, hustled them back to their mother. He followed them to the porch. By leaning around Sean, the crutches and the bottle of sunscreen, he managed to give Cecelia a quick kiss on the cheek.

"Gross." Kevin rolled his eyes. "Just like Mary Beth and Roger."

Much to Adam's surprise, Cecelia's face flushed.

"Mom's blushing," Sean announced.

"I am not. Stand still while I get this sunscreen on the back of your neck."

Adam grinned. He realized that none of Cecelia's children had ever seen any show of affection between them. Thoughtfully, he studied Kevin and Sean, trying to remember how it felt to be thirteen years old. As he recalled, his knowledge of sex had been limited to what he'd learned in the locker room and from furtive glimpses at men's magazines. So maybe Kevin and Sean hadn't put two and two together. If so, it was just as well.

"Are the boys dressed all right?" Cecelia asked. "I knew you'd be wearing your uniform and they might be meeting a lot of people...."

Adam looked them over. They were wearing striped polo shirts and jeans that must be fairly new, he noted, because the knees weren't worn. Except for their red high-top shoes with the trailing laces Kevin and Sean looked pretty clean-cut to him. "We're going to be doing a lot of walking. You guys better tie your shoes so you don't trip."

"Everybody wears these shoes untied," Kevin explained. "Nobody trips."

"Well..." Adam took another look at the high-tops. He was definitely skeptical.

"I suggested that for this particular occasion some other shoes might be more appropriate," Cecelia said, "but I was outvoted. Sorry."

Adam shrugged. "Okay, guys, go get in the car."

The twins let out a loud whoop and raced down the driveway to the Bronco.

Cecelia put her hand on Adam's arm. "I suppose I could have insisted the boys wear their leather shoes, but I try not to interfere too much. There are so many things that are more important than clothes."

"Are you trying to give me some advice about Danny?"

Cecelia smiled and kissed him lightly. "Maybe. What matters most today is that everyone have a good time."

"I have the day pretty carefully planned," Adam answered confidently, "and I've never known anyone who didn't like the Thunderbirds."

"I hope you're right."

"I know I'm right," Adam replied. "I'll have the boys back in plenty of time for dinner," he called over his shoulder as he headed toward the Bronco.

"Angela's fixing chicken pie and you're invited," Cecelia called back.

Adam waved his acceptance and pulled out of the driveway. Kevin and Sean couldn't contain their excitement, and as Adam drove they asked him question after question about airplanes. Adam was impressed at how well they understood some of his technical explanations and found himself thoroughly enjoying the exchange. If Danny were only half as enthusiastic as the twins, today would be terrific, Adam decided as he pulled the Bronco into his reserved parking space in front of wing headquarters.

"Wow, your own name on a sign!" Kevin's eyes opened wide as he read aloud: "Colonel Adam Campbell, Commander 92 Bomb Wing."

"Are you the most important guy on the base?" Sean asked, climbing out of the car.

Adam laughed. "Well, I am up there, but do you see those airmen across the street?" He pointed to several young men in fatigues, and the twins nodded. "They're jet engine mechanics, and they keep all the planes in topnotch condition."

"Even if mechanics are important, I'd rather be a pilot," Kevin stated.

"Keep on getting those As in school and playing on that allstar basketball team, and you might be able to get an appointment to the Air Force Academy." Adam put his hand on Kevin's shoulder, guiding him in the direction of the main gate where Danny was to meet them.

"Me, too? Or does the Air Force Academy only take one person from each family?" Sean looked worried.

"I think the academy would take both of you, if you both qualify." And they might, Adam thought. The idea gave him a deep sense of pride.

The boys, one on each side, stretched to keep pace with Adam, and grinned every time an airman in uniform saluted. The base was packed with people, mostly young families with small children and babies in strollers. Adam felt less a commanding officer and more a part of the crowd with the boys along. As they turned a corner the main gate came into view, and they spotted Danny, slouched against the guard house with his hands shoved into the front pockets of his jeans.

"Hey, Danny," shouted Kevin.

Danny cocked his head, but made no move. He felt like a traitor joining up with them.

"Maybe he doesn't see us," Sean said.

But as Adam and the boys drew nearer, it was apparent Danny could see them quite well.

"How are you, Danny?" Adam asked.

Danny shrugged. "Not bad, I guess." His eyes traveled from the silver eagles on the shoulders of Adam's uniform to the command pilot wings and the rows of ribbons on his chest. "All decked out for war, I see."

"No," Sean objected. "He would wear his flight suit if he was going to war. This uniform is like his regular suit. Right, Adam?"

"Something like that," Adam replied. Danny was also wearing his usual uniform—the bandana around his shaggy blond hair, the peace symbol earring, the faded vest over the thin white T-shirt, and the ragged jeans. Only the shoes were different. Instead of scuffed boots he had on rubber thongs, which were probably no worse than the twins' red high-tops, Adam told himself. Anyway, he was not going to make clothes a major issue. But the differences between his son and the twins were glaring.

"Well, what do you say we head for the flight line? The show starts in less than half an hour." He started to clap Danny on the shoulder and then thought better of it.

The bleachers were nearly full when the group arrived at the flight line, but the commanding officers had a reserved section. The twins climbed to the very top row of seats, and Adam and Danny followed. As Adam paused on the way up to greet several friends, he was conscious of the disapproving glances cast in Danny's direction. Only George Lathrop seemed oblivious to the young man's appearance.

"Nice to meet you," Lathrop said, extending his hand.

To his credit, Adam thought, Danny took Lathrop's hand and muttered a reasonable pleasantry.

"So, are you a college student in the area?"

"Yeah, I go to Eastern Washington State in Cheney."

"Is that so?" Lathrop remarked. "I've got a son down at Texas A & M. Studying chemical engineering, pollution, that sort of thing. What are you interested in?"

Adam saw Danny visibly relax. "Environmental science. **Biology.** I get into a lot of pollution things, too."

Lathrop nodded. "Good field, especially if you're planning to live in the northwest. We need people out here like you."

Danny's eyes shone. "Thank you, uh, sir," he added awkwardly.

Lathrop moved down two rows to join his wife, and Danny sat down next to Sean.

Damn, Adam thought. *Lathrop had a more meaningful conversation with that kid in two minutes than I've been able to have with him in two hours.*

"I didn't know you were into environmental science," Adam said.

Danny shrugged. "Guess I never mentioned it."

"You like to camp, get out in the woods, that kind of thing?"

"Yeah, I do."

"So do I," Adam said. "Backpacking especially." It sure would help if Danny would elaborate a little. Talking to him was hard work.

The spectators broke into applause as the Thunderbirds' narrator came to the microphone in front of the six red, white and blue F-16 fighters. After a brief history of the crack team, the pilots walked to their planes. They snapped their canopies down in succession, and the jets rolled off. Necks craned and cameras snapped as the Thunderbirds soared into their breathtaking Diamond Opener followed by the Pass in Review, trailing smoke all the while.

"This is great," Kevin shouted.

Sean didn't say a word, but his grin stretched from one side of his face to the other. Adam looked carefully at Danny. Although he did appear to be watching the show, he didn't respond with anything that could even be remotely called enthusiasm.

"Well, what do you think?" Adam asked his son during a lull in the engine noise.

"You really want to know?"

Adam nodded, but he wished he hadn't asked.

Danny stuck his chin out defiantly. "These are nothing but a bunch of hotshot fighter pilots practicing war games."

"I'm sorry you feel that way, Danny." Adam applauded with the rest of the crowd as the fighters streaked by in a Knife-Edge Pass.

"Worse yet, the Air Force is billing this as entertainment." Danny's eyes narrowed as he watched the planes. "These are the same formations planes fly when they're going to drop bombs."

The roar of the engines prevented Adam from answering immediately and gave him a moment to control his irritation. "You're right," he agreed in an amicable tone when the noise subsided. "These so-called stunts are the same types of maneuvers all pilots learn when they're in training. Nevertheless, most people think they're pretty good entertainment."

"Now I suppose you're going to give me the pitch about how we need all these fighter planes and other weapons as a deterrent. That's a bunch of crap." Danny stared straight ahead, deliberately ignoring the Thunderbirds' Clover Loops in the clear blue sky high above the crowds.

Adam worked to control his temper. Next to him, Sean and Kevin were clapping and cheering with excitement. Why couldn't Danny just cool off and enjoy the show?

For the next half hour the noise from the F-16 engines and the shouts from the spectators made conversation impossible, effectively preventing Danny from provoking an argument. Finally the Thunderbirds landed and taxied to a stop on the runway.

"That was the greatest air show I've ever seen," Kevin said as they climbed down from the bleachers.

"That was the only air show you've ever seen," Sean reminded his brother. "What did you think of it, Danny?"

"I suppose it was okay if you don't mind watching war planes."

Kevin grimaced. "You sound just like Angela." He turned to Adam. "I'm starved. Can we get a hot dog?"

"Sure thing," Adam agreed, handing the boys some money. "We'll meet you at the snack area." The twins took off at a run, and Adam focused his attention on Danny. "Maybe there are some things you don't understand about the philosophy behind military strength," he began.

"What's to understand?" Shoving his hands in his pockets, Danny walked several feet away from Adam. "You military types don't give a damn about what happens to humanity. You don't care if some third-world power gets hold of a nuclear bomb and wipes out a few million people. If you have it your way, the United States will always have more bombs and more missiles than anybody else. You never think about what would happen if we really used them."

"You're missing the point." Adam returned a passing sergeant's salute, not missing the look of contempt that crossed Danny's face. "Just because we have nuclear weapons doesn't mean we're going to use them. I'm sure you've studied the balance of power. When the world is out of balance, when one country is stronger than all the rest, it would be easy for the strongest country to take advantage of its power. That's why we're negotiating with the Soviet Union to cut back on nuclear weapons. If we just throw ours out, we have nothing to negotiate with.''

"So we just keep building more and more nuclear weapons to have something to negotiate with? That stinks.''

Two clean-cut airmen, about Danny's age, apparently overhearing the heated discussion, turned around. When they recognized their wing commander, they quickly looked away.

"Listen, why don't we continue this debate later?'' Adam said in an attempt to mollify Danny. "We can join Sean and Kevin for a hot dog and then catch the end of the parachuting demonstration.''

"You can do whatever turns you on, Colonel Campbell. Personally, I'm going to split.'' Danny disappeared into the crowd.

As he watched Danny go, Adam's disappointment grew into cold rage. If that was the way the kid wanted it, that was the way it would be, Adam decided. Finding him had been a mistake from the very beginning.

"We got you and Danny hot dogs,'' Kevin said as Adam approached the concession stand. He looked around curiously. "Where's Danny?''

"He left.'' Adam offered no explanation. "Come on,'' he said, taking two hot dogs from Kevin. "We'll eat these on the way to the car.''

Adam was grateful for the twins' banter on the way home. Their exuberance about the air show meant he didn't have to talk. He genuinely liked Sean and Kevin, which made the situation with Danny that much more difficult. How could he relate to Cecelia's boys so easily and not be able to exchange a dozen civil words with his own son? Adam shook his head. The twins were like

him, and Danny wasn't. The longer he stayed in Spo
kane, the harder it was going to be for all of them.

Cecelia was waiting when Adam and the boys ar
rived. Both Sean and Kevin leaped out of the car, and
gave their mother an immediate rundown on the Thun
derbirds. Adam held back, wishing his report could be
as enthusiastic. Cecelia didn't deserve this mess with
Danny. None of them did. He watched her smile as she
listened to the twins, and it occurred to him that she
looked sexy even with that bulky cast on her leg. Her
cheeks were pink, probably from spending the after
noon outside, and her tousled hair had settled in a mass
of curls around her face. In fact she looked very much
as she had that weekend in the woods. But there would
be no more weekends like that.

As he walked up the front steps, Angela appeared on
the porch to announce that dinner was ready. Realizing
he couldn't leave gracefully, Adam stayed to eat with
them. The meal was chaotic and spontaneous, with the
twins again relaying the exploits of the pilots, this time
for their sisters who seemed appropriately impressed.

Cecelia threw out questions, too, and was acutely
aware that none of the answers came from Adam. She
sensed an uneasiness about him, and during a lull in the
conversation asked the question that kept bothering her.
"Did Danny meet you at the air field?"

"Yeah, he was there," Sean said around a large
mouthful of chicken pie.

Ignoring her son, Cecelia looked directly at Adam. "I
thought he might come back with you for dinner. Did
he seem to enjoy himself?"

Adam didn't meet her eyes. "Not particularly," he
answered in a carefully controlled voice.

No longer hungry, Cecelia laid down her fork. "What happened?" she asked bluntly.

Adam shrugged. "Nothing. He just didn't like it."

"It isn't his thing," Angela volunteered. "I could have told you that.'"

Kevin frowned at his sister. "He didn't have to be such a pain about it. Your piano recitals weren't my thing, either, but I sat through them."

"Is there any more hot bread?" Sean asked.

"In the oven," Angela told him. "Get it yourself."

The conversation drifted to a concert scheduled in the park the next weekend, and Cecelia made no attempt to turn it back to Danny. She didn't need anyone to spell out the details to know the day had been a disaster. If Sean, who tolerated almost anything, was complaining about Danny's behavior, then Danny must have been both vocal and antagonistic. No wonder Adam seemed withdrawn. She knew he'd had big hopes for the day, and now she couldn't tell if he was angry or simply disappointed. Probably both, she decided.

"I need to be getting back to the base," Adam said, as they finished dinner. "I've got some paperwork to do tonight."

"Surely you can stay long enough to have some coffee," Cecelia responded quickly. "We can take it outside." Even as he agreed, she could feel his hesitation. Maybe he did have a lot to do, she told herself, but she suspected otherwise. Adam had pulled away from her after his first confrontation with Danny, and all indications were that he was about to distance himself again.

"Was Danny really hostile today?" she asked quietly as they sat in the gathering darkness under the oak tree.

"You could put it that way."

Adam was sitting half-facing her, his chair farther from hers than she'd have liked. She could feel the wall that had gone up between them again. "I know it's hard, Adam," she said gently, "but Danny's angry and confused. We'll just have to keep trying."

"I have been trying," Adam snapped. "Quit defending him, Cecelia. He's dogmatic and ill-tempered and our 'trying,' as you put it, isn't going to change a thing."

"He's young, Adam, and all caught up in himself. He'll come around, but it's going to take time."

Adam sipped his coffee. "I wouldn't bank on it. Not this kid."

"I know there aren't any guarantees." She paused. Adam was even more upset than she'd realized, but at least he was expressing his feelings. If she could only keep him talking, they'd come up with something. "We have to keep working with him, Adam. It's our only option." She started to explain that teenagers need love the most when they're the most unlovable, but Adam cut her off.

"No, it's not the only option."

She met his eyes and saw the rising storm inside him. Her confidence that they could work things out began to waver. "What do you mean?"

"Exactly what I said. It's like the old adage about beating a dead horse."

"So you're suggesting we just abandon Danny? I can't do that. Not now." Her voice grew quiet and steady. "And neither can you, Adam. He's our son, our own flesh and blood, and he needs us. We can't just turn our backs on him."

"I'm not suggesting you turn your back on him. I'm saying that as far as I'm concerned, there's no common ground between Danny Mitchell and me. I realize that's a problem for you, Cecelia, and I've caused you enough problems already."

Adam's words sent a chill through Cecelia. The night air was suddenly cold, the chair hard and unyielding under her, the cast heavy on her leg.

"Exactly what are you trying to tell me?"

Adam stared into the darkness. A profound sadness gripped him as he thought about what he had to do. As long as he stayed in Spokane, he was going to make her life miserable. Cecelia would be constantly buffeted between him and Danny, always trying to mend the rift that was too wide to be mended. He wouldn't put her in that position. He loved her too much. He knew she sensed what was happening, and for the moment that was probably enough.

"You establish whatever relationship you can with Danny," he said finally. "Leave me out of it." Abruptly he stood up. "I have to get back to the base."

"Adam, don't do this." Cecelia leaned toward him. "Don't push me away because of Danny."

Her words hurt, but he was going to do what he had to do. "Do you want me to help you take the coffee mugs inside before I go?" he asked.

Cecelia closed her eyes. She wanted to reach out and grab him, as if that somehow could keep him from slipping away. "No, thank you, Adam," she answered. Her voice was so low it was nearly lost in the night.

After Adam was gone, Cecelia went up to her bedroom, struggling with the dilemma he had left her. She would not abandon Danny. She couldn't. After so many

years of separation, he was part of her again in a way
only a mother would understand. But she wouldn't give
up Adam, either. She loved him; maybe she had always
loved him. That wasn't important now. The past was
over and she had survived it alone. Now the future
stretched before her, its hazy images all bound up in
Adam. She reached in the bedside table for her journal
and pen:

> Adam and Danny have both become part of me,
> each in his own way. I can't bear to let either one
> of them go. There are no answers. . . .

Her words trailed off as her mind searched first in
one direction, and then in another. But she couldn't al-
ter what she'd written. There were no answers.

POP WASN'T THE LEAST BIT surprised when he saw
Danny's old Ford pull into the gravel driveway. When
he had told him about the antique guitar at Cecelia's
Memorial Day shindig, he'd known that Danny would
eventually show up to take a look. No musician worth
his salt could resist the lure of a fine, old instrument.
Pop set his hoe against the back fence and stepped
carefully over the rows of tender, young vegetable plants
he had been weeding. Danny waved at him from across
the yard, and Pop waved back. Then he stood and
watched his grandson walk toward him.

He wasn't a bad looking boy. Had a little of both
Cecelia and Adam in him, and if he wasn't mistaken,
Danny was built like his own father had been. Patrick
Riley had been tall and lean and a rebel, too, leaving
Ireland as a young lad to make his way in America. Af-
ter raising hell for a while, he'd finally settled down with

a good woman on a fine piece of land and produced nine healthy children, including himself. Danny would turn out all right eventually. True, he had some problems to work out, and that was going to take time. But he'd make it. The boy came from good, strong Irish stock.

"Well, what brings you out to my neck of the woods?" Pop settled his hand on Danny's shoulder and walked toward the house with him.

"I kind of thought...that is, if you aren't too busy..."

"You've got a hankering to get your hands on that old guitar I told you about, haven't you, boy? Well, come on inside with me, and we'll take a look in the attic." Pop pushed open the porch door and bent down to take off his muddy gardening boots, grunting from the effort. "I'm getting too old for all this digging and weeding, but I like getting my hands in the dirt. I suppose I'll keep at it until the Good Lord comes to take me. Do you work outside, Danny?" He led his grandson into the kitchen.

"I don't garden, but I backpack and fish. I like being out in the wilderness." Danny's gaze travelled around the comfortable, cluttered kitchen. He could almost imagine the boisterous Riley clan gathered around the big table—all those aunts and uncles he'd never met except for his Aunt Jeannie. He picked up a faded old photograph in a silver frame and studied it. The young woman looked very much like his birth mother. "Who is this?" he asked.

Pop took the photograph from Danny and smiled at it. "That's my Maggie, your grandmother. She was just sixteen when that picture was taken." Pop took out his handkerchief and carefully wiped off the silver frame before he set it back on the chest. "Passed on now, a year ago Thanksgiving," he added in a husky voice.

A grandmother, Danny thought. He'd had a grandmother, too. All of these connections, all of this past, and he'd never known about any of it. "Was my grandmother Irish, too?" he asked.

"Maggie Sullivan was as Irish as they come. Only seven years old when she came to this country. I met her a couple of years later, when she was ten and I was sixteen. Right that very day, she said she was going to marry me. And I laughed and told her she was only a little girl and I was nearly a grown man. But she just smiled that wicked smile of hers, and answered that she'd be grown up before I knew it, and I'd just have to wait for her."

"And you did?" Danny knew the answer before he even asked the question. But the story, any story about his own family, was fascinating.

"I did wait," Pop answered solemnly. "And I never regretted it for a single minute. Now come on, let's get up on to the attic, and see if we can find that guitar."

Danny followed Pop through the cavernous front hall and up the stairs to the second floor. There Pop pulled on a chain hanging from the ceiling, and a set of stairs dropped down. "Why don't you go on up and take a look around?" he suggested. "If I recall rightly, the guitar is at the far end, near that little round window."

Danny was up the stairs and inside the attic before the words were out of his grandfather's mouth. Brushing the cobwebs away from his face, he stood for a minute to let his eyes adjust to the dim light.

"Have you spotted the guitar yet?" Pop called from down below.

"No," Danny answered. His eyes traveled around the dusty room. "But there's a funny looking dressmaking dummy with no head standing right in front of me."

"That would be your grandmother's. She never used it much after the babies started coming because the waist was too small, but for some reason she had to hang on to it. Now look over to one side. Do you see an old steamer trunk?"

"Yes." Danny stroked his hand across the fine leather bindings, wondering what was inside the trunk, and who it belonged to. Next to the trunk was a wicker baby carriage, with big old-fashioned wheels, probably the carriage his grandmother had used for his mother and all his aunts and uncles.

"Are you having any luck, boy?"

"I'm still looking." Danny set aside several round hat boxes and a set of pink doll dishes and made his way down to the end of the attic, stepping carefully on the widely spaced wooden planks. Then, underneath a pile of musty clothes, he finally saw the old guitar. "I've got it," he shouted triumphantly to his grandfather.

"Bully!" came the response. "Bring it on down here so we can take a good look at it."

Danny descended the attic stairs, holding the guitar carefully out in front of him. "I think it's in good shape. The strings are rotted, but look, the wood's not cracked and the joints seem to be tight."

Pop adjusted his glasses and leaned over to get a better look at the old instrument. He was pleased to hear the excitement in Danny's voice. "Yep, I think you're right. A little elbow grease and some new strings and you'll be in business, son. Maybe you can strum us a few tunes at the next family gathering."

"Maybe. But not if Adam is there. I don't think he'd like folk music." Danny's jaw set stubbornly.

"Now, you might be surprised." Pop patted Danny on the back. "Adam isn't a bad fellow. I think if you two spent some time together, you might find you have a few things in common. After all, he's your father and blood is thick."

Danny followed Pop silently into the kitchen, and set the guitar on the table. He would never accept Adam Campbell as his father.

"You're mighty quiet for someone who just got himself a family heirloom," Pop observed.

"Yeah, well, family takes some getting used to, I guess. All the stuff you've been telling me about my grandmother and everybody this afternoon...that's all right. But some of the other people—"

"Like your father?"

"He's not my father!" Danny's eyes hardened. "My father is dead."

"You're right, son. And you're wrong, too." Pop patted Danny's back again. The boy was so angry and hurt that he couldn't see reason right now. Speaking gently, Pop continued, "The father who raised you is gone, but there's another one who'd like to get to know you. Don't you think you should give him a fair chance?"

"I tried," Danny said. "I went to his air show and I watched all those war stunts. They're not my kind of thing—"

"And you didn't act too appreciative, I suppose." Pop poured two glasses of lemonade and handed one to Danny.

"I acted just fine. I was polite to his friends."

"But were you polite to Adam? That's the basis for relationships, you know, being nice to each other."

Some of the conversation between himself and Adam passed through Danny's mind. All that stuff about war planes and nuclear weapons had been pretty heavy. But that was how he'd felt. "I was reasonable with Adam," he said defensively. He looked away when he realized Pop was watching him closely. "Well, maybe I wasn't always reasonable," he admitted.

"That's the first step, boy. Knowing where some of the problems are. Now, maybe the next time you're with Adam you can ease up a little bit and things will be better."

"If there ever is a next time," Danny muttered.

Pop smiled at his newest grandson. "I know there will be a next time, boy."

CHAPTER THIRTEEN

LATE FRIDAY AFTERNOON Adam sat brooding over a scotch and water in the Officers' Club bar while he waited for George Lathrop. The club was nearly full, as it always was during happy hour on Fridays. Adam had purposely chosen a chair at a corner table facing the window because he didn't want to engage in casual conversation with people passing by. He was edgy and irritable after too many nights without sleep, but he finally had made a decision, or at least half a decision. Lathrop was the man to help him implement it.

"You look as though you need a vacation," Lathrop noted, as he eased into the chair across from Adam. "I thought you were going to take some time off to help, um . . ."

"Cecelia."

"Yes, Cecelia. How's her leg?"

"Getting better." Adam realized he'd fallen short there, too. He'd been so preoccupied with the mess he'd made with Danny that he'd been virtually no help to Cecelia.

Lathrop ordered a drink and settled back in his chair. "I take it you two are having some problems?"

"You could put it that way." Adam knew Lathrop was giving him an opening to talk if he wanted it. He also knew his friend wouldn't press the issue.

"Too bad," Lathrop sympathized. "Were those her boys you had at the air show?"

"Yeah."

"Fine looking pair of twins. I noticed the other one had a different last name. Is he related?"

Adam took a long gulp of his drink. He did need someone to talk to and Lathrop was a good friend. He wasn't one to pass judgment. "They're half brothers," Adam answered matter-of-factly. "Danny is my son."

"Your son?" Lathrop stared at him.

"Cecelia got pregnant during my last year at the academy."

Lathrop drained his drink. "Damn good thing nobody found out. You could have been out on your ear."

"I realize that." At the time it had been one of his major concerns but now...now it seemed far less important than so much of the rest of what had happened.

Lathrop frowned. "Cecelia's had the boy all this time?"

"No, we gave him up for adoption." Adam was surprised at how easily he could explain, as long as he stuck to the facts. "We didn't know where he was until a couple of months ago," he added.

"And now that he's in the picture things aren't going too well?"

"That's putting it mildly." Adam ordered another drink for both of them. "He and I have exactly zero in common—you could probably figure that out from taking a look at him."

Lathrop's eyes wandered to the window and for a few moments he was quiet. Then he turned back to Adam. "How long has it been since you've seen my son, Charlie?"

Adam tried to remember. "Not for years. He was maybe ten or eleven. Nice looking kid."

"He's in college now," Lathrop said. "Danny reminds me of him."

"Danny?" Adam couldn't imagine George Lathrop having a son who looked like Danny. "You're stretching it, George."

"Actually, no, I'm not. I always thought having an Air Force colonel for a father contributed to his rebellion. Maybe not."

They sat in silence for several moments, each man caught up in his own thoughts. "Where did things go wrong?" Adam asked finally.

"I don't know that they have," Lathrop answered slowly. "Kids his age are in the process of finding themselves, and I know a lot of grown men who haven't done that yet."

"Maybe." Adam wasn't quite so forgiving. "But how do you talk to him? Danny can't even bring himself to be civil."

"Well, with Charlie it works best to get him on neutral ground doing something we both like. That way if the conversation gets tense we can focus elsewhere."

Adam sat back in his chair and thoughtfully swirled the ice cubes in his glass. "That seems like a lot of trouble."

Lathrop chuckled. "You obviously don't know much about teenagers. They're always a lot of trouble. Charlie's basically a good kid, except he's got some weird ideas. But I must admit he makes me think once in a while."

Adam found himself listening carefully. "What do you mean about getting your son on neutral ground?"

"I don't bring him to the base and he doesn't take me to St. Elmo to hang out with his friends. Actually we do a lot of fishing."

Adam considered Lathrop's solution. It made sense, except that Lathrop was dealing with an entirely different set of circumstances. While Lathrop and his son had a lifetime of memories to build on, he and Danny had nothing but shared animosity. "I'm afraid that wouldn't work with Danny," he said. "The kid's really hostile."

Lathrop didn't seem impressed. "They're all hostile. That's the way they get people to pay attention to them."

"But why?" Adam raised his voice so that Lathrop could hear him above the rising din in the bar. "We weren't that way," he argued.

"Weren't we?" Lathrop grinned. "Remember the chug-a-lug contests and the drag races?"

"That was different."

"Yeah, Campbell, that was different. The world was different then. And besides, some kids don't follow the crowd. They're into their own thing."

Adam finished his drink. Lathrop made it all sound so logical. "You really think it would do any good to take the kid fishing?"

"Couldn't hurt," Lathrop answered.

"Maybe I'll try it," Adam mused. "In the meantime, I'd like you to follow up something else for me, George. That job you mentioned at the Pentagon—"

Lathrop's expression told Adam he understood. Adam was considering the traditional military escape, a transfer that allowed a swift exit from sticky personal problems.

"I'll make a few calls," Lathrop said. "I need a favor from you, too. I'm taking off later tonight and I'll be gone until sometime Monday. Can you stop by the office late afternoon tomorrow and see if my broken air conditioner is fixed, and if it isn't get CE on the stick."

"Sure thing," Adam agreed. "I've got no plans at all, except maybe a fishing trip, and there's no way that will take all day." He glanced down at Lathrop's empty glass. "You want another drink?"

Lathrop checked his watch. "Better not. My wife is expecting me early tonight." Shaking his head, he stood up. "That's one of the drawbacks of being married. Somebody always wants to know where you are."

Adam didn't think that sounded like much of a problem. He went back to his room in the BOQ and sat alone for an hour, resenting the stark walls and the military issue furniture. Things would improve after his permanent quarters were ready, he told himself. But not much, not as long as he was alone. He thought about calling Cecelia to see if she was busy. That way they could discuss the possibility of his taking Danny fishing. Then he rejected the idea. If he decided to take the job at the Pentagon things would be hard enough for her without him hanging around any more than he had been already.

Finally, after fixing himself another drink and a cold ham sandwich, he picked up the phone. He'd give it one more try with Danny, and then no one could say he hadn't made an effort. It was Friday night. The kid probably wasn't home anyway.

To Adam's surprise, Danny answered the phone.

"Danny, this is . . . um . . . Adam." They hadn't discussed what Danny would call him, but the Mahoney kids called him Adam. "How are things going?"

"All right," Danny answered after a moment's hesitation.

Even the two words sounded suspicious. Obviously there would be no small talk. Adam decided to get right to the point. "I thought I might go fishing on Saturday. As I remember, the fishing around here used to be pretty good. I thought you might like to go along."

Danny hesitated again. Fishing sounded fine, but with Adam Campbell it could be a miserable trip. He was about to say he was busy when he remembered all that stuff Pop had said to him about the past and all the lineage and the connections. It was new to him and he'd thought about it a lot. Not that it made him like Adam Campbell any better, but it forced him to think about the man differently.

"Danny, are you still there?"

"Yeah," Danny answered. "I guess I'll go."

The reply wasn't enthusiastic, but at least it was affirmative. "I'll pick you up at eight o'clock," Adam said. "Is that all right?" Adam asked, when there was no response.

"Yeah," Danny answered. "I'll be ready."

After hanging up, Adam remembered what George Lathrop had said about teenagers and tried hard not to be irritated by Danny's sullenness. At least he'd agreed to go. Adam picked up the phone again and dialed Cecelia.

"Taking him fishing sounds like a wonderful idea," she said enthusiastically. "You'll be out in the woods, by yourselves. That'll be perfect." She paused, and then her voice changed to a low, intimate tone. "People can get really close to each other out in the woods, you know."

Adam chuckled. "I know."

But where Danny was concerned, he wasn't counting on anything. He'd allowed himself to get his hopes up when he took Danny to the Thunderbirds, and he wasn't going to make that mistake again.

Still, Adam was in good spirits that bright, crisp Saturday morning as he and Danny headed north out of Spokane. "Looks like it's going to be a good day. Not a cloud in the sky," Adam observed. He took a sip of coffee, steaming hot from the thermos. He'd spent all the previous evening gathering together equipment, and by the time he'd finished, he had been really looking forward to a day of fishing.

Danny removed another doughnut from the box Adam had put on the seat between them, but didn't answer.

Adam frowned and tried again. "Angela says you do a lot of trout fishing." He flipped down the visor to cut the glare from the sun. "I used to know some good places around here when I was a kid, but I've been gone a long time. You got any ideas?"

Glancing sideways, Adam caught a flicker of interest in Danny's eyes. Knowing Danny was weighing his answer carefully, not wanting to get too involved, Adam waited. Finally Danny spoke.

"There's some nice streams running off the Little Pend Oreille river, about twenty miles from here, where I go sometimes," Danny answered, still looking straight ahead. "But sometimes in the spring the roads wash out. I don't know whether we can get back in there."

"Tell me which way to go and we'll give it a try," Adam answered. "The Bronco can take pretty rough terrain." They were off to a good start, he decided. He was doing exactly what Lathrop had suggested, going to a neutral place—actually a place Danny had chosen.

Maybe this time they could do something besides argue.

When they opened the doors of the Bronco at the end of an old logging road that wasn't much more than mud ruts, Adam felt a sense of victory. Danny had talked to him more in the preceding half hour than in all the other times they'd seen each other. Granted, he'd only been giving directions and scattered comments about the area, but at least he was talking.

Each of them carried a small tackle box and a fly casting rod as Adam followed Danny down an overgrown path to the sandy bank of a narrow stream. Looking around, Adam figured about the only thing they'd catch there were bullheads. But, after all, he hadn't come for the fishing.

"We have to walk upstream a ways," Danny informed him. He set off at a steady pace along the edge of the water.

"How'd you find this place?" Adam inquired, keeping up with him easily.

"I usually go hiking in the spring," Danny answered, "as soon as the weather warms up enough so I don't freeze my ass off sleeping out at night. I like the wildflowers."

"The wildflowers?" Adam questioned.

"I suppose you think that's wimpy, like everything else about me."

The glimpse of insecurity beneath Danny's tough facade surprised Adam. "No, Danny, that's not it at all," he answered quietly. "I used to tramp around in the woods every spring, too. It was sort of a ritual."

Danny muttered something Adam couldn't quite hear. They rounded a bend, and the stream widened into a clear, deep pool. Overhead the early morning sun filtered through the leaves on the trees, casting patches of sunlight on the quiet water.

"Well, this is it," Danny announced with a shrug, setting his tackle box on the wide trunk of an uprooted willow lying along the bank.

Adam surveyed the scene with the practiced eye of the outdoorsman. He noted the marks of beaver teeth on the logs that spanned the stream and the deer prints in the mud. One set of prints was larger, different from the rest and he bent over to study it.

"Probably an elk," Danny said, watching him. "I saw one when I was camping out here a few weeks ago."

Adam wondered if this might have been where Danny had disappeared to after their disastrous first meeting. "I've never seen an elk in the wild," he replied, setting his own tackle box beside Danny's. "They stay pretty much away from civilization."

Without comment Danny took a hand-tied fly from the tackle box and meticulously attached it to his line.

"You're good at that," Adam observed, as he fitted together the sections of his own rod. "You catch much here?"

"A rainbow or two on a good day," Danny answered, closing his fly case. He flipped his rod tip back to cast, letting his yellow line loop back and forth above his head until he expertly dropped the fly alongside a large log partially visible above the surface of the water.

He didn't say anything more, and neither did Adam. For nearly an hour nothing but the zing of fly lines through the air broke the morning stillness. It was a neutral silence, neither comfortable nor uncomfortable, Adam decided. A good time to talk.

"You come here often?"

"Sometimes."

"Seems like a good place to think."

"Yeah."

Adam watched his fly land lightly on the surface of the pond barely disturbing the water around it. "What do you think about when you're out here alone?" He saw Danny stiffen and realized he was moving too fast.

Danny flipped his rod hard and the line slapped the water. "I should have known," he muttered. With hostility in his eyes, he turned toward Adam. "Is that why you brought me out here? To have a philosophical discussion?"

His bluntness caught Adam off guard. "Yes, I suppose it was, partly," he replied slowly.

"And what's that supposed to accomplish?"

"Maybe a measure of understanding. Maybe not."

"I understand you just fine, and there's no way you're going to ever understand me. You live in a different world, and in your world they don't listen to people like me because they don't want to hear what we have to say."

"That's quite an indictment." Adam leaned over to untangle his line from a dead branch along the water's edge. "We don't see eye to eye on national defense, but that's one issue in a whole life. There are probably a hundred other things we feel the same way about."

"Name one."

"Well, how about fishing?"

"Right. Try something important."

"Okay, then the environment. I'll bet one of the reasons you like to come up here is that there's no sign of man. No gum wrappers, no styrofoam cups. You probably think it's important we take care of the environment because there are no replacements available. I agree with you. It's one of the areas I've been really tough on in every command I've had."

Danny shook his head. "You tell me you care about the environment. Yet you still want more nuclear weapons and you don't even see the contradiction." Again Danny cast too hard and the fly landed on the water with a resounding splash. "Did you ever think about all the nuclear waste we're creating and what that's going to do to the environment? My father said that could wipe out civilization even if we never dropped a nuclear bomb."

Adam paused, methodically drawing in his line as he considered what Danny had said. Danny was smart, and more perceptive than he'd expected. He worded his answer carefully. "Your father was right, unless we can figure out some better ways to dispose of the nuclear by-products. Some engineering studies are being done right now on a mountain out in the middle of nowhere to try to solve that problem."

"That's no solution. My father—" Danny stopped and looked at Adam, anger burning in his eyes. "But you don't want to hear about my father. Anyway, he's dead. Now you say *you* are my father."

Adam met Danny's eyes. He began to understand some of Danny's resentment. "I'm your *natural* father, Danny." He struggled to keep his tone firm, his voice even. "We're linked biologically. That's all, unless we choose to make it more."

Danny stared at Adam for a long moment before turning away.

Suddenly Adam saw him differently from before. Danny was straddling the gulf between boy and man, trying to reconcile his beliefs, which were still rooted in idealism, with cold realities he couldn't quite accept.

Adam could still remember himself at Danny's age,
haunted by self doubts and yet full of bravado, so sure
he knew all the answers. He'd been going to reform the
world once, too, but he couldn't quite remember anymore how he'd planned to go about it.

Suddenly Danny stepped back and reeled in his line.
"Fishing's lousy," he muttered. "I shouldn't have
brought you here."

Adam didn't move. "I thought you were a fisherman."

"What's that supposed to mean?"

"Nothing. Except you're pretty impatient for a
fisherman."

"I suppose you want to sit here all day and wait?"

"I'm willing to give it more than a couple of hours.
After all, you tell me there are trout here sometimes.
That's a better recommendation than a lot of places I've
fished."

Danny sat down. "All right, you want to wait, we
wait. But let's cut the deep discussion."

"Suits me." Adam dragged his fly tantalizingly across
the surface of the water. He brought the line in and
stood up to cast it out again, letting it drop in a shadow
about two-thirds of the way across the stream. He
wished he'd at least get a bite or, better yet, that Danny
would.

"Look, Colonel Campbell—"

"Now, just a minute!" Adam reeled in his line and
balanced the rod on a good-sized rock. Then he sat
down on the uprooted willow and faced Danny
squarely. "Let's cut the Colonel Campbell routine. Call
me Adam. Maybe that will get rid of part of the problem."

"All right, *Adam*," Danny said, "but the name doesn't change what I was going to say. You want to talk, we'll talk. But the simple fact is we're on opposite sides of the fence. You're not going to change your position and neither am I."

"You're probably right," Adam acknowledged. "But tell me this, Danny, what are you really after?"

"We've been all through this. We've got to stop this nuclear buildup—"

"No, that's not what I mean. I want to know what your goal is, not how you're going to accomplish it. In the final analysis, what is it you really want?"

Danny hesitated.

Adam waited patiently. This was his last shot, the only way he could think of to build a bridge between them.

"I'm not sure what you're getting at," Danny answered after several minutes. "In the final analysis, as you put it, I want a peaceful world without the threat of nuclear war, where the environment is clean, and people can live good lives."

"Very well put, Danny. Now tell me, what do you think I'm after—in the final analysis."

Again, Danny was silent, staring thoughtfully into the woods beyond the trout pool. Finally he said softly, "I don't know."

"Well, I do know," Adam answered. "And I can't say it any better than you did. It isn't where we want to go, Danny, it's the way we propose getting there that's different. I don't think I quite understood that before today."

"You're trying to tell me that you and I have the same goals?" Danny shook his head. "No way can I buy that."

"What do you think I want? War? Do you really think I spent all that time in Viet Nam just so I could come home and send a new generation of kids off to die in another senseless war?"

"Well, no, but—"

"Of course not. I want peace. Any thinking man does. I want people to be free to live good and productive lives. And I'm working damn hard, every day of my life, toward that end."

"You make it sound easy," Danny answered. "The problem is you're wrong, and that could destroy us all."

"I could say the same thing about your approach, you know. But I respect you because you're fighting for something that's important."

Danny didn't answer. He threw a stone into the water and they both stared at the widening ripples that spread toward the shoreline. Adam wondered whether there was any hope for the two of them. Maybe he should have agreed to go home. Maybe they'd come as far as they could. Somehow he didn't believe that. The more he knew about Danny, the more he liked him, and the more he realized how shallow his first impressions of his son had been. But even as he found himself drawn to Danny, he wasn't sure the feelings could ever be reciprocal.

Time passed quietly, marked by the drumming of a woodpecker and the zing of the fly lines. Danny didn't say anything more, and Adam couldn't tell whether he was thinking about their conversation or whether he was withdrawing into himself. For the next hour, Adam fished without enthusiasm and even when Danny caught a nice-sized trout, nothing changed.

On the way home Danny was more open than before, talking mainly about water quality in the streams and antipollution efforts that were beginning to show results. Adam's mind wandered to the hours he'd spent with Cecelia's sons and he thought about the easy, comfortable relationship he had with them. He could hear Cecelia's warning. *"Danny's different. He's not like you."* At first he'd thought that wouldn't matter, but now he wished he'd listened to her.

"Thanks for the ride," Danny said as he took his gear out of the Bronco. "I know a couple of other places where the fishing's good sometimes."

Danny's cautious invitation brought Adam back with a start. "We'll have to try again one of these days," he replied, but he wasn't sure he really meant that. He'd seen fishing as a simple answer, but there weren't any simple answers. The gulf between him and Danny stretched so wide he couldn't imagine how they'd ever bridge it. Maybe they could call a truce and even achieve a mutual tolerance, but why? What was the point? Adam couldn't see how that kind of relationship was going to improve life for either one of them.

After dropping Danny off, Adam forced himself to stop by Cecelia's. He knew she'd be anxious to find out how the fishing trip had gone, but he wasn't sure what to tell her. Finally he settled on a brief summary of the facts.

Cecelia studied him carefully as he talked. They were sitting in the kitchen drinking iced tea. When he'd been reluctant to come in, saying at first he was too grubby from fishing and then that he had to get back to the base, Cecelia had known the day had been another disappointment. But as he talked, his reaction seemed to be a contradiction. The day had obviously been at least a moderate success. Maybe Adam expected too much, or maybe there was more she didn't know.

"What's wrong, Adam?" She rested her hand lightly on his arm. "Is there more you haven't told me?"

"That's all of it." He shook his head and leaned back in his chair. "I guess when I take a look at Danny and me, I can't see that we're headed anywhere good. You were right, Cecelia. We're just different."

He seemed so discouraged, Cecelia thought, but he was making progress. He simply had to keep trying. "Adam, you can't be so impatient. These things take time," she reasoned gently.

Time. Adam couldn't believe time was going to solve anything where Danny was concerned. What was more likely to occur was a continuing tug-of-war between him and Danny that would leave Cecelia in the middle. That wasn't going to work out well for any of them. Her life would be so much easier if he weren't there, actually if he'd never come at all. He couldn't change what had already happened, but at least he had some control over the future.

After declining Cecelia's dinner invitation, Adam went back to the office to check on the air conditioner Lathrop had asked him to take care of. He passed through his own office and, on top of the stack of papers that had been left on his desk, he found a memo from Lathrop. He scanned it quickly, his eyes catching on the last paragraph:

You're due at the Pentagon in the office of the joint chiefs of staff at 0900 Monday unless you call to cancel. Ask for General Porter Jackson. He's an old friend of mine and he's expecting you. With your record and the POW background, you're a natural for the job. Good luck.

Adam reread the entire memo thoughtfully. The job was topnotch. Careerwise the move would be a step up, and from a personal standpoint ... He thought about Cecelia in his arms that day by the waterfall and about sitting with her on the steps of the cabin listening to the sounds of the forest. He was going to have a hard time leaving her.

But then he thought about Danny and about the mess he'd made of Cecelia's life. She was better off without him. Once he was across the country, her memories of him would fade, and she could get on with her life almost as though he'd never come back.

He folded Lathrop's memo and put it in his pocket, but he put off telling Cecelia about his plans until Sunday. When he stopped by her house on his way to the airport, he was in full uniform.

"This trip to Washington seems a bit sudden," Cecelia observed. "Is something wrong?"

"No, nothing's wrong. I have an appointment in the morning with some people at the Pentagon."

"When will you be back?"

"In a few days."

Although Adam's words were no doubt true, every instinct warned Cecelia that something he wasn't saying was far more crucial.

"There's something you're not telling me, Adam," she said quietly. "Is it because you can't, or because you don't want to?"

He looked distinctly uncomfortable. "I'm not sure this is the best time to discuss it. I have a plane to catch."

"You could have come sooner. I've been home all day." Her eyes searched his face. He looked gaunt and tired and very unhappy. "What is it, Adam?" she prodded. "Why are you going to Washington?"

He couldn't meet her eyes. He hadn't wanted to tell her now, but he knew later wouldn't be any easier. He swallowed hard. "There's a job opening up at the Pentagon, Cecelia. I'm going to talk to them about it."

"Oh, Adam, no." She reached out and gripped his hands, expecting him to take her in his arms. But he stood ramrod straight, watching her. "You don't have to go, do you?" She let go of his hands and stared at him in disbelief. "You *want* to go."

"It's for the best, Cecelia."

"Dammit, Adam!" She took a step backward, reeling from the flash of anger that shot through her. "You're running away. The going got tough so you're running just like you did before."

"I'm not running—"

"You most certainly are. You can't face your son so you're running away from him, and you're leaving me in the process. I love you, Adam. Doesn't that make any difference at all?"

"Cecelia, you don't understand."

"Then why don't you try explaining?" she challenged. "That's something you haven't bothered to do so far."

Adam checked his watch. "I'm sorry. I know I should have talked to you, but if I don't leave now, I'm going to miss my plane." He took a step toward the door. "I really have to go."

Cecelia wanted to scream at him to stop, not to throw away everything they had together. Instead she covered the distance between them in three short steps, nearly falling as she dragged the heavy cast. She wrapped both arms around his neck, and held him for a moment before she leaned up and whispered, ''Think about it, Adam, before you do anything. And just remember, I love you.''

She felt his lips brush her cheek and then he was gone. Cecelia didn't watch him go. She hobbled as quickly as she could toward the bathroom and was barely safe behind the locked door before she dissolved into tears. She couldn't believe it was over—not now when it had only begun.

CHAPTER FOURTEEN

TWO DAYS LATER CECELIA wrote in her journal:

My cast is finally off but Adam isn't here to celebrate. He's at the Pentagon, and I don't know if
he's ever coming back.

As Cecelia wrote the words, she realized she had only
one blank page left in her journal. Maybe that didn't
matter. The entries were getting harder and harder to
write. She missed Adam so much. When Jeannie had
taken her to the doctor that morning to have the cast
removed, he was all she'd wanted. And when Jeannie
had left her at home, she'd sat alone in her bedroom
and cried.

Slowly she put the journal back in the drawer and
limped to the bedroom window to watch the breeze
ripple through the leaves of the old oak tree outside. At
the sound of the back gate opening, Bingo barked
sharply.

"It's just Pop," Cecelia reassured the dog. "He's
coming to help plant the flowers." She pulled on her
oldest jeans and a sweatshirt, shoved her feet into her
gardening shoes and went downstairs.

"You're looking mighty fit with that cast off," Pop
said, setting a flat of marigolds on the patio and bend-
ing over to pat Bingo, "but you don't look very happy."

He scrutinized Cecelia carefully. "Matter of fact, you look like you don't feel too good. Does the leg hurt?"

Cecelia managed a smile. Pop could always tell when something was wrong. Just being with him made Cecelia feel better. "My leg aches a little bit," she admitted. "But I don't think I'll have any trouble planting the flowers."

After closing Bingo in the kitchen, she picked up her gardening gloves and followed her father to the oak tree where flats of impatiens were waiting. Walking without the cast felt fine, even though she was very slow. And being able to wear jeans was an unexpected pleasure. She hadn't been able to get into her jeans since... Cecelia swallowed hard. Since she went backpacking with Adam.

"You want to mix the pinks and the whites, or are you gonna make those two fancy circles again?" Pop picked up a hoe.

Cecelia laughed. "You obviously didn't think much of my attempts at landscape design, so we'll do it your way this year and mix the colors."

Pop raised an eyebrow as if he was going to ask Cecelia something, but handed her a rake instead. "Come on, we have to get busy. Haven't got all day, you know."

Cecelia moved alongside her father, raking an area of soil smooth as he finished hoeing. Gardening together was one of their traditions that went back as far as Cecelia could remember. It was also a time when she shared her feelings with Pop. Twenty years before, on a chilly day in early spring when they were raking leaves from the tulip bed, Cecelia had told him she was pregnant.

Pop grunted as he whacked at a large dirt clod. "I've been meaning to tell you. Danny stopped by to see me last week to pick up my old guitar. Remember, that day at your picnic I told him he could have it."

"Danny came out to see you?" Cecelia was surprised.

"Yep, said he'd been to the air show with Adam. Seems like the two of them didn't do real well together."

Cecelia stopped raking for a moment. "That's how it sounded from what Adam told me. He seemed so discouraged after they got back. Then they went trout fishing, and that seemed to go a little better than the air show, but not as well as Adam had hoped."

Pop leaned on his hoe. *So they'd gone fishing together.* Maybe Danny had listened to some of what he'd said. But young people were so impatient. "These things take time," he told Cecelia. "You got a boy who's hurting for a father who just died, and a man who's never been around kids, and they're not gonna turn into father and son overnight. Those two will have to work at it."

"Adam has been working at it, Pop, so much that it's nearly tearing him apart."

Pop looked steadily at his daughter. "And tearing you and him apart in the process?"

Hot tears welled up in Cecelia's eyes. "That's exactly what's happening. Adam's at the Pentagon now, interviewing for a job. If he gets it—and I'm sure he will—he'll be moving to Washington."

"Without you?"

Wordlessly Cecelia nodded.

Pop shook his head. "The man's running away from his problems. Do you love Adam?"

"Oh, yes." As the words came out, the tears spilled over.

"And does he love you?"

"Yes."

Pop reached in his back pocket and handed her his handkerchief. "Now Cecelia, crying isn't gonna help. You're telling me you love Adam and he loves you, and at the same time you're telling me you're just gonna sit back and let him take off to live in Washington. Does that make much sense to you?"

"No, I suppose not." Cecelia blew her nose and stuffed the handkerchief in the back pocket of her jeans.

"You know," Pop said. "It's time for you to do something."

"I've tried everything!"

Pop began hoeing again. "No you haven't, because the problem's still there. If you'd tried everything, you would have solved it. Now, you've talked to Adam, and he understands this thing with Danny is going to be slow, right?"

"Well, yes, but—"

"Now give me a minute." He chopped vigorously at the dirt. "Have you talked to Danny about any of this?"

Cecelia pondered for a minute. "No, now that you mention it, I haven't."

"Well, no wonder the boy's acting the way he is. There's a lot he doesn't understand. Why don't you have a talk with him?"

"Me?"

"You're the boy's mother aren't you?"

Thoughtfully Cecelia picked up her rake. "Actually, I guess I'm the only one who can really explain everything that's been going on, now and when he was born. Maybe if he understands how Adam feels. . . ."

"Now, don't go into this expecting miracles." Pop patted her on the shoulder. "The best you can hope for is another step or two in the right direction. But at least that's a start." He patted her again and reached for the trowel.

By early evening, impatiens filled the flower bed around the oak tree, multicolored zinnias lined the back fence and bright yellow marigolds were planted in the window boxes. Pop stayed for dinner, a simple meat loaf, but one of his favorite meals. After he left and the children had filtered off to their various activities, Cecelia took her coffee to the patio and settled back in a lounge chair. From the street in front of the house she could hear a group of little boys calling to each other while they finished their regular evening baseball game.

As she gazed at the deep purple sunset, she thought of how unbearably lonely her life would be without Adam. Her children were growing up and in a few more years would be off living their own lives. But she and Adam had many, many more years to share. Wonderful years, filled with love, if only Danny weren't in the way. Somehow both Adam and Danny had to come to grips with the problem and learn to accept each other. A close relationship was probably too much to hope for, but if they could only achieve some measure of understanding— The back gate creaked and Cecelia turned around. "Who's there?"

Two figures appeared in the shadows between the gardening shed and an evergreen.

"Hi, Mom," came the subdued answer.

"Mary Beth! I thought you were spending the week at Priest Lake with the Hamiltons." As her daughter came closer, Cecelia could see she was pale and her eyes were hollow with exhaustion. "What happened?" Cecelia asked. "What are you doing home? And who's with you?"

"It's me, Danny, Mrs. Mahoney." He moved into view behind Mary Beth, carrying her suitcase and shuffling uneasily from foot to foot.

With that deep maternal instinct, so finely tuned in women with several children, Cecelia knew something was wrong. A dozen possibilities ran through her mind, each one worse than the last. Apprehensively she gazed from Mary Beth to Danny and back to Mary Beth again. "Maybe the two of you better sit down and tell me what's going on."

With a furtive look at Danny, Mary Beth sank into a lawn chair in front of her mother. Danny set the suitcase on the patio and sat down on the back stoop. Neither one said a word.

Cecelia directed her attention to her daughter. "Well?" she asked.

Mary Beth hung her head and studied her hands which were knotted in her lap. "It's my fault," she began. "It was all my idea."

"What was all your idea?"

"Going to Seattle to find my mother." The sentence spilled out like one long word.

Cecelia inhaled sharply. Of all the possibilities, this was one she hadn't considered.

"But she never got to Seattle," Danny broke in. "She changed her mind and she's been with me all day."

"Danny changed my mind," Mary Beth said.

Cecelia looked from one to the other, her adopted daughter, her natural son. Raised in different families and yet so alike. When would they ever understand that they were not rejected at birth, but given in love? When would they ever accept love from all those who cared so much? "Start from the beginning," Cecelia said quietly, "and tell me everything that happened."

"I'm afraid you'll be so angry." Mary Beth's voice trembled.

"That's true. I might be very angry, but I'll still love you both. Neither one of you could do anything to destroy that." From the deep corners of her mind Cecelia could hear her father telling her the same thing, many years ago. Now she understood what those words truly meant. Her children might hurt her, or disappoint her, or make her angry, but no matter what she would never stop loving them.

"Well..." Mary Beth looked at Danny. "I wasn't at the lake, and I never was going. This morning I emptied out my savings account at the bank—I had two hundred and seventy-eight dollars—and I was going to go to Seattle to find my real mother."

"How were you going to do that? You don't have any information about her."

"Yes, I know her name and the hospital where I was born."

"That's not possible!" Cecelia leaned forward. "I'm the only one who has that information and it's—"

"Locked up in the safety deposit box at the bank," Mary Beth finished. "Remember when Angela turned eighteen and you gave her a key to the box and took her down there and showed her all those insurance papers and stuff?"

"Yes." A sick feeling began to spread through Cecelia.

Nervously Mary Beth continued. "I figured out if there was any information about me it would be in that box. So I practiced signing Angela's name, and one day last week I took the key from her top drawer and I went to the bank and signed out the box. That's when I found my birth certificate.'' Mary Beth looked over at Danny again.

"Go ahead. Finish the whole story," he encouraged.

"I copied the information..." Mary Beth paused. "Mom, my mother was only fifteen years old, younger than I am now. I could tell from her date of birth on the paper. I couldn't believe it.''

"That's right." Cecelia could see the shock in her eyes and perhaps the beginning of understanding.

"Then I put the box back and called Danny and told him what I found. He and I have been talking about all this adoption stuff, and he knew I wanted to go to Seattle and look for my mother.''

"I told her it was a bad idea," Danny said. "I mean, look what's happened to us since I found out about you and Adam. Everything's a real mess, and nobody's happy.''

"Especially you?" Cecelia reached over and put her hand on Danny's knee.

"Yeah," he muttered, avoiding her eyes. "Especially me.''

"I didn't listen to Danny." Mary Beth's voice lowered. "I didn't care. I just wanted to go to Seattle and find out for myself." She stared at the ground. "Except when I got to the bus station this morning I got scared. I wasn't exactly sure what I was going to do when I got to Seattle. I began to wonder if my mother would want to see me even if I found her. Probably nobody knows she had a baby, like nobody knew you had Danny. The more I thought about it, the more mixed up I got and I didn't know what to do anymore. Finally I phoned Danny and he came and picked me up at the bus station. Then we went for a long drive and talked about it a lot.''

''And what have you decided?''

Mary Beth looked at her mother for the first time. ''I decided I'm not ready to find out about my birth mother yet. Maybe someday, but not right now.''

''That isn't all,'' Danny said.

''I feel stupid about the rest,'' Mary Beth said.

''But it's the important part.''

''I know.'' Mary Beth hung her head again. ''I love you, Mom,'' she whispered. ''I'm sorry about everything.''

Cecelia felt her eyes brimming with tears. She ached to gather her daughter in her arms, the way she had when Mary Beth was little. But the bond was too fragile right now. Instead she lifted Mary Beth's chin and looked into her eyes. ''I love you, too,'' she said. ''Very, very much. I'm glad you came home.''

Mary Beth lowered her eyes and pulled away. ''This is getting too emotional for me. I'm going upstairs to unpack.'' She picked up her suitcase and started toward the back door. Then she stopped and turned around. ''Is there any dinner left? I'm starving.''

''Cold meat loaf in the refrigerator,'' Cecelia answered.

''It sounds as though she's going to be okay now,'' Danny said after the screen door banged shut.

''I'm sure she will,'' Cecelia answered. ''She grew up quite a bit today, Danny. Thank you so much for helping her.''

''It's all right. I understand her pretty well, I think. I wish I could figure myself out as easily.''

Cecelia watched her son's face grow sober and she felt him retreat inside himself. *How very much like Adam,* she thought. "What do you mean, Danny?" she asked gently. Would he open up and talk to her?

"All this adoption business. You know, I never gave it much thought until Adam showed up in my living room that day. I was adopted, my folks loved me, and that was that. I didn't care where I came from or any of that stuff like Mary Beth. I was pretty happy most of the time except for missing my dad after he died."

"It's really hard to lose a parent. The sadness lasts a long time."

Danny shook his head. "I was kind of hoping it would go away pretty soon. That feeling inside, I mean."

Cecelia watched him swallow and look across the back yard.

"No one can ever take his place," Danny said in a low, determined voice.

"That's true, Danny. No one will ever take his place."

Danny stood up and began to pace back and forth across the patio. "But that's what Adam's trying to do. He's trying to take my dad's place, and he's not my dad. He's not anything like my dad. He's nothing but a macho warmonger."

"Those are harsh words, Danny. Is it possible you're having trouble seeing past his uniform to the real man who's wearing it?" Cecelia watched her son's reaction carefully, waiting for an explosion. But he simply continued pacing, his hands jammed in his pockets. "Danny, if you'll stay a few minutes, there are some things I'd like to show you."

He looked at her warily. "I guess so."

"Good. Make yourself comfortable and I'll be right back."

When Cecelia returned a few minutes later, she was carrying a small brown cardboard box with a tray of food balanced on top. Danny came over to her immediately, took the carton and helped Cecelia into the lawn chair with his free hand.

"That was a pretty neat maneuver," Cecelia told him as Danny set the carton on the ground next to her and sat back down on the steps.

Danny grinned, a good sign, Cecelia thought.

"Is some of this food for me?" he asked, eyeing the meat loaf sandwich, chips, cookies and milk hopefully.

"Everything except the coffee," Cecelia answered, handing him the plate. She'd learned years before that there was no point in trying to reason with a hungry kid. She opened the carton and pulled out a thick high school yearbook. After blowing off the dust, she flipped the pages casually, waiting for Danny to show some interest.

"Is that your yearbook?" Danny craned his neck curiously. "It looks pretty old."

"Over twenty years. If you promise not to laugh, I'll show you a picture of me when I was fourteen." She turned the yearbook around so that Danny could see a group of ponytailed girls in their drill team uniforms lined up on the football field.

"Hey, there you are, right in front. You haven't changed all that much, except your hair is short now."

"You do know how to flatter a woman," Cecelia remarked. She reached into the carton again and took out a second yearbook. "This one belonged to my brother,

Jim," she explained, turning to the senior section. "Let's see if you can pick out Adam."

Danny washed his sandwich down with a slug of milk and scanned the page. By the look on his face, Cecelia knew that he had found the picture.

"He looks just like me," Danny finally said in a strained voice. "The same eyes, the same chin. It's eerie, like I'm a clone or something." Aloud he read the list of activities under the picture. "National Honor Society, band, basketball—" Danny stopped reading. "That surprises me. I'd have thought Adam would have been a football jock."

Cecelia shook her head. "But he wasn't." She turned several pages. "Can you pick him out here?"

"This is a bunch of kids demonstrating in front of the state capital," Danny said in surprise. "Here's Adam holding a sign that says something about fish and pollution. I can't quite make it out. What was he doing?"

"Trying to get some antipollution bills passed in the state legislature."

"No kidding!" Danny grinned and studied the picture for a minute. "So how come this kid, who looks like a normal human being, someone I might even like, wound up in the Air Force?"

"Well," Cecelia began. "Adam was smart, athletic, a natural leader, but he had a tough time growing up. His father walked out when Adam was eight or nine and never came back. His mother tried, but it's tough to raise a boy alone on a skimpy hairdresser's salary."

Danny nodded his understanding and Cecelia continued. "Adam's basketball coach took a liking to him and concluded pretty fast that there wasn't going to be any money for college. So he encouraged Adam to explore some possibilities like scholarships, grants, that

ort of thing. In the process Adam found out about the
Air Force Academy and realized it offered a topnotch
education that would give him unlimited opportuni-
ies. When he got accepted, he decided to go.''

Cecelia dug in the cardboard box and handed Danny
picture. "This is Adam in his cadet uniform his first
Christmas at home." She laughed quietly. "That was
when I fell in love with him, but he didn't know I was
alive." She pulled out another picture. "And here he is,
four years later, on graduation day. Can you see his gold
second lieutenant bars on his shoulders?''

"I see them." Danny took the picture. "Were you at
the graduation?''

"No," Cecelia answered quietly. "That was only a
few months before you were born. I was in Portland at
home for unwed mothers.''

Danny was silent for a moment, putting the pieces
together in his mind. "Then Adam went off to pilot
training and Viet Nam, right?''

"That's right," Cecelia replied. "He was shot down
toward the end of his tour of duty. At first he was listed
as missing in action, presumed dead. Later on his sta-
tus was changed to POW, prisoner of war, on the basis
of some coded information that came out of one of the
camps.''

She handed Danny a flat, silver bracelet. "Have you
ever seen one of these?''

Danny shook his head as he examined the bracelet.
"Adam's name is on this," he said in surprise. "'Lt.
Adam J. Campbell.' With the tip of his finger he traced
the letters. "What is this thing?''

"It's called a POW/MIA bracelet. Thousands of
them were sold by the League of Families of POWs and
MIAs during the war. Each one had the name of a POW

or MIA engraved on it, and by wearing a bracelet you showed concern for the POWs. They were treated very badly, you know.''

"Yeah, I've heard some things about that." Danny studied the bracelet he was holding. "But Adam came out okay, didn't he?" His tone was more anxious than his words and seemed to imply he wanted reassurance.

Cecelia hesitated. "Yes and no. He doesn't have many visible scars, but he does have some that don't show."

"Like what?"

"He's sterile now, Danny. He can never father another child." Cecelia spoke quietly, without any trace of emotion in her voice, but she never took her eyes off her son's face.

Danny stared at his mother in disbelief as he absorbed the meaning of what she had just told him. Then came the explosive reaction. "Are you telling me that I'm the only kid Adam will ever have?"

"That's what I'm telling you."

Danny came to his feet in a rage. "Great, just great. Here I am thinking all this time that we're having this good conversation about Adam and maybe he isn't such a bastard, after all, and then you try to put me on a guilt trip. You're just trying to make me feel sorry for Adam so I'll buddy up with him and do a big time father and son routine—"

"No, I'm not, Danny. Please sit down and let me finish—"

"No! I'm not sitting down and I'm not listening to anything else. I've heard enough." Danny wheeled around and headed for the gate.

"Danny!" Cecelia's voice rang out in the night.

Her son paused and looked back at her. "Yeah?"

Cecelia thought quickly. In the glow of the moon-light she caught a glimpse of the silver POW bracelet Danny was still holding. "I just wanted to tell you to keep the bracelet," she said.

Danny looked down at the bracelet and back at Ce-celia. Without another word he shoved the silver band into his jeans pocket and kicked open the gate. Cecelia could hear his angry footsteps echoing all the way down the walk. But he had the bracelet. Later, when he cooled off, he'd take another look at it, run his fingers over Adam's name again, and do some serious thinking. Danny was that kind of kid. A lot like his father.

That night when Danny was tossing his jeans into the laundry basket, the bracelet fell out of his pocket and hit the floor with a clanking sound. He bent to pick it up, intending to stuff it in the top drawer of his dresser, but then he took another look at it. Turning the brace-let around several times in his hand, he watched the light from his desk lamp reflect off the polished sur-face.

It wasn't much of a bracelet really, just a flat piece of metal, less than an inch wide, curved to fit someone's wrist. Methodically he traced each letter of Adam's name and the numbers of the date he was shot down. After some calculations he realized that Adam had been very young when he was a POW—in his early twenties.

Still holding the bracelet, Danny sat down on the bed. He was almost twenty himself, not much younger than Adam had been when he was captured. He wondered what it must have been like to have been caged like an animal for months, or even years. The idea was incom-prehensible. He was willing to spend a few hours in jail if he got arrested during a demonstration, but years—

A man would have to be damn committed to what he was doing to take a risk like that.

Danny thought about his own father and realized grudgingly that his father would have admired Adam. He wouldn't have agreed with him, either, not for a minute. But his father respected anyone who stood up for what he believed, no matter what it was. "Stick by your values, son," Danny remembered him saying. But his father had also said that part of becoming a man was learning how to give and take without compromising yourself.

Again Danny traced the letters on the bracelet with his finger. "Lt. Adam J. Campbell." His biological father. Not a substitute for the father he had lost, but rather a different person in a different role. Except neither he nor Adam seemed exactly sure what that role was. He thought about being the only son Adam would ever have. Danny knew that wasn't his fault, but it bothered him.

He laid the POW bracelet on his desk next to Pop's guitar. In a way they were both symbols of the family he was trying to get used to. He stroked the newly polished wood of the guitar. Some parts of finding a new family were easy, and other parts were hard as hell.

SHORTLY AFTER DAWN on his last day in the nation's capital, Adam walked up Constitution Avenue, relishing the silence of a city not yet awake. Within hours the streets of Washington, D.C., would be choked with cars. Long lines of tourists would have queued up outside the White House and the Washington Monument. He'd be contending with all that on a daily basis soon, assuming his final interview went well. He had no reason to think it wouldn't. His reception at the Pentagon had been cordial at every turn. The job with the joint chiefs of staff was just what Lathrop had said, a step up, and no doubt a star in a year or two.

Adam turned onto Twenty-third street. Just a few more blocks to go. Over the past three days, several people had asked him if he had visited the Viet Nam Memorial and he'd had to admit that he had not. Like almost everyone in America, he'd heard and read about it, but during his brief visits to Washington he'd avoided going to see it, always telling himself there wasn't time.

His pace slowed as he neared the memorial, and he was aware of the rising cadence of his heartbeat and a light mist of perspiration inside the rim of his hat. Stupid, he thought. Fifteen years had passed since he came back from Viet Nam. That was half his adult life. He walked on, slower still, against an invisible resistance pressing on him like a rising tide.

The path ahead of him sloped gently downward and on its left-hand side the wall seemed to rise out of the earth, unimposing at first like a low, thin marker, and then growing higher until the polished black granite stood ten feet high. He paused in the morning stillness, staring at the stark black wall which held the weight of more than fifty thousand lives.

Slowly he walked forward, past a woman who stood alone, her hands clasped in front of her and her head bowed. All the time his eyes were fixed on the endless columns of names that covered the face of the wall. There were names he knew, men he'd served with, men he might have died with. He stopped at the panel where deaths were recorded from the months just before he was shot down and reached out to run his fingers over the names engraved there... Krueger, Holmes, Jenkins, Garcia, Ross... Waves of emotion rolled over

Adam as he stopped and carefully traced the letters etched in stone. Williams. That had to be Pete. Memories came back of the day at the river when the chopper medics had been airlifting out a bunch of wounded soldiers. Pete had thought he heard a man cry out back in the brush. Everyone had warned him to be careful, but he'd gone to check anyway, determined not to leave anyone behind. The explosion came a few minutes later. He'd always hoped that somehow Pete got out alive. Apparently he hadn't. Adam's eyes ran on down the column of names and up the one adjacent: Jones, McFarland, Johnson, Cochran, Jankowsky... He stopped again. Walt Jankowsky's two kids were grown up now, and he never even got to see the younger one.

An extraordinary feeling of helplessness gripped Adam as he faced the empty death embodied in that stark black wall. Finally he stepped back, past a battered helmet, a single red rose, and half a dozen American flags stuck in the ground, all part of the memories that people had left in front of the wall. But Adam's eyes never left the endless columns of names etched in the stone. The enormity of the loss they represented flowed into a question Adam had never asked himself before. What did all those lives mean for the others, the ones like him, who had come home?

With his head high he held his hat across his chest in a silent salute. What they'd died for was what he had in the palm of his hand and was about to throw away. The love of a woman, the reality of a child, the welcoming warmth of a family. The men listed before him were gone. For them it was over. But it didn't have to be over for him.

A gentle breeze brushed his face as he turned away and walked back up the path into the raucous sounds of the city. His steps were swift and sure, his eyes fixed straight ahead, looking beyond the warm June morning. Finally he knew what he wanted and how much it was worth to have it. First he had to undo the damage he'd done in the past three days. Then he could go home to Cecelia and straighten out the rest of his life.

CHAPTER FIFTEEN

WHEN THE PHONE RANG that Thursday evening, Cecelia knew it was Adam. She wasn't sure how she knew; she just did. Hurrying across her bedroom, she picked it up before the second ring and answered with a breathless, anxious hello.

"My plane just got in," Adam said without preamble. "I'm on my way there, if you'll see me."

"If I'll see you?" Cecelia echoed. "Oh, Adam, please come home."

Her heart pounding, she hung up the phone. He might be coming to say he got the job and was leaving immediately, she reminded herself. *But he might not,* a voice inside her whispered. He might really be coming home. She looked at the clock on her bedside table. Seven-thirty. He'd be there in half an hour, and either way—however he felt—she wanted to greet him alone.

"Hey, Angela, can I borrow your hair dryer?" Mary Beth's voice pierced her closed bedroom door. Someone turned the stereo volume up. The phone rang again, and Cecelia picked it up.

"He's not here," she said in a response to a female voice that asked for Sean. In a few minutes, she decided, that would be absolutely true. Instead of hanging up, Cecelia slipped the telephone receiver under her pillow. There would be no more phone calls, either.

Quickly she summoned all of her children to the up-stairs hall.

"In a few minutes, Adam is going to be here," she announced to the surprised group. "I have some things I want to discuss with him alone." She saw a surreptitious look pass between Kim and Mary Beth.

"Does that mean you want us to evaporate or something?" Kevin interrupted.

"Not exactly," Cecelia answered, "but close. I want you all to go to the movies."

"You mean that horror film you've been saying for two weeks wasn't appropriate?" Kevin asked.

"A horror film!" Mary Beth exclaimed. "Oh, gross. Besides I only go to the movies with Roger."

"Tonight," Cecelia said in a voice edged with steel, "you go to the movies as a family. You will leave in exactly ten minutes and you will go to the movie. You will then go to the pizza parlor next door and eat pizza, and none of you *under any circumstances* will leave there before eleven o'clock. At precisely eleven-fifteen you will return home and go to bed. Do I make myself clear?"

They all stared at her. Cecelia realized she hadn't ordered them around like that for years—maybe never. No wonder they were startled.

"But, Mom," Kim began, "I was just about to shampoo my hair—"

"So was I," Angela seconded, "and I've got a summer job interview in the morning."

"I realize going to a movie may not be what some of you had in mind this evening," Cecelia said evenly. "But I often do things for you that weren't what I would have chosen, either. Tonight, I expect you to do exactly what I've told you."

"But, Mom—"

"Shut up, Mary Beth," Kevin intervened. "She's right. She never asks stuff like this. We've got to do it."

"Just because you want to go to a stupid horror movie," Mary Beth groused.

"I'll get the car keys," Angela said, looking at her mother. "And I'll make sure we're home at eleven-fifteen, not a minute before."

The children were gone and Cecelia was upstairs in her bedroom, when she heard Bingo bark. She fumbled with the buttons on her blue silk blouse and then quickly tucked it into a pair of white slacks. Then she heard the faint sound of the doorbell ringing and a cold chill swept through her. Fearing the worst, she hurried down the stairs and, with Bingo prancing around her feet, she pulled the door open.

Adam didn't stop to say hello or ask how she was or what had taken her so long. He swept her into his arms and held her so tightly that she gasped for breath. When he loosened his grip it was to kiss her—a long, deep kiss that said more than any words.

Cecelia rested her head against his chest and closed her eyes. "Thank God, Adam," she whispered. "Have you really come home?"

"Yes, Cecelia. I've come home. I was a fool to consider leaving. Will you forgive me?"

She tipped her head back and met his eyes, full of passion and longing and an overwhelming love. "There's nothing to forgive," she answered softly.

He shook his head. "You don't understand. I was about to chuck everything and move to Washington. You were right. I was going to run away."

"But you came back? What changed your mind?"

He looked past her, wondering how he could ever explain what had truly happened to him as he stared at that black wall full of death. He wasn't sure he really knew himself. "I guess I finally grew up, Cecelia," he answered slowly. "I finally figured out what's really important and I realized it's worth any price."

She wrapped her arms around his neck and held him, feeling a bond so strong that nothing would shake it again. "Come upstairs with me, Adam," she whispered.

He drew back startled. "But the kids—"

"They've gone to the movies. They won't be back for several hours."

A broad smile spread across his face. "We're alone?"

"Yes!" Gripped by pure joy, she laughed, a soft, melodious laugh that rang through the empty hallway. "We're absolutely and completely alone."

"Then let's go," he answered, his arm around her shoulders.

The bedroom was just as she had left it, lighted only by the glow of a small lamp on the chest across from the bed. Hearing Bingo's footsteps padding up the stairs behind them, Cecelia closed the door and locked it. Then she turned to Adam and saw the dark passion in his eyes.

She expected him to scoop her up and tumble onto the bed with her, but he didn't. He stood facing her, caressing her as though he'd never touched her before. Cecelia stood perfectly still, understanding suddenly the commitment they were about to make to each other.

Adam studied her face, its gentle contours softened in the dim light. He'd known her forever, and yet he'd never really seen her, not like this, not as a part of himself. Her eyes had never been quite so blue, nor her hair so soft as he twined his fingers in it. The total trust he saw as she gazed upward made him want to give her everything she'd ever dreamed of. She loved him. She'd told him so a dozen times and he'd thought he understood what she said. Now he knew there was more.

His hands moved downward from her shoulders to the first button on her blouse. "You'll never know how much I need you, Cecelia." His voice was husky with emotion.

Almost afraid to speak, Cecelia trembled at his touch. "I need you too, Adam," she whispered. "I need you to be a part of me." As he touched her, waves of passion washed over her. She closed her eyes and then opened them again to watch the sense of newness, almost wonder, in his face. He'd seen her body before, and she knew he thought it was beautiful, but tonight she knew he saw her differently. Tonight she was his.

When they came together, the passion that drove them carried a new and deeper meaning that bonded them as one.

"I LOVE YOU, CECELIA," Adam whispered. They lay side by side, still joined together. "Until today I don't think I understood what love was."

"I thought I did," Cecelia answered. "Now I'm not so sure."

They stayed together in the soft glow of the lamplight, listening to the ticking of the clock and the whisper of the curtains fluttering in the breeze from the open window. Deeply satisfied, she let her thoughts drift into the future and found she wasn't afraid anymore.

Adam stroked her cheek. "You realize we haven't solved our problems."

Cecelia sighed contentedly. "Maybe not, but we've sure made them easier to deal with."

"For the moment at least." Adam kissed her lightly on the nose.

"No, I meant that, Adam." Her tone was serious. "We can deal with almost anything if we do it together."

"You believe that, don't you?'"

"Of course." She drew her head back so that she could see him more clearly. "Don't you?"

He hesitated. "I want to believe it. But then I think about Danny..."

Cecelia studied him, remembering that Adam knew nothing of Danny's reaction to the day they'd spent together fishing. Adam had gone away decidedly apprehensive, unaware of the inroads he'd made with his son. And yet, even dogged by that uncertainty, he had come back.

"If Danny can't deal with me, I can handle that, Cecelia," Adam continued. "I don't like it and I'll keep trying as long as he'll let me, but I can accept it. I can't accept losing you."

"Oh, Adam." Cecelia held him close. "You didn't have to make that choice. There's more you don't know."

As she held him in her arms, she told Adam about Danny's visit to her father and about showing him Adam's POW bracelet. "I won't pretend it's going to be easy," she admitted. "Nothing with kids that age is easy, and you and Danny had two strikes against you before you even started. But he's beginning to be receptive, Adam. He's beginning to see you as a whole person instead of a symbol of everything that makes him angry."

Adam shifted his weight and propped himself on one elbow, his eyes meeting Cecelia's. ''If you're right, we've come a lot farther than I thought we had.''

''I am right,'' Cecelia assured him, knowing as she spoke how volatile and unpredictable teenagers could be. ''But sometimes you're going to have bad days,'' she added cautiously.

He grinned. ''That implies a good day once in a while. From what George Lathrop told me about his son, I gather those are a rare gift.''

''Oh, come on, teenagers aren't that bad.'' Cecelia playfully wiggled against him and nuzzled against his neck.

Adam rolled her over and kissed her soundly. ''We're going to be here until morning at this rate. When are the kids due back?''

Cecelia groaned and checked the clock. ''At eleven-fifteen. I'd forgotten all about them.''

''In that case, maybe—''

''Right. Maybe we'd better get dressed.'' She raised her hands to his cheeks, wishing they had more time together.

He answered as though he'd read her thoughts. ''I love you, Cecelia. I don't want this to ever end.''

''I don't either, Adam. I'm so sorry they're coming home.''

''No, you don't understand. I want to marry you, Cecelia. I want you to be my wife.''

''Oh, Adam, yes,'' she answered with no hesitation at all. ''And I want to go to bed with you at night and have you with me when we wake up in the morning, and I want to plan together and dream together, and I don't ever want to be apart again.''

He kissed her again, a gentle kiss that sealed the pact they'd made.

"Do you realize that we've just changed our whole lives?" Cecelia asked softly.

"Yes, I do," Adam replied, holding her tightly in his arms. "I also realize that I want to stay here with you forever, which is a damn good reason for us to get up right now unless you want to announce our engagement in the bedroom."

Laughing, Cecelia stood up. "You're absolutely right."

As they dressed, Adam told her about the interviews at the Pentagon and his complete change of heart after visiting the Viet Nam Memorial. "I had a little trouble explaining such an abrupt about-face," he said, smiling at the thought. "I barely got to the airport in time to make my plane."

"Did you have dinner tonight?" Cecelia asked as he buttoned his uniform shirt.

Adam looked up. "Come to think of it, I guess I didn't. With the time change, we only had lunch on the plane, and once we landed, I really wasn't thinking about food."

Cecelia laughed. "Neither was I. Can you handle grilled cheese and tomato soup?"

Adam hugged her. "As long as I share it with you."

DANNY STOOD HESITANTLY on the Mahoneys' front porch, shifting from one foot to the other. It was almost eleven o'clock, too late to visit anybody, except all the house lights were on, so they must be up. He'd tried to phone earlier, but kept getting a busy signal. Gripping the handle of the guitar case tighter, he tried to decide what to do. He really wanted to show them how good Pop's old guitar looked now.

He reached for the doorbell and then pulled back. He'd been told he could come anytime and not wait to be invited. He'd never done that before, but each time he'd come here, he'd felt more as if he belonged. He wished things could be as easy with Adam. Adam did try hard. Danny had to give him that. And he did seem to know a thing or two about trout fishing.

Danny caught his foot on the mat, and from inside the house he heard Bingo bark. Too late to change his mind now. The dog had heard him, and now the whole family knew someone was at the door. He rang the doorbell.

The sandwiches were on the griddle and the soup was heating in the microwave when Bingo raced out of the kitchen barking furiously. Cecelia checked the clock, frowning. "They're early."

"Only a few minutes," Adam noted. "But why are they ringing the doorbell?"

"Maybe they forgot to take a key. You watch the sandwiches and I'll let them in." Cecelia grinned, as she handed him the pancake turner.

The doorbell rang again and Cecelia hurried to answer it. Secretly she suspected the bell was Angela's way of announcing their arrival so they wouldn't interrupt anything embarrassing. Cecelia wished her oldest daughter would at least pretend she didn't know what was going on.

"Come on in," Cecelia said as she pulled open the front door.

"Thanks," Danny answered as he stepped across the threshold.

"Danny!" Cecelia stared at him.

"Is something wrong?" Danny drew back. "If you don't want me here . . . or if it's too late—"

Cecelia swallowed hard. "No, nothing like that, Danny. You just startled me. I thought you were the kids coming back from the movies."

"They're not here?" He looked disappointed. "I can come back some other time. I had something I wanted to show them."

Cecelia weighed the situation. She could let Danny go, which for the moment might be easier. Or, she could urge him to come in and take a chance that things would go well with Adam. She made her decision quickly, silently praying it was right.

"They should be home anytime now. Why don't you come on in, Danny? Adam's here, and we were about to eat a sandwich. You can have one with us."

Cecelia felt him tense when she said Adam's name. He took a step toward the door and leaned over to pick up a large, black guitar case Cecelia hadn't even noticed until that moment. "I'll come back—"

"Please don't go, Danny." Cecelia put a gentle but restraining hand on his arm. "I want you to stay. I want you to feel at home here."

He hesitated, meeting her gaze with eyes that looked very much like Adam's. "I can't stay long," he said slowly. He knelt down to pat Bingo and then rubbed the dog behind the ears. Bingo wagged his tail and rested his head on Danny's knee. "I think he's beginning to like me," Danny said softly.

"I'm sure he is," Cecelia agreed. When he stood up, she put her hand on his arm and propelled him toward the kitchen. "One grilled cheese coming up—or do you want two?"

"You don't need to go to any trouble," he said, and Cecelia knew immediately he was hungry.

"We need a couple more sandwiches," Cecelia announced cheerily as they entered the kitchen, hoping to somehow warn Adam so that he wouldn't appear as startled as she had been when she saw Danny. He looked up and, to her surprise, broke into a cautious smile when he saw his son.

"Good to see you," he said casually to Danny, as he put a round of cheddar on the cutting board and picked up the cheese knife. "What have you got there?"

Danny's eyes dropped to the guitar case, and she sensed him relaxing. With that single comment, Adam had turned the attention to something concrete that everyone could handle. That was the key, Cecelia realized. Go on living and focus on all the normal everyday things, and the rest would take care of itself.

"This is what I came to show everybody," he said with obvious pride. "I've fixed up the guitar Pop gave me." He placed the case on the kitchen table and carefully opened the fasteners. "I still want to put some more wax on it but it's coming along."

As he took the instrument from the case, Cecelia stared at it in amazement. The mellow glow of the deep-brown wood highlighted the intricate stenciling on the face of the guitar. The instrument looked as though it had been preserved under glass in a museum for the last hundred years. "That can't be Pop's guitar!" Cecelia exclaimed. "Not that old thing that has been in the attic all these years."

"Sure is." Danny grinned. "And it's got a great tone." He ran his fingers lovingly across the strings, producing several rich, haunting chords.

Adam stopped cutting cheese and walked to the table, standing for several moments in silent admiration and then rubbing the back of his hand over the smooth wood. "You've done an incredible job on that," he said with obvious sincerity. "What did you use on the wood to give it a finish like this?"

Danny launched into a detailed discussion of his craftsmanship, spurred on by Adam's questions.

With relief surging through her, Cecelia set the microwave to reheat the soup and put two more sandwiches on the griddle. But the food wasn't important anymore. What mattered was the relaxed cadence of those male voices behind her. A sudden realization swept through Cecelia. She and Adam, the man who was about to become her husband, were comfortably together in the kitchen with their son, a new family slowly rising from the ashes of the past. Suddenly Cecelia understood how important it was that she and Adam make Danny a part of their plans from the very beginning.

As soon as the sandwiches were done, Cecelia piled them on a plate and poured three cups of soup. She approached Adam and Danny the same way she would have if Adam had been talking with Sean or Kevin. "Okay, guys. Time to get the guitar off the table if we're going to eat."

"Women always seem to insist on clearing everything off the table," Adam said to Danny in a low voice, and Danny nodded as he put the guitar back in the case.

"Otherwise you'll get grease on the guitar," Cecelia answered pragmatically, delighted with their response.

As she set a plate in front of Danny, she let her hand rest briefly on his shoulder, and as she gave Adam his plate she hugged him. Danny looked at her gesture of affection toward Adam and then averted his eyes. "You actually couldn't have picked a better time to come," Cecelia said to Danny. She took a drink of her soup. "Adam and I have some news and we wanted to share it with you first."

Both Adam and Danny looked at her. Danny appeared suspicious and Adam surprised. Cecelia wondered if she was making a mistake. She and Adam hadn't talked about how to tell the kids and maybe he didn't want to talk to Danny. She also hadn't considered the possibility that instead of being happy for them, Danny might become very angry. As the silence stretched out, Cecelia took another drink of her soup and tried to decide how to proceed.

"We hadn't really discussed this." Her eyes helplessly met Adam's and then he seemed to understand.

"What your mother is trying to say, Danny, is that we're going to get married. We're a little slow about these things..."

Danny stared from one to the other of them. Cecelia could feel his hostility. "I guess I'm supposed to congratulate you," he said.

Cecelia lowered her eyes, deflated. "Not necessarily," she said to Danny. "It depends on how you feel."

"What do you expect of me?" he challenged. "Are you trying to make us into a happy family twenty years too late?"

Adam set down his sandwich and looked Danny in the eye. "It's about time you and I got a couple of things straightened out," he said firmly. "First of all, I don't expect anything from you. I love your mother. Twenty years ago we weren't ready to get married. Now we are. But you need to understand that my relationship with her is totally separate from my relationship with you.''

"Then why are you spending time with me and taking me places? It can't be because you enjoy it.''

Adam half laughed. "At least you recognize that. Actually, Danny, I've tried to get to know you because I hope some day we will enjoy each other. You make me think. Maybe I make you think. And maybe that's enough.''

"That's all you want?'' Danny was still suspicious.

Adam shrugged. "It's a place to start.''

Danny took a long drink of soup, all the while watching Adam. Bingo nudged his leg, and Danny reached down to pat him. "Maybe you're right,'' he answered slowly. "Maybe it is a place to start.''

The front door opened, sending Bingo scampering out of the kitchen to welcome the children home. "Mom?'' Angela called from the hall.

She was evidently the forward scout, making sure everything was safe, Cecelia realized. "We're in the kitchen, Angela,'' Cecelia called.

Angela appeared almost immediately, followed by her brothers and sisters. "Danny,'' she said in surprise. "I thought Mom got rid of us so she could be alone with Adam.''

Adam gave Cecelia a look that made her blush. He'd thought it was a little odd that all the kids had just happened to be at the movies. Now he realized what had happened. She was obviously embarrassed. He wished he could lean over and kiss her, but that would only make things worse.

"Your mother and I had some matters to discuss,'' he told Angela. "We'd taken care of them and we were just having a sandwich when Danny stopped by.''

"You should have come earlier," Kevin told Danny. "You could have gone with us. We saw an awesome horror flick."

Mary Beth made a face. "It was gross just like I said it would be."

"That's just because you weren't in the back row making out with Roger," Sean teased her.

"Cut it out!" Mary Beth retorted.

"What's there to eat?" Kevin asked, opening the refrigerator.

"Grilled cheese, if you fix it yourself," Cecelia answered. She felt Adam reach over and idly stroke the back of her neck. She tried to imagine what it would be like to have him with her all the time. No, she corrected herself, with *them* all the time. He wasn't just marrying her; he was marrying a family. He knew that, but suddenly Cecelia wondered if he truly realized what he was getting into. She looked up to find Mary Beth watching them as Adam touched her hair.

"Obviously you and Adam worked out whatever your problem was," Mary Beth observed bluntly.

Cecelia could have killed her.

"Actually we did," Adam answered.

"Does that mean you'll be around next winter when basketball season starts?" Sean asked.

Cecelia realized that a considerable amount of discussion had occurred on the way to the movie. No doubt the girls had done an in-depth analysis of her relationship with Adam. She hoped the speculation hadn't been too graphic. The best thing to do, she decided, was not to even think about it.

"I expect to be around for lots of winters," Adam said. "We'll work on that fast break until you've got it down perfectly."

Kim, who had been listening quietly, walked across the kitchen toward the table. "I think Adam's trying to tell us something," she said, zeroing in on Danny. "They've already talked to you, haven't they?"

"Depends on what you're getting at," Danny said noncommittally. "We had a conversation."

"Wait a minute!" Kevin interrupted, looking from Adam to Cecelia and then back to Adam. "Are you going to marry our mother?"

Suddenly the kitchen was silent. No one moved. Every eye was riveted on Adam. Slowly he pushed his chair back from the table and stood behind Cecelia, his hands on her shoulders. "Coming home on the plane this afternoon, I gave a lot of thought about what to say to all of you if your mother should agree to marry me."

He paused, and Cecelia felt his hands, strong and warm, grip her shoulders. This must be hard for him, she realized.

"I knew it would mean a change for you," Adam continued. "You've had your mother to yourselves for a long time. It won't be easy to share her. And then there's the question of how I fit in. I can't come into your lives—any of you—" he looked directly at Danny "—and suddenly act like your father. That kind of relationship is something that grows with time."

Adam's eyes moved around the room, resting on each of them individually and finally stopping at Kevin. "But the answer to your question is yes, I am going to marry your mother."

"All right!" Kevin responded, glancing sideways at his brother, who looked as happy as he did.

The others were quiet, no doubt weighing the pro
and cons, Cecelia realized. They were older, and the
understood their lives were going to change. She fe
Kim's hand slip into hers and her youngest daughte
hugged her tightly. "I love you, Mom," she whis
pered, and Cecelia blinked back tears.

"When are you going to do this wedding thing?"
Danny asked.

Adam and Cecelia looked at each other. They hadn'
discussed when, or how, or any of the details.

"I haven't cleared this with your mother," Adam
said, his eyes still on Cecelia, "but do you suppose th
gazebo is free a week from Saturday?"

"A week from Saturday?" Cecelia repeated.

"Sure, Mom, that's perfect," Angela broke in, "a
long as you do it in the afternoon. That night Danny
and I have tickets to a concert."

"Our baseball games are all in the morning, so we'
be free," Sean offered. "How about you, Kim?"

"I've got a tennis match Saturday morning, but I'
leave early if I have to because I'd rather go to a wed
ding any day."

"Roger and I were going on a picnic," Mary Beth
began—"

"Mary Beth!" Angela broke in.

"But I guess we could go on Sunday instead," she
finished, grinning. "I suppose getting married is prob
ably more important than a picnic."

"Then it's settled?" Adam asked, looking slightly
confused.

Cecelia laughed. "This sure is a strange way to pla
a wedding."

"If you're going to have a wedding, you'll need music," Danny observed. "How do you feel about a guitar?"

Cecelia reached across the table and took his hand. For the second time in five minutes, her eyes misted with tears. Whether he realized it or not, Danny's offer was for more than music. He was offering approval, however tentative, and hope, which was all she could have asked.

"Thank you, Danny," she said simply. "I can't think of a better new beginning for Pop's guitar."

"Yeah, well, I was thinking about this song," he continued, easing his hand away. "You know the one, Angela, about the green fields?" As he talked, he knelt down and opened the guitar case and took out the guitar. Ignoring the chorus of admiration it stirred, he began to play.

Angela moved over beside him, her clear voice soon joined by his deeper one. The others recognized the familiar melody one by one, and their voices blended in the chorus: "We'll walk hand in hand, through the unfamiliar land, with a love that will bind us together."

While the children gathered closely around Danny, and the singing continued, Adam took Cecelia's hand and they slipped away quietly. With the soft strains of music all around them, they walked across the backyard to the gazebo. Once they were alone, Adam took her in his arms. He looked down at her, and in the pale light from a crescent of moon, he could see the happiness shining in her eyes.

"I think it's going to work, Cecelia," he said softly.

"So do I," she answered. "So do I."

That night she filled the last empty page in her journal:

As I finish this journal, I am closing one chapter in my life and opening another. I have found the man I love and the son I'd lost. My life is finally complete.